MECHANIQUE

A TALE OF THE CIRCUS TRESAULTI

MECHANIQUE

A TALE OF THE CIRCUS TRESAULTI

GENEVIEVE VALENTINE

PRIME BOOKS

To My Family

1.

The tent is draped with strings of bare bulbs, with bits of mirror tied here and there to make it sparkle. (It doesn't look shabby until you've already paid.)

You pay your admission to a man who looks like he could knock out a steer, but it is a slight young man who hands you your ticket: printed on thick, clean paper, one corner embossed in gold ink with a griffin whose mechanical wings shine in the shivering mirrorlight.

Tresaulti, it says, and underneath, Circus Mechanique, which is even more showy than the posters. Their bulbs are bare; who do they think they are?

"Go inside, take a seat, the show is about to begin!" the young man shouts to the crowd as he hands out the tickets, his hinged brass legs creaking. Above the noise the food vendor is shouting. "Come and have a drink! Beer in glasses! Beer in glasses!"

Inside some invisible ring the circus people have drawn in the muddy hill, there are the dancing girls and the barkers and jugglers. The musical man is playing within the tent—a cranking, tinkling mess of noise from this far away. The dancing girls shimmying outside the tent doors have metal hands or feet that glitter in the lights, and calling above it all is the young man with the brass legs who had come through the city a day ago and put up the Tresaulti posters.

Inside, the tent is round and bright, dozens of bulbs hanging from the rigging. Some of them have paper lanterns over them, so the light is a little pink or a little yellow.

The trapezes are already hanging from the topmost supports, stiff brackets of brass and iron, waiting for girls to inhabit them. The poster says "Lighter than Air." The mood in the tent is, *We'll see.* Not that you're hoping for someone to fall—that would be morbid—but if you say something is lighter than air, well, the bets are on.

(These trapezes are imposters; they are for practice, they are for the beginning of the act. For the finale, the real trapezes walk out. Big George and Big Tom are lifted into place by Ayar the strongman, and they lock their seven-foot metal arms around the poles and hold themselves flat as tables. The girls scamper up and down their arms, hook their feet over Big George's feet, and dangle upside down with their arms spread out like wings. When Big George swings back and forth, the girls let go, flying, and catch Big Tom's legs on the other side.

But you do not know that this first trapeze is a false front. You have not yet been surprised.)

The tent comes alive as those who bought tickets file in; some of them have stopped at the food wagon, so the beer-smell cooks slowly under the bulbs. People talk among themselves, but carefully; the government is new (the government is always new), and you never know who's working for whom.

A drum roll announces the beginning of the show, and the tent flaps open up for the entrance of an enormous woman in a black-sequined coat. Her curly dark hair springs out over her shoulders, and she wears red lipstick that seems unnaturally bright when she stands under the pink paper lanterns.

She raises her arms, and the crowd noisily hushes itself.

"Ladies and gentlemen," she calls.

Her voice fills the air. It feels as if the tent grows to accommodate the words, the circle of benches pushing out and out, the tinny Panadrome swelling to an orchestra, the light softening and curling around the shadows, until all at once you are perched in a tiny wooden seat above a vast and a glorious stage.

The woman's arms are still thrown wide, and you realize she has not paused, that her voice alone has changed the air, and when she goes on, "Welcome to the Circus Tresaulti!" you applaud like your life depends on it, without knowing why.

2.

THE MECHANICAL CIRCUS TRESAULTI
FINEST SPECTACLE ANYWHERE
MECHANICAL MEN beyond IMAGINATION
Astounding Feats of ACROBATICS
The Finest HUMAN CURIOSITIES
the World has ever SEEN
STRONGMEN, DANCING GIRLS
& LIVING ENGINES
FLYING GIRLS, LIGHTER than AIR
MUSIC from the HUMAN ORCHESTRA
BARGAIN ENTERTAINMENT for ONE and ALL

☞ No Weapons Allowed ☜

3.

The Circus Tresaulti has six acts.

All of them are set to Panadrome's music. He is the most complicated of all Boss's machines—he is a true marvel—but one look at that human face above the mechanized band is enough for most. The music seems to seep into their blood, turning them to metal from the inside out, trapping them inside some brass barrel they can't see.

They press their hands hard to their chests until they feel their hearts beating, and they don't look at him again.

It begins with jugglers, who move into the tent from outside. They toss clubs and glasses of water and torches. For their finale, each torch falls flame-first into a glass of water, extinguished with a hiss that's lost in the applause.

The jugglers are human. You can see one with a false leg, but these days there are so many bombs and so many people to re-make; one shiny leg is no surprise.

(They could be mechanical, too, if they chose, but the three jugglers have formed a little union against it. God knows if a false arm would be fast enough to catch anything.)

The dancing girls come next. They are all muscle under their filmy skirts—once they were soldiers or factory workers, they pack and unpack as much rig as the tumblers—but the audience demands dancing girls, so they make do. Over the years they have all learned the profit in the curled hand and the cocked hip.

Their eyes are rimmed with kohl and their lips are painted purple; they uncover as much as they can of their skin (you have to cover the scars, of course). They dress in whatever spangles they can come by. Their dancing names are Sunyat and Sola, Moonlight and Minette. (Their real names don't matter; no one in the circus is real any more.)

For their finale, the strong man enters. The four of them climb onto his shoulders and his arms. They sit—legs crossed, arms raised—and he carries them off the stage as if they were no heavier than four cats.

The strongman's name is Ayar. He was strong before he joined the circus. Boss made him stronger. He never asked for more strength; he didn't want it when it was offered. He accepted only on condition—Jonah.

Jonah was injured fighting—a lung collapsed—and he had been getting worse, worse, worse, until the doctor used a bellows on him and told Ayar (who wore a different name then) to expect the end.

The Circus Tresaulti was in town. Ayar stood in the city square and stared at the picture of the Winged Man for a long time.

Then he carried Jonah out to the camp and asked the first person he saw, "Where is the man with wings?"

The boy was young, but he looked at Ayar for only a moment before he said, "You'll want Boss. Wait here."

Negotiations took an hour—a long hour, an hour Ayar remembers only in brief moments of shouting, of crying, of wanting to hit her but still holding Jonah—and then the worst was over.

When Ayar woke up, he had a new name that went with a body made of gears and pistons and a spine that could carry anything, and Jonah was standing over him, smiling, turning to show Ayar the little beetle-glossy hatch Boss had built for the mechanisms that powered Jonah's new clockwork lungs.

(Boss made Ayar stronger, but Jonah she saved.)

Ayar doesn't regret it. He is of a temperament to be liked, and of all at Tresaulti he has the least urge to complain. He struck a better bargain than some.

He lifts the dancing girls; he lifts benches from the front circle with five rubes from the audience on them. At the end of Ayar's act, Jonah drives the small red truck through the opened flaps into the center of the ring. He climbs into the bed and turns around slowly, so everyone can get a look at the brass hump sticking out of his back. Then Ayar sets himself under the flatbed and lifts the truck with Jonah still standing on it.

Ayar is supposed to call when he is ready to lift, so Jonah can prepare, but it is always Jonah who calls, as if he knows when Ayar will be ready better than Ayar will.

(It had been Jonah—when he was so ill—who said, "You will just not let this go, will you?" knowing Ayar wouldn't. Ayar got a new spine and new shoulders and new ribs, and his comrade back again.

"Your comrade," Boss had said. She looked them over and raised an eyebrow and said, "Sure, we'll call you that.")

Outside, Ayar sets down the truck, and Jonah jumps off the flatbed, smiling, and cuffs Ayar lightly on the shoulder.

"Nice lift," he says, every night.

Then it is Ayar's turn to smile, though he doesn't return the gesture. What can he do with his pile-driver arms, cuff Jonah back?

The next act is a duo. Stenos is the thin man in black who stands and offers his arms, who tosses the woman into the air, and catches her again. Bird is the woman, the one in grey, who flies. He is tall and graceful; she is like a skin-covered spring. They should be lovely to watch.

The audience does watch them—they are impossible not to watch—but what they see is rarely lovely.

MECHANIQUE: A TALE OF THE CIRCUS TRESAULTI

The light in the tent seems to change as they go on, the dark creeping up around them. To focus on them is painful; sometimes it's difficult to look at them directly, and their bodies become only impressions.

It is two acrobats performing. No, it is two acrobats dancing. No, it is two dancers fighting. No, it is two animals fighting.

After their act there is no applause.

The tumblers roll out just as the silence gets uncomfortable.

The tumblers are wild and bright, and have made their own family even within the circus troupe. They love more than anything to hear Boss call out, "The Grimaldi Brothers!" (It is only because of the Boss's voice that anyone believes the name for a moment. *Grimaldi Brothers*; as if anyone would have eight grown children in days like these.)

Their names are little jumps: Alto, Brio, Spinto, Moto, Barbaro, Focoso, Altissimo, Pizzicato.

(Boss gave them the names. She never told them what they mean; they never bothered to find out. They make a living, almost, and they would be fools to ask questions.)

The aerialists are the finale.

The girls swing from the trapeze thirty feet above the ground. When a girl lets go, the audience gasps. When she twists and manages, impossibly, to grip the outstretched arms of the girl waiting to catch her, the audience roars.

When Big Tom and Big George walk out into the ring with their arms raised, people scream; applaud with relief.

Ayar hoists both men into the air like batons, and their mechanical hands close with sharp clicks over the rigging bars. The girls have locked up the trapezes and are perched on the rigging, their weight on the balls of their feet, their hands wrapped tightly on the bars.

There are six aerialists, even though it seems like more, like ten or twelve or twenty girls leaping into thin air. Elena is the captain; Fatima and Nayah are her lieutenants, and then there are Mina and Penna and Ying. They dress in shabby spangles and paint their faces to look the same, though if you know what to look for you can make them out: the captain; the girl with the strongest feet; the girl who will be first to jump down onto Tom; the girl who trembles.

They are swift and sure, and they don't need to call warnings. After enough time, it's easy to see when a body is preparing to leap; it's easy to be ready.

By the end, Big Tom and Big George are swinging so far back and forth that a girl can hold his ankles on the upswing and just touch the upper edge of the tent. When she swings back to the center of the tent, reaches the other apex of the pendulum and lets go, there are two seconds in the air when she is weightless; the audience can feel it, and holds its breath.

They finish the act posed triumphantly: four of them wrapped around Big Tom's and Big George's arms; Ying and Mina, the smallest, hang by their knees from Tom and George's feet, upside down and smiling.

The audience is never sitting at the end of the Circus Tresaulti; it is always on its feet, whistling and pounding the boards, knocking beer glasses into the dirt. They don't notice the glasses; their eyes are on the golden lamplight, on the aerialists who shimmy down the rigging and take their bows on the ground, on the men who can only smile because their arms are still locked on the crossbars. It's magic, and the audience applauds for as long as their stinging palms can stand it. (Who knows if something beautiful will ever come again?)

Later, after all the rubes have gone home chattering at one another about how fast the tumblers are, how agile the aerialists, Little George will step out of his brass legs and collect the beer glasses, even the ones with cracked sharp edges; glass these days is hard to find.

There was a seventh act, years ago.

He was the Winged Man, and when he swooped from the rigging and spread his wings the crowd would go wild, screaming and shouting, straining in their seats to reach for him as he sailed just over their outstretched fingers. Sometimes a woman would faint. Sometimes a man would faint.

There were always tears of joy; a man so beautifully married to machine was something that people needed to see after a war like they had been through. The technology in those days was weapons and radio signals; people needed to remember the art of the machine.

He landed after the applause shook the bleachers and the rigging so hard they looked ready to collapse; the light around him was tinged gold from the feathers in his wings, and he stood in the center of the ring and let them applaud him, that most amazing specimen of man.

That was before he fell.

4.

We're the circus that survives.

Boss claims we were always around; she shows me glue-paper posters with the edges singed and flaking. The circuses are owned by a series of brothers with names I don't know, and peopled with acts I've never heard of. (I recognize *Grimaldi*, the brothers' false name.) Other than that, there's nothing much to them but worn-out pictures. I don't even know where she's found them.

Some of the circuses have an eagle mascot; some have a lion, or a flaming hoop, or an eight-point star. The emblem of Tresaulti Circus is a griffin in profile, her hinged wings outstretched. A tattoo of that crest covers the top half of each of Boss's wide, pale arms. You can see them in the ring, though the tattoos look like lace sleeves in the lantern light; you wouldn't guess if you didn't already know.

You have to really know what you're looking for, when it comes to her.

The names of the other circuses are different from ours, so I know they can't be our circus still going, but the only time I ask her about it (when I'm still young and stupid and too slow to get out of the reach of her arms), she clips me on the ear.

"The name changes, Little George," she says, "but the circus is always the same." She flicks the tattoo on her right arm as if to prove her point or wake the animal. Her nail slices her skin, and where the griffin's metal wings have been grafted, the blood pools like oil.

For a moment I'm frightened, but I don't know why. Nothing to worry about.

No one has wings like that any more; not since Alec died.

5.

This is what happens when you take a step:

Your first leg moves out from underneath you. By now your chest is already moving, your back foot ready to push.

(You will not notice, but here you are the tallest you will ever be, poised on one foot and ready for motion.)

Your first leg sweeps ahead, and your back foot powers you. Your weight is propelled forward, inertia dragging you back.

In this instant is the body-terror; here you are unbalanced, unable to rest or move back. Your arms are swinging, trying to keep the mechanism in motion. Here you are at the lowest point. Here is the danger of falling.

Your first leg hits the ground, heel first, and the worst is over. The chest is following, finding balance in this new place. Now if you lift the back foot, you keep hold of yourself. Your back leg swings to meet its brother, and you are standing still.

This is what happens when you take a step: you are moving closer to what you want.

This is what happens when an aerialist lets go of the swinging trapeze:

She swings with her legs forward and lifted, feet pressed together and toes pointed, for momentum.

By the time she lets go of the bar, her legs are already touching her chest, and she is in the pike position of a diver; she is already pulling her torso away, arcing backwards as fast as she can. Her arms are close to her chest like the folded wings of a bird, for speed.

Then her arms are straight, arms extended. Her spine is

parallel to the ground. Her eyes are fixed ahead, and her path is clear; she is the bird in flight.

But the legs are coming up behind her; gravity has hold of her, and her legs are weights dragging her down to the floor forty feet beneath her.

Here, someone catches her. (Or they don't.)

She wraps her hands around her partner's wrists, and her momentum drives the swing. Her legs snap down, under her and forward; now the power of the pendulum has hold of her, and she will swing out, her toes just brushing the fabric of the tent. She will spend a moment weightless, motionless; a state of bliss.

This is what happens when an acrobat lets go of the swinging trapeze: the bird or the ground.

6.

I don't know if it was cold or not the day Bird auditioned; I remember looking at her and going cold, but that's not the same thing.

(She had another name back then, but I don't remember it. It doesn't do to hold too tightly to the old life.)

She approached the campsite with her head high and her hands visible—no weapons. She was in a dirty coat that must have looked sharp, once.

I was on watch, but I could only stand dumbly and gawp into a face that was so spare it hardly seemed she had one, just an expanse of skin with two gleaming eyes set in it.

"I would like an audition," she said.

She said it without ego, as if I were the one who would audition her, as if I would know exactly what to do.

And I did; I got Boss.

Boss picked up a drill and came back holding it at her hip like a pistol. She carried something with her whenever someone came asking after work. "Scares the cowards off," she said, and it was true. Most people just looking for a job balk at seeing a woman with a brass elbow in her hands.

But this time it was Boss who balked. When she caught a look at Bird's face she stopped in her tracks, and for a moment I thought Boss was actually going to take a step back from her.

(Some moments are endless and terrifying, even if they turn out all right. Most moments with Bird in them are like that. This one was the first of many.)

Finally Boss said, "What do you want?"

Bird said, "I want to audition."

Another long silence before Boss said, "Inside." The griffin on her arm was trembling.

They went inside the tent. I got a "You keep busy, nosey," from Boss, so I fetched tent spikes and coils of rope and kept looking over at the closed entrance of the tent, waiting for some sound, any sound, that would tell me what was going on.

It was the first time anyone had gotten inside the tent before being in the Circus. Usually people auditioned right in the campsite, so the rest of the troupe could come and watch. You could get a feel for most people by the way the troupe took to them or not.

When they came outside, Boss looked as if she'd seen a ghost. Bird was behind her; she had chalk on her hands, and something about her expression made her hard to look at.

"We have a new aerialist," she said. "Get the girls."

I made a run for it, circling the camp in under a minute, shouting at Panadrome and Barbaro and Jonah and Fatima to get the others and bring them to the tent where Boss was waiting.

Bird stood with her arms at her sides, her palms making chalky handprints on her coat, and looked at them all as they approached. Jonah smiled at her, as usual for Jonah, but everyone else seemed to hang back as if smoke was coming off her. Panadrome seemed surprised Boss had auditioned Bird alone; he looked back and forth between them, his face clouded.

Elena, small and stretched tight as a drumhead, pushed her way to the front, frowned, and folded her arms.

"Too tall," she said. "Who could catch her?"

"She'll have hollow bones put in, like the rest," Boss said, in that voice that doesn't allow argument.

(Boss didn't look at Bird either, that whole time, and I should have known then what she had seen in the tent that frightened her, but I was young. You ignore a lot of warnings when you're young.)

Elena didn't argue, but she looked at Bird with narrowed eyes, and you could feel her setting her heart against this strange woman with the shoddy coat and the smooth, expressionless face.

"She won't last," Elena said.

Elena is a bitch, no mistake—she'll slap you as soon as look at you—and I'm the last person to think cruelty about Bird, but even the broken watch on Ayar's back tells the time twice a day, and it was Elena's turn to be right.

7.

Boss always tells the rubes that her late husband made us all.

"Oh lord," she says when they wonder about our mechanicals. She lifts her hands and trills, "I can barely oil the things, let alone!"

She doesn't say what she lets alone, and no one asks. She's wearing her long dress with the sparkling coat over it, looking like an enormous sequin. She looks like looking good is all she can manage.

I think she says it so they get the feeling we could break at any moment. It's always more exciting to watch something you know could backfire.

"We saw the last performance," they would be able to say. "We saw the final act of the Circus Tresaulti, before everything went wrong."

But there's no mistaking what she can do, not among us real folk, no matter what she tells the crowd.

(I didn't understand her. I had been with the circus too long; I felt too safe to know why it was better to make some things seem breakable and frail. I didn't know who might come looking for us, if they thought we were strong enough to take hold.)

The workshop truck is the first truck behind the passenger trailers. Boss keeps it locked, with the key around her neck. Whenever I catch a look inside it seems a useless mess, one table and some tools and some scrap in a pile in the back, but she works magic with whatever she's got. (With metal, with audiences, with us.)

All the aerialists have skeletons of hollow pipe. It's tougher than bone, and lighter, and easier to fix when it breaks. For them it's all under the skin, though—Boss wants all her girls to stay pretty.

"No man pays to look at an ugly woman," she says.

Ayar is laced with metal bands that weave inside and outside his chest like a second set of ribs, and at the shoulders are the two gears that help him lift the small truck when it's that time in his act. (It would have looked awful on a paler man, but Ayar's bronze to start with and even his eyes are sort of golden, so this looks more like him than when he was human. That happens, sometimes.)

The teeth of the wheels are visible in back, so you can see him working. His spine, though, is the draw they put on the poster. It's melted together from bits of copper and brass that Boss has found; there's a watch face in the middle. It was still going when she welded it on him.

"It'll stop on its own," she said, when he complained about it. "Don't whine. It looks just like the garbage pile."

That was his angle—she wanted him to look as if he had risen from a trash heap stronger than the men who had buried him beneath it. It was meant to inspire and to frighten—the junk-man resurrected. (Boss makes freaks, but she knows what she's doing.)

But the watch didn't stop. Jonah finally had to send a chisel through the case to turn off the ticking.

She's done something to almost everyone, except the jugglers and the dancing girls. For them it's a pretty brass glove that hinges on and off, or a filigree plate strapped onto the skull—something to titillate, not something that stays.

(I think the filigree plates are a mean joke, because of Bird, but nobody asks me anything.)

And there's Panadrome, whom nobody but Boss looks in the eye. Poor soul. He makes such pretty music that you'd think he'd be better liked. Though even here there's the hierarchy—there always has to be one, it's how you know who you're better than—and Panadrome is last, because there's hardly any man left of him. He's just a one-man band with a soul attached.

The brass-man angle gets us the crowds, though, I can't deny it. Whenever I walk through what passes for a city these days and slap a poster on some bombed-out wall or other, people sneak out from behind their bolted doors just to get a look edgewise.

They're nice posters, in the style of the old ones she's shown me, huge and glossy and bright—a holdover from the days before the war. Boss got them printed up in New Respite, where the printer could still use colors, so the posters have little flourishes of green and gold.

It takes ten seconds for me to get the paste over it to where it will stick, but that's always plenty of time.

"Mechanical men," someone whispers, every time the poster goes up. They're not impossible to find—here and there you see someone who's been patched up with wires and cogs—but that's a homemade business. Looking at me makes them all think there must be some artistry in that circus.

They glance at my legs, ask how much the show is, make plans to leave their weapons at home.

My brasses aren't real, just leg casings with seams up the sides and a gear at the knee that draws blood, but brass brings the crowds, every time.

The poster has a fancy frame drawn around the announcement, studded with little illustrations of our acts. It's genius advertising, except when people ask me about Alec, and I have to tell them he's gone.

(I asked Boss if she didn't want to cut him off the poster. "They'll forget about him by the time they see the circus," she said. Maybe he's the real emblem of Tresaulti now, and I'm just the last to know.)

Ayar is in the top left corner, drawn with his back turned, looking over his shoulder at his spine. The watch is there, frozen at a quarter to six. Under his picture: FEATS OF STRENGTH.

Top right is a cameo of the aerialists wrapped around each arm of the trapeze, one hooked onto each bar. (Big Tom and Big George aren't there; they stay a surprise.) THE FLYING SPRITES, it reads, which is fine as names go, so long as you don't know them.

Top center is Alec, wings out, grinning like he knew what the score was; he was invincible. THE WINGED MAN.

The tumblers are left side (THE GRIMALDI BROTHERS), eight of them piled on top of each other, scrambling to get into the drawing and not be chopped out by the frame.

Panadrome is on the right side. His brass barrel chest is ringed with piano keys and valves; he holds the accordion bellows straight out with one arm, tucks a ratty top hat under his elbow with the other. He's got a dignified expression. I always wonder if he was a businessman before, or if that's just how you have to look when you're more metal than man.

The jugglers don't have a place on the poster. Boss has never bothered to name their act; they come in and out so much there's no point in marking them down.

Jonah is bottom center, his pose matching Ayar's; his brass hunch is hinged open, so the printmaker could sketch the cogs and gears and pistons that keep his lungs going. THE MECHANICAL MAN, it says.

Bottom left is a trio of the dancing girls, the ones wearing the brass skull plates and the metal gloves and hardly a thing else. EXOTIC DANCING GIRLS, the poster says, though it's only exotic because they've had to make it all up as they went along, so it's foreign stuff even to them. They laugh about it during load-out—each of those girls hauling her own weight in timber. (None of those girls lasted long, and the printmaker seemed to know it; their faces are vague sketches, nothing to hold on to.)

Stenos and Bird are on the bottom right like an afterthought. You can hardly see their faces, because the scale has to accommodate their pose: he's holding her aloft with one arm, her hands wrapped tight around his hand, her legs with their pointed feet stretched impossibly apart—one along her spine, one pointing out like a weather vane.

Underneath them it says, FEATS OF BALANCE, and oh, it's a lie, it's a lie.

8.

The Circus Tresaulti travels a wide circuit. These days there aren't the sort of borders there used to be, so anyone with the courage and the means can cross from ocean to ocean.

It's decades before they return to a city, where a new generation will come and watch the circus and roll their eyes at anyone who says that it's the same, it's just the same.

(Most people don't live long enough to see the circus twice. These are ragged days.)

9.

The war brought the world to a halt.

There were the bombs and the radiation that cleared out whole cities, but that passed. What was worse were the little wars that drove everyone back behind the makeshift walls of sudden city-states, too locked in stalemates to step outside, to step forward.

But the government man has, at last, managed to create a city that functions (a long time coming, he thinks whenever he looks out on the market in the town square, the only legitimate market he can remember). He knows the roads are open and the world is wide; now he can start to stretch out his fingers over the landscape, along the roads, just to test his reach.

It's slow and careful going. Too fast and you falter, he knows; he saw it in his predecessor, just before he came to power.

He knows, however, that he can succeed at last. He has lived long enough to take the measure of this world; this world hungers for any man of vision who can drag it up out of the mud.

The government man is on his way back from a city in the east, in the back of his black car newly painted with his crest, when he sees it.

The government man has the car pull over. He gets out and picks his way over the last of the debris into the city; he studies one of the posters plastered to a crumbling concrete wall that might have been part of a building, once.

It's tinted in rich greens and black and cream (he could see it from the road, he knew at once what it was), and he looks at it for a long time, peering at the faces inside the cameos. He frowns and taps the bottom corner of the poster absently; then he's back in the car, and the driver is pulling back onto the dirt road.

(The government man has plans to fix what's left of the pavement, when he has enough reach to hold out his hands and touch the ocean on either side.)

The paste on the poster still smells, so he knows they can't be far away. There are two cities between them, maybe. Maybe three.

The government man's heart races, and he rests an open hand on the empty seat beside him, like he needs the balance.

The duo acrobats are new, he thinks. He doesn't remember them from the first time; he looks forward to a pleasant surprise, when he sees the circus again.

10.

Stenos was a thief when Boss found him.

You'd think he was too tall to be a thief—he stood a head taller than Boss, and she's almost six foot—but he was skinny for a guy with broad shoulders. Usually by the time they get that tall they look like Ayar, with muscles like bricks, but not Stenos. He looked just like anybody, right up until he jumped five feet in the air to catch some edge on a wall that looked perfectly smooth.

Boss had caught him trying to sneak wallets from the rubes during the aerialists, just as people were standing up to applaud, so they wouldn't notice until they sat down that something was gone.

She disappeared into the workshop with him, and we all stood around like a pile of idiots. I stood around mostly because I was afraid Stenos would never come out again and I'd have to carry the body out.

Boss doesn't allow stealing, not from anyone.

We barter for tickets—we take blankets and oil and sides of meat we can't identify, shoes and coins and peaches so hard you crack them on the trailers—but we never take more than a show is worth, and we never lift anything from the rubes once they're in their seats.

Whenever anyone asks why, Boss says, "It's good business. I want to come back here someday."

She took Stenos into the workshop, and when they came out they pretended she had blackmailed him.

"It was the circus or prison for me," he said, and Boss walked him around the camp introducing him, saying, "Look what I've caught us."

But one look at him and everybody knew he joined up because it was better than sneaking around under bleachers and hoping that desperate people had anything worth taking. He looked well and truly worn out the day he fell in with us. He would have died in another year of working alone.

That first night he shook my hand as he passed.

"Stenos," he said after a beat, like he wasn't used to giving the name.

(I don't know what his name was before he came to us. Maybe it really is Stenos; mine's really George. Maybe each of us has been wearing their real name all this time, with nobody else knowing. Wouldn't that just be the way?)

"George," I said. "I'm a barker."

"Acrobat," he said. "Someday. I suppose."

I laughed. "Me too, someday, I suppose."

He looked me up and down, and then he let go of my hand as he said, "You'll do well if you try."

I didn't know what that meant, and I didn't feel like asking. I made myself scarce so as not to give him any more passes at me. I gave him a week until he was screwing Elena. Mean finds mean.

On his way to the trucks he passed Bird, who was dressed for her night's training on the trapeze. Stenos and Bird both slowed down as they passed, looked one another over, and shrank back like a pair of fighting snakes; they passed on without any other sign of recognition.

(I should have known what it looks like when people are fighting over something precious; that, for sure, I should have known.)

The year Stenos joined up, I got permission from Boss to try out for the trapeze after the girls had finished practice.

"Sure," Elena said when I told her. She was sitting on the trapeze like a girl on a swing, feet curved like a pair of sickles.

Maybe they were frozen that way after so many years. Maybe it hurt her to walk flat-footed on the ground.

She passed back and forth overhead a few times, lazily; she was on the trapeze just for fun.

"What do you want me to do?"

She shrugged and pointed. "You take that one, I'll take this. Jump, and I'll catch you."

She was grinning, and I shivered.

After a long time I said, "Maybe I'll just stick to tumbling," and she swung back and forth above me, laughed like a handful of nails.

Some people think Bird fell. I never have.

Stenos didn't talk much. He carried lumber and strung up canvas and kept to himself. He didn't drink, he didn't smoke, he never sat with us in the tumblers' trailer—he was as bad as Bird for keeping away from the rest of us. (Even Elena sat at the night fire, for God's sake, and if she was on fire none of us would piss on her to put out the flames.)

He wasn't my idea of a friend. He seemed to be waiting for something better all the time.

(I feared he'd take my place in the tumblers and leave me out in the cold; it was my biggest worry, then.

You don't see as far as you should.)

I should have paid more attention; Alec fell when I was very young, but you'd think something like that would give you a sense of who was out of their mind.

But I was still young, and Fatima was so lovely in the firelight when she smiled, and the tumblers told me they'd give me a name of my own someday, and what did I know that I was a fool?

How was I to know he had seen the wings?

11.

This is what the wings are like:

They arch just over the wearer's head when they are closed; they brush the calves of a tall man. When they are open, they are wider than a man is tall, the primary feathers half again as long as an arm; the tops of the arches nearly meet.

Of all the mechanical pieces in the Circus Tresaulti, Boss has taken these into her heart. Here there is no iron cage, no grinding supports. The ribs of these wings are made of bone. (The dead don't need them any more, and what should she do, let them go to waste?)

She has wrapped them in brass so they shine, and so that no one thinks too long about what makes these wings seem so warm, so real.

Each feather is jigsawed and hammered and smoothed so thin that when it strikes another feather it rings out a clear note. She has constructed them so that, when the wind passes over them, it rings out a triumphant G major seventh. (She knows the chord by heart. She had a life before the drill and the saw; she was the first of them to leave her name behind.)

The gears are small-toothed, and the edges burned with a smoky pattern that looks like the shadow of leaves. (She thought, a long time ago, about adding jewels to look like water drops, but Alec laughed and said, "They're flashy enough already, don't you think?" and shook himself like a bathing bird until their bedroom filled with the sweet, clear notes.)

Though they have knobs of gears that attach to the shoulders, though it takes hours to set the joints so the nerves and muscles can move them, everyone sees the wings are not really a machine. They are art; they are skill; they are proof that the world has not abandoned beauty.

Alec was handsome, and had the air of a man who knew he was destined for great things. As soon as Boss saw him she knew what a find she had come across. When Alec was alone in the tent, she approached him and spoke, which is all it has ever taken for her to draw someone in.

Not that any of the rest of them would know it; most of them came looking for her. Alec was the first one of them she ever chose. (The only one, until Stenos, lifetimes later.)

It was for Alec she made the wings.

It was the only gift she ever gave him; it was the only gift she has ever given to someone without a new name attached, the only gift she's ever given without killing someone first.

With the wings on he was more than whole, and felt it. He dropped from the ceiling and basked in the applause, in the wondering gazes, in the sharp intake of breath when people saw what he was.

He was magnificent. Until.

When Boss ran out from behind the curtain and saw the mess that had been Alec, the wings were bent from the impact, and it looked as though he had tried to cover his face, as if he were shy; as if he no longer wanted to be seen.

Boss does not know when that change happened in him. She was not looking at him when she might have seen it; she assumed he would be happy to be perfect.

In the warehouse, after they had carried the body out, she closed the wings, locking the joints, lacing tight the ribs to hide the copper petals as much as she could.

They are almost the same as any other bundle of pipes and scrap in her workshop. Half a dozen performers have joined the circus since; none of them has given the wings a second glance.

But if you are as single-minded as Bird, or as hungry for glory as Stenos, then you see them.

If you are like them, then when you enter the workshop there is no pile of scrap, no steel table wiped almost clean of blood. There is no terrifying rack of drills and ratchets, no coils of cord to lash your bones back in place. There is no Boss to inflict her will on you, to build you up and wake you with a new name and a body she knows will look good at the center of the stage.

For you, the world narrows to a single point as you step inside the workshop. (This is what happens when you take a step; you are moving closer to something you want.)

For you, the workshop is only the roof that has been pitched over your waiting wings.

12.

The knife thrower was a soldier in the last great war.

"Unofficially," he says, which sounds like he was a resistance fighter, but truly means he was on the wrong side when the dust settled and the other government was in place.

He has an answer ready, though, when people ask him where he learned to throw. "There were lot of rats in my neighborhood," he will say, and laugh.

His assistant's name is Sarah (he thinks; she changes it a lot). She hardly speaks—she's a little simple—but she's thin enough that it's almost impossible to actually strike her with a knife no matter where on the wheel you aim, so he pays her enough from his takings to keep her around. His knives get awfully close to the skin, sometimes; he doesn't want to imagine what might happen if his next assistant is tubby.

The Circus Tresaulti is camped two miles outside town the day he decides to audition, so he loads the wheel and Sarah in the truck, and drives out into the hills until he reaches the camp.

The camp is a half-circle of two dozen vehicles fanned out behind the tent, vans and trailers and painted wagons lashed down to truck beds. He unloads the wheel carefully—paint is hard to come by if something chips—and Sarah, and pops on the top hat he's managed to protect from two wars since his soldiering days (the hat collapses, so he can strap it to his back and carry it anywhere). By the time he has the hat on and Sarah is all strapped in, the circus folk have made a little audience around the wheel.

He starts with the patter; he doesn't believe in wasting time.

"Ladies and gentleman," he calls out, "prepare to enjoy a feat of death-defying dexterity!"

"We've all enjoyed them," says the brass-covered hunchback, and the strongman says, "You can tell because we're not dead yet."

There's a ripple of laughter among the watching crowd that the knife thrower does not like.

"For the owner of the Circus Tresaulti, I will give my finest performance," he goes on (no use wasting all his rehearsal). He gives the crowd a quick scan; he sees the tall, slender man who looks like a leader and nods curtly. The man raises an eyebrow, half-smiles, nods back.

The knife thrower clears his throat and throws five knives, one by one, near Sarah. It's child's play for him; it's just a chance for him to make sure the blades are balanced. The first round can go on for ages if the crowd claps after every knife, but this group is just staring at him, so he gets it out of the way.

After the first round he collects the blades from the board, spins the wheel, and walks five paces. Then the knives fly from his hands all at once, thunkthunkthunkthunkthunk into the wood. The last knife slices through the end of Sarah's ponytail and pins the lock of hair to the board.

Silence greets the big finish, and the knife thrower looks at the tall owner and squints, not understanding.

After what seems like an hour of quiet, a fat woman emerges from the crowd like a puddle of oil. She walks past the knife thrower without looking at him, straight to the board.

"You want a job?" she asks.

Sarah nods.

The woman waves her hand as she turns to go, and a boy jogs forward and starts to undo the straps.

The knife thrower warned people off the Circus Tresaulti every night of the run. "A pile of thieves," he said. "They took my assistant! They're a den of tricksters!"

It didn't stop anyone from going. The knife thrower knew because he bought a ticket every night—you have to check out the competition—and the tent was always full.

People have no loyalty; that's what it is. That's the real pity.

13.

When Bird came to Tresaulti, there was nothing wrong with her.

"Well, not to look at," Boss says when anyone mentions it, just to let everyone know something must have been wrong elsewhere. Her spine, they guess. Her innards. Maybe her bones were rotting out.

It must be something, because Boss says she doesn't like to put metal into those who are perfectly good. She's refused me a dozen times.

("You just put on your brasses and shut up," she says, every time I even open my mouth to ask.

Once I say, "Bird wasn't broken, but you did her!"

"The ones I fix were all broken," she says, and waves her hand. The griffin on her arm flaps its wings.)

I think Bird must have been mad, and that's why Boss did it. You'd have to be mad, to ask.

I think Stenos must be mad now. You'd have to be mad, to keep her.

Bird let Boss put hollow bones in, like the rest of them, and she trained alone at night to learn the routine; she did the flips close to the ground, the strength work on the bars to get used to the height, swinging back and forth on the trapeze with her feet pointed out, for hours after the shows were over.

She lasted a few years with them, letting go and spinning, snapping out her arms for the catch, bringing her knees to her chest to be swung up to the rigging. She was elegant, powerful, powder-handed, and weightless. For her, it was the bird and the bird and the bird.

Then it was the ground.

Ying slid down the rigging to go warn Boss what had happened, but the act went ahead without her—Boss's orders are that the act goes ahead, no matter what.

("What," she said, "war without end, and one more body will worry them?")

Only after the act had finished and the tent was empty did Boss take Stenos to go scoop Bird up from the sawdust and bring her out of the lantern light to the workshop to see what could be done.

(It was a good thing about the bones, after all; Boss was able to put her back together, unbending what was mangled, putting in new pipes where they were needed. Now Bird's got a thin iron plate over the skin of her left temple, and a glass eye, but it could have been worse. She could have been Alec.)

Sometime after Boss had fixed Bird, while she was still asleep, Boss must have had enough of worrying about people falling. Or she was angry at Stenos about something; there's never any knowing, with Boss.

Boss hauled Bird onto her shoulders, banged her way outside the workshop, marched across the yard where we were loading out, and dropped her right in front of Stenos.

He had to crouch and shove his arms out flat to catch Bird before she hit the ground. He was so tall and carried her so easily that, knocked out in his arms, she looked like a roll of leftover canvas.

Stenos looked at Boss like Boss had lost her mind.

"The problem's yours now," Boss said, with the air of someone delivering a punishment. "Your duo act goes live in the next city."

Boss disappeared into the maze of the camp, lost among the little pools of lantern light.

Stenos looked down at the sleeping woman in his arms, his gaze unblinking. After a long time, he curled his fingers inwards, holding her tighter.

I left him alone. There's no talking to some people.

But my skin was crawling the whole time I walked away, and at the edge of the camp by the feed truck I stopped and looked back.

I wondered if they had ever spoken. I remembered their meeting, when they had recoiled from one another, but since then they hadn't exchanged so much as an angry look.

I thought Boss had gone mad in putting them together. It wasn't right, the two of them. I could feel it in the air just looking at them, like winter had suddenly come, like we had fallen into some shadow and nothing would be the same again.

Even Ayar's back tells the right time twice a day, and it was my turn to be right.

14.

The women start calling her Bird while she's still on the ground, before they even know how badly she landed.

(Before this she had another name, but she wore it like a bad suit, and as soon as the words are uttered, the old name dies.)

"Poor bird," one of them says (Elena), and one of them laughs (Penna), and one of them is biting back a scream (Mina), and one of them is running for Boss.

The one who runs is Ying; she moves so fast that she scrapes the skin off her palms sliding down the tent pole. She performs in bandages for two weeks after.

Bird has never thanked her. No point; it would only make Ying somebody's enemy.

"She fell," Ying calls, which is a lie.

Bird wants to give over—it's easier, surely, just to die—but she can't. Her eyes are nothing but blood, and she feels sick, presses her face to the dirt, but her lungs are pushing in and out, sucking up blood and dust and whatever air is left.

Around her, muted, people are applauding. The tent goes dark.

When everything is quiet again, someone picks her up; she feels strong hands shaking under her. She thinks, *Soon it will all be over.*

(But she knows better; Boss told her what would happen when she gave her the bones, and so Bird knows this is not the end. She must wait, and bear it. Someone is holding her.)

In the workshop, Boss's hands pass over her body. She feels the motion (it's pain, it's all pain, the air is beating against her), but doesn't move. One eye is gone; she doesn't want to open the other. Best not to move. Best just to die.

(She can't die; she fights; she pulls breath through the holes in her copper ribs.)

"I should have known better," says Boss, like an apology. "Elena can tell about this kind of thing."

Her throat is too full of blood to answer. The pain is like a brand.

Boss says, "Stop fighting it," and there is the ring of a hammer on copper, then nothing.

Bird doesn't wake up until the next night, and knows from Panadrome's waltzes that the show is happening without her. She sits on top of one of the lighting crates, her legs folded under her, and listens to the rubes shouting and stamping until the ground shakes.

After the show, Little George tells her that Elena performed with a black eye.

"It was Boss's present to Elena for letting you fall," he says, making fists at his sides and rocking on his heels. His metal casts creak. "She slapped Elena right in the face."

The other one says, "Some people have all the fun."

His name is Stenos; Stenos whom she has never believed about anything. But he was holding her when she woke up, carrying her through the camp like a dangerous animal that had been found asleep.

Now he is sitting beside her, on her left side; she cannot see him. The heat of his leg bleeds through her skin, warms the metal in her left hand where she grips the edge of the crate.

(The wings. He is after the wings.)

They have managed, so far, never to speak to one another. But now she does not try to break away from him. She lets the heat of his skin fan out through her hand, soak into her wrist. She leaves her hand where it is.

You must live in the place that has been carved for you; this much, now, she understands.

You must live in the wagons with the aerialist girls and their slippery hands. You must sleep in an upper bunk with your face close enough to the roof that the rain leaks onto your neck, with Elena lying across the narrow aisle, sleeping the sleep of the just.

You must live in the crook of the man's arm when you walk through the towns, giving the illusion that you are a pair; when you are not ready to jump and he is gathering the strength to throw you; when you are tired from practice and cannot walk.

You must live on the ground.

Now, she is Bird. If she remembers some other name, she wouldn't think to answer to it.

She must live with the name that has been carved for her, because of the fall; because of the height of her twists and leaps; because of the wide, bright eye that never closes.

15.

Everyone paints up. Boss believes in a real show.

The aerialists are pink and brown and gold, and Boss makes them paint up all alike—round white faces like a set of dolls, thick black lines along the eyelids, gold shadow from the brow to the cheek and all the way out to their pulled-back hair. Their mouths are plastered white, so if their lips tremble no one can tell.

Tumblers get red for their mouths, to match their jackets, and black pencil for their eyes. It gets frightening as the act goes on and the sweat leaves streaks of grey and red over their faces, but Boss doesn't mind if they look scary, I guess.

Ayar and Jonah don't get anything except a little kohl. ("No one's looking at your faces," says Boss, pushing her work goggles back into the frizz of her hairline and looking at one or the other. "What would you two do with a clown's face? Hopeless, both of you. Now come in here, Ayar, your right shoulder is bent.")

Bird makes up, too. Somehow she found silver shadow the same color as the iron plate, and she makes wide gunmetal smears over her eyelids and her good temple, staring defiantly into the trailer mirror, like she's doing something she's not supposed to.

Stenos doesn't wear anything but the kohl, not on his own. Sometimes Bird will turn from her seat at the big mirror and find where he's standing (he's within arm's reach of her before a show, always), and she'll look him right in the eye and draw one finger over his brow, or across his mouth, and leave a trail of grey on his skin.

Stenos always looks upset afterwards, though you'd think he'd just tell her not to do that if he hates it so much. But he must be a glutton for punishment, because he's there every night in his black costume, standing quietly just behind her, accepting whatever she gives.

(Sometimes she holds out her hand like she wants to make him up, and when he leans in she takes hold of his throat and looks him in the eye like she's settling some private fight. He never fights back—never even pulls away—and every time she holds out her hand he leans forward, no matter what. He performs some nights with a silver neck. I try not to look at them.)

Bird's the only one in the place who looks better made up. When she's barefaced it just draws attention to where she's been mended. It's better when the paint is on, and you can take in her face like something she's had done on purpose—I don't know why Boss made the face plate iron. It just reminds the others what happened to her, and Bird doesn't need any favors when it comes to being cast out.

It's best if you glance at her all made up and just let her gaze go. No point in looking deeper; if you look past the greasepaint at her left eye, you'll get nothing back; it's all glass.

She's gone cold mad over the years. The wind blows right through Bird.

She scared even the government man, when he came to take Boss away—for all the good it did her.

16.

After the posters went up in a city, we waited a day for people to make up their minds. In the meantime, we set up the tent, dropped beer barrels in the nearest cold water, and made the dancing girls run a lot of errands.

They suited up in their shirts and spangles, draped themselves in scarves, snapped their metal casts over their hands. (Sunyat's metal foot was shaped too pointed to walk on. She wore long skirts in the city, so no one would be suspicious when her feet came flashing into the ring.)

"Right," said Moonlight to me as they headed out of camp. "Anything you need, little man?"

They were carrying coils of rope and a sack of rice, and some wiring Boss had decided she didn't need. They'd barter in the city; drum up a little excitement by looking mysterious.

I grinned. "Anything more valuable than what you pay for it."

She laughed and swiped idly at me, and the four of them smiled all the way down the hill toward the city.

Boss never went into the city herself until the parade (she thought it looked common), and she wouldn't let me go except to put up the poster ("You'll go into the city and wind up your mouth and the next thing we know we'll be in for it," she said, every time I asked).

She was in the workshop, fixing something on Panadrome. They stopped talking when I knocked, and there was a little pause before she opened the door.

"They've gone to the city," I said. "Should we send the brothers?"

A pair of Grimaldis sometimes followed the dancing girls. They were stronger than the crew, and faster, if it came to it.

"No," Boss said, looking out towards the city. (Maybe she could see the dancing girls; with Boss, you could never tell.) "What did you think of it?"

"Not bad," I said. Sometimes we set up outside cities that were little more than rubble and tents, but here the dirt paths were clean, and there had been only one soldier guarding the open square where I pasted the poster.

Boss nodded. "Let's hope they don't tear anyone apart for looking at them sideways, and leave it at that."

Panadrome said, "I don't like it."

"You don't like anything," Boss said as she closed the door, and then it was just the muffled sounds of the two of them arguing it back and forth.

When the dancing girls came back, they weren't smiling any more, and Sunyat went right to Boss's trailer.

"What happened?" I asked, but Moonlight only shook her head and handed me a burlap bag of slightly rotten fruit.

By the time I got back from Joe at the food wagon, the crew was taking down the tent poles, rolling up the canvas for Ayar to throw into the trucks, and Boss was standing outside her trailer talking with Elena. Elena had her arms crossed over her chest, and once or twice she cast dark glances over her shoulder, down to the city.

I hung back until Elena was gone, and went inside.

"What's happened?"

"We're going," Boss said, "don't you have eyes?"

"Did something happen in the city?"

Boss looked into her mirror, then sighed as if she'd lost an argument and said, "Someone was asking about us."

I wanted to laugh, but something about the way she said it made me nervous, so I shut my mouth and waited.

But Boss only said, "Make sure we all go on to the next city. No crew stay behind this time."

I frowned. "Fuck, who was asking about us?"

"Probably no one," Boss said. "And watch your mouth."

I caught Minette outside the dancers' trailer just as the engines were starting.

"I heard about what happened," I said (half the truth will get you everywhere). "Are you all right?"

She shrugged. "I still don't think it was a government man; some people are nosey, is all." She shot me a smile that was meant to reassure, and I closed the door and ran to give the driver the Go signal.

I took that leg of the trip in the trailer with the Grimaldis. I didn't know what to make of it yet, and I was afraid Boss would find me out if she saw me. She had a way of guessing what your game was just by glancing at you.

(I didn't believe anything else terrible could ever really happen to us after Alec died; you think strange things, sometimes.)

17.

Every performer in the Circus Tresaulti has a costume. The show must deliver real showmanship even in hard times; mechanical people are never as marvelous as mechanical people in suits.

Ayar and Jonah wear dark pants and high leather soldiers' boots, and nothing else. Their costumes are their bodies; their adornments are the brass hump and the gleaming ribs, the clockwork lungs and the spine.

The tumblers dress in red pants and jackets. (Spinto and Altissimo look sick in theirs—too blond to fight the color.) Boss has had the jackets lined in yellow; when they jump or cartwheel, the tails fly out and up, and the tumblers look like little flames.

The jugglers wear green and grey and red and blue in parti-color, so their arms are a blur of color as they throw and catch. These costumes are easy to maintain. You can make them with scraps; you can make them up for anyone out of whatever you find.

The girls on the trapeze wear blue—grey-blue for Elena, ice-blue for Nayah to set off her dark skin, navy for Ying ("You look young enough without wearing a girl's blue," said Elena). Each girl has made her own, fighting for the personality the greasepaint takes away. Sometimes they wear white stockings, the feet cut off for movement; when times are lean, they powder their legs white instead.

Bird wears a dove-grey tunic laced tighter than a mummy, and cast-off stockings from the girls on the trapeze. ("It doesn't matter about the tears," said Boss when she handed them over, before Bird could protest. "They won't clap no matter what you wear, so we might as well save the money.")

Sometimes in the summer she ties strips of canvas to her feet, so Stenos can hold her without slipping.

Stenos wears plain black, head to toe. Against the pale floor he stands out more than she does; he tosses and catches her in sharp silhouette, and she hovers above him like a ghost.

Alec wore plain canvas pants; not that anyone ever noticed them.

18.

I'll never understand how there could have been a fall for Alec.

He had wings.

He came in at the grand finale. He swooped from the rigging where no one was watching, hovered in place for as long as the applause lasted. Every night, Alec flew from the ceiling. Every time I saw it—every time I even heard it from the yard, his feathers singing inside the tent—I stopped breathing.

When he fell, I saw it.

I had fought for a space in the front of the crowd, and even as I watched him plummeting I couldn't believe it. I waited for him to open his wings long after he had been flattened.

The girls were up on the bars when it happened. In those days they crawled up Big Tom and Big George at the end of their act, and each girl threw one arm out to frame his descent for the big finish, and they were all poised with their flourishes when he slid off the bar, wings closed, and dropped.

Elena saw it happening a moment earlier than anyone else— she twisted and jumped for him in a single motion. She didn't reach him in time, and if Big Tom hadn't caught her feet with his feet there would have been two corpses.

(Why she helped him, I didn't know. She'd never moved a toe for any of the rest of us.)

Ying scrambled down the rigging so fast that it looked to me like she and Alec hit the ground at the same time. Ayar was already running inside from the yard; the crowd, realizing something was wrong, was already on its feet, trying to get a better look at who had died. A few screams floated through the tent like in a bad dream.

Now, everyone says it must have been loud—"A panic," Ayar

would say later, shaking his head, and if the aerialists ever talk about it they say the noise was deafening.

That's not what I remember, though I don't know if it's just because time has made some sounds fade and some sounds clearer. Who knows what it was really like. People can remember anything.

I only remember the notes his wings made as the feathers scraped against one another when he crashed, as they sliced through the dust and pierced the ground.

Ayar carried him out of the tent, and Ying and I ran out with him, past the dancing girls and out into the yard where Boss was already waiting.

Jonah was still near the flatbed truck, and he opened the back gate so Ayar could lay Alec's body out.

We crowded the back of the truck. By then Elena was outside also, her face flickering into view from between people's elbows as she cut through the crowd and hoisted herself up onto the truck bed fence with one hand. Someone had unhooked Big George from his long arms, and he was there with bare shoulders, resting against the side of the truck for balance. He looked like he had just been sick. (They found Big Tom long after the show, still hanging on the rigging, too stunned to move.)

The crowd parted for Boss, and she approached the truck and looked down at the body.

"What can we do?" Big George asked.

"Go finish," Boss said.

Elena turned to her. "What?"

Boss snapped, "Go finish the act and bow. They're turning into a bunch of cattle in there."

"We have to do something," Ying croaked. "Alec is dead. He's dead! You have to fix him, he died in front of everyone, they're frightened!"

Elena's only protest was, "We've been out here too long. Can't go back in now. We'll look like fools."

"If someone falls in the middle of the act," Boss said, "then you point at them like they intended it and you finish. Nobody wants to see you fail a man. Anyone can fail a man. They pay money to see us do things they can't."

(Later Ying would cry in the trailer and ask, "How could she be so cruel? About Alec, it's not right," and fall apart into tears so loud I could hear her outside.)

"They won't swallow that," I said. "They saw him falling."

She looked at me with hard little eyes. When she folded her arms, the griffin tattoos on her shoulders stretched their wings.

"If the girls had finished, they would have." She looked at us as if we were unruly kids. "Rubes don't want the real. Deliver the illusion, and they'll clap."

After what seemed like a long time, Elena turned for the tent, and one by one the other aerialists followed, and even Big George.

Finally, when I couldn't take the quiet any more, I asked, "What do we do?"

"Take him to the workshop," she said. "I'll do it."

From the tent came the beginnings of applause.

19.

For them it is not, "When Alec fell."

For anyone who sees it, a moment like that is never in the past; it is always happening, just out of your sight. Behind Elena's eyes and Little George's eyes, Alec is always falling.

When Ying jumps from Big George to Tom, flying under the center of the tent roof, she knows when she passes the spot where Alec fell, the awareness slicing through her like a blade.

When Bird falls, Alec is falling.

When the acrobats or the aerialists do any trick that frightens the audience into holding its breath, Alec is falling, and their ears fill with the sound of his feathers singing.

20.

This is what no one knows about Alec:

Boss could have saved him.

She can replace a skeleton without harming the soul inside. She could have fashioned him a clockwork heart. She had done the same for Jonah.

It was harder not to save him. When she stepped into the workshop, a little of his smoke crept into her lungs (a breath she has never really let out again), and when she touched him she had to fight not to breathe it back into him and wake him. It was not a problem of skill.

If Alec had fallen, he had wanted to fall.

So when she was alone in the workshop with him, she unscrewed the shoulder joints from his tanned smooth back. She wiped the wings clean of blood, and she folded up the copper petals and lashed tight the bone-and-plate ribs, and when she had cleaned up the damage from the fall, Boss called for Ayar and Jonah.

"We have to bury him," she said, wiping the oil off her hands.

There's no telling what happens within someone after so long, but she remembers the bright, wild look in his eye every night just before he stepped off the rigging. She remembers sleeping beside him at night. He never settled down, even in sleep; whenever she touched his hands (twitching like a bird's claws as he dreamed) she got an electric shock just from being so close to him, just because of what he was.

(He slept with his face mashed flat into the pillow, snoring gently, his wings folded tight along his back like a resting dove. This is what no one knows about Alec.)

This is why Boss recognizes Bird when she sees her. This is why it feels as if Boss has been expecting her; the dread is replaced by the knowledge that this is the other shoe that has dropped at last.

"I saw your poster," Bird says. "I want wings."

Boss says, "Well, don't stand there jawing. Show me something."

The hair on her neck is standing up. She waits by the tent flaps, and does not come any closer to Bird.

Bird goes through the motions, bends and flips and turns with all the adequacy of any other nimble soldier, but she betrays herself; every time she holds out her arms Boss recognizes the spread of those hands, the arch of her fingers, the tilt of her head, the half-closed eyes. She's another of Alec's kind.

"Earning wings takes time," says Boss, later, and crosses her arms over her chest as if it's gotten cold. "I'll give you the bones made of pipe. You can do the trapeze, if they'll have you."

There is a long silence.

"And the wings?"

Knowing it's a lie, Boss says, "We'll see."

Even then Bird does not agree; she just follows Boss to the workshop, steps inside without making a sound.

This is what no one knows: all the while Bird's bones slide in, Boss's fingers tremble.

21.

The government man followed us.

It took him nearly a week; by the time we saw the black sedans coming the tent was already staked, and there was no way to avoid them.

"Set up," Boss said when she saw them coming, and we scrambled.

By the time the two black cars had pulled up to the camp and the government men slid out of the back seats, everyone was ready. Ayar and Jonah were standing with the crew men, in shirts and too-big jackets. Panadrome was locked inside one of the trailers. The dancing girls were out in force, the aerialists behind. The jugglers were practicing (100% human act, just in case).

Boss stood a little behind the first ring of performers, a little in front of me.

(The crest on the car doors was an orange lion; it faced forward, and from where I was standing it seemed to be rearing back from her griffins; recoiling, or preparing for a fight. I didn't move. I knew a bad sign when I saw one.)

Four of the five men stopped at the nose of the first car. The fifth man, in a suit that matched his grey hair, kept walking towards us, and even though the whole camp was assembled, some fifty strong, he walked straight for Boss like she was all alone.

"Lovely circus," he said.

Boss said, "Nice car. It must be hard to manage."

"It's worth it," he said, "so I can get to know my country."

Boss smiled thinly. Her griffins were trembling.

"I'm fond of the circus," said the government man.

His eyes were almost as pale as Bird's glass one, and it was hard to look directly at him.

He examined Boss, his gaze drifting up and down. "I'm glad I saw the poster," he said. "I haven't been to anything as grand as your circus since I saw you back when I was a boy."

He had to be sixty years old. There was no way he could have seen us when he was young. Elena had been here ages, and even she couldn't be over thirty. I'd been here since I was five, and I was a young man still. The Circus Tresaulti couldn't be half as old as the government man was. He was mad.

Boss said, "You flatter me."

He smiles. "I don't think I do," he said.

(This is no regular government fool, I realized, going cold. This is a man who knows something.)

Boss waited him out.

Finally he said, "You're right. Forgive me; I should never ask a woman's age. We're not barbarians yet, are we?"

"I hope not," she said. "For my own sake."

He laughed, and I shivered.

"I've half a mind to see it again," he said. "It's been a long time since I've had an evening out."

My heart pounded in my ears. I felt sick.

"Be my guest," said Boss, and her voice carried the grind of the workshop drill.

The government man's face went grim, and he drew himself up inside his suit and turned back for the car. He walked slowly, carefully, like a man without a care in the world.

The men folded themselves back inside the cars—one or two with their hands on their guns—and then there was a wall of dust, and they were gone.

As soon as the cars disappeared, the jugglers ran for Boss; behind them, there was a brief rain of clubs. Stenos reached her, too, and the dancing girls followed, like Boss was a magnet for their worries. Some of the crew began to inch forward, just to listen.

I had some courage back by that time, enough to turn to look at her.

"What do we do?" asked Moonlight.

"We've got to move on," said one of the jugglers. "We can't stay here."

"There's nowhere we can go," I said, though why I felt that way I didn't know. We were travelers; surely there was somewhere he couldn't find us.

"He found us once already," said Minette. "Better to get it over with. Maybe he just wants a cut, that's all."

"We can stay here," I said. "We just have to hide Ayar and Jonah." I was glad no one had wings any more. "As soon as he's come and gone, we'll pull up stakes and set down in a new city, and everything will be—"

"We change nothing," said Boss.

Sunyat, whose costume jingled because she was shaking, made a choked noise. "But they'll see Ayar . . . Panadrome . . ."

Boss didn't answer, though she had to know it was true. Everything we were gave us away to anyone smart enough to look past the show.

Boss wasn't looking at any of us who were close to her, and I thought maybe she was too scared to think straight (I was), but then I saw she was looking over at the other group of that had gathered, farther away.

For a second I didn't see what she saw, because the difference just seemed to be people who were eager to help and people who weren't, but then I realized she was looking at Ayar and Jonah, the aerialists, the tumblers, Bird; those who were metal. They were standing tightly together watching Boss without expression (Fatima might have been crying, but I couldn't be sure). They were standing a little away from the crew, not speaking.

They knew something the rest of us didn't know—about Boss, about the man with the orange lion on the side of his car;

they knew what might happen, without even looking at one another.

I looked back at Boss, more frightened of her than of the government man.

"Get into your legs," she said, without looking at me. "We have a show tonight."

On the way to the trucks I passed Ying, who reached out and grabbed my hand hard enough to hurt. We hadn't talked in a long time, maybe not since Bird had fallen, and I was so surprised by it that I stopped and looked at her. I heard her suck in a breath, like she was going to tell me something, but then some small sound startled her, and she vanished into the tent.

Panadrome struck up his first song of the night, tinny and too-happy, like he knew something, too, and was doing his best to drown it out.

22.

When they parade through the cities, Little George and the aerialists go first. (People are less likely to shoot at women and a kind-looking boy with brass legs.)

Next come the dancing girls, grinning and waving with bracelets jangling over their bare arms; they make sure that wary men will stop thinking of their guns.

Panadrome walks with them, playing lighthearted music with the one-armed accordion and the tinny brass keys, and the girls smile and pick up their skirts and wave their metal-gloved hands.

Next come Ayar and Jonah walking side by side (and here the men shrink back from the doorways, looking around for a weapon; there is nothing you can do to sweeten Ayar). The jugglers appear behind them, tossing clubs and knives back and forth.

("Just in case they're thinking of trying us," says Boss, "let them know we have blade-throwers.")

After the jugglers come Stenos and Bird. Stenos carries her sitting on his shoulder like a parrot, her good eye scanning the crowd, or she curls into herself, folded up like a sack of flour, and Stenos carries her tucked into the curve of one arm from one end of the city to the other. Her feet never touch ground.

Next come the Grimaldi brothers, who flip and twist and cause a commotion among the kids.

The parade ends with Boss in a painted wood throne on the smallest flatbed truck, which is apple-red and covered with banners proclaiming: CIRCUS TRESAULTI. Big George and Big Tom (their daytime metal arms the length of a normal man's) are driving; Boss sits in her sequin cape, waving and calling out, "The show begins at sundown!" in that voice that carries over the roofs.

The trailers wait just outside the city center, on any road that can't be gated shut. The rest of the crew drives the supply trucks along the back roads and parks outside the city, waiting to set up camp. If the performers walk out of the city limits, the crew starts to unload the tent. If the performers come out running from the city square, they leap into the trailers' open doors and make a run for it. Boss, in her own truck already, will regroup with them outside gun range.

This is a habit learned from a close call; this is a rescue they still sometimes need. No matter how much time passes, there are some people who don't like a crowd made of metal, no matter how much they smile.

23.

Stenos and Bird practice away from the others. Neither one of them likes closed spaces.

(Sometimes they practice in the rain rather than go inside the tent, her feet wrapped in canvas strips to give him something to hold on to.)

He kneels, his hand extended; she steps into his waiting palm. He lifts her with one hand, his fingers tight around the sole of her foot. She stands over his head, looking out over the circus yard, unconcerned. Her balance has always been perfect.

She did not slip from the trapeze.

Suddenly she bends in half, her head to her knees; he is almost late in raising his other hand, but he is never too late, and by the time her legs are straight above her in a handstand and she is pressing her hands into his palms, he has found his footing and does not tremble.

She splits her legs front and back, a line so straight you could rest a table on it. He holds the heels of his hands together and watches her.

(Sometimes, during practice, she will hold a position as long as she can, as if she can punish him by forcing him to bear her weight until he folds.

He waits for her. She must know it's no trouble to him to carry her; she's made of hollow bone. He can hold her as long as it takes.)

When she gives in, she shoves her arms apart; his arms follow hers, and in the open space she has created her body plummets toward the ground.

He braces himself and grips her wrists—not a sound out of him, never a finger out of place—and she jerks to a stop with her legs curled over her back like a shrimp's tail, her face four inches from the ground.

She does this often.

He has never dropped her.

(She keeps hoping.)

He leans back, pulling her with him; as she rocks back up she opens her legs around his waist, presses her feet into his spine. Later, he will have two marks below his shoulders, angled out like wings.

He keeps hold of her right wrist as he wraps his left arm around her to keep her from sinking, his palm splayed over her sternum, his fingers just touching her throat.

His hand burns through to her bones.

24.

First, I loved Fatima.

I'd loved her since the moment she walked out of the workshop when I was just a boy. I worshipped her dark eyes, her brown skin, the way she rolled her feet heel-to-toe as she walked from the workshop to the tent, even though the first days of walking on the pipe-bones were never anything but agony and she must have wanted to faint. She was out to prove everything, and I loved her.

I was young.

Fatima never gave me the time of day. She spent most of her time in the air, practicing under Elena's sharp eye, and she spent her time on the ground inside the trailer with the others, fighting whatever little battles a group of false siblings have. (The Grimaldis seldom fought that way, but then, they didn't have to live with Elena.)

Ying didn't like Fatima. "Too much like Elena," she said, whispering—we were unloading the trapezes, and she was at the far end of the long bars.

"I think she's beautiful," I said.

Ying didn't like her chances of being overheard, I guess, because she didn't answer me.

Fatima came to us in better shape than most. The only scars on her were the small ones Boss makes when she's putting in new bones: behind the knee, the small of the back, the top of the neck, the wrists. Back at the beginning, I thought Fatima must have had a pretty easy life until she came to us, to be without any scars.

I was young.

I was in love with Fatima for years before I got up the nerve to speak with her.

I waited outside the tent for her to leave practice; Elena walked ahead, and I ran to catch Fatima while she was alone (I would never speak in front of Elena). The words were out of my mouth before I could even greet her.

"I love you."

Fatima looked over her shoulder, lowered her gaze from her full height down, down, down until she met my eyes.

"I'm sure you do," she said, and while I was still blinking through her answer she had caught up with Elena and was out of hearing.

I thought she was being cruel. I found Barbaro and Focoso and nagged them for a real drink until they gave me one, and they toasted me for going above my station.

"A woman like her," said Barbaro, "a woman like her . . . " and when his words gave out he made a low, half-afraid whistle.

"A man must look to his own kind," added Focoso, and nodded over at the mens' trailer, where Ayar and Jonah lived together. "Don't aim above your head, boy. Water finds its level."

It wasn't the kindest advice I ever got. I only took it because it came with drink, and the advice burned more than the gin.

Of course, like most unkind advice, it was correct, eventually, somehow.

I don't speak much to her now. "Will it hold?" when she's testing the lock on the trapeze. "Look out, it's snowing," when she leaves the tent in winter.

She's as beautiful as ever, has hardly aged, but I long ago stopped thinking of her as mine, thank goodness. I see men on the road who do it, and it's never pretty.

("No one is anyone's," said Boss, when I told her, but it was a lie, and we both knew it. She had a pair of wings tied up in her workshop that gave her away.)

Fatima at least believed I loved her, which was more than I deserved.

I fell in love with Valeria when the knife thrower cut off her hair.

Something about her unconcern touched me as much as Fatima's pride had done; when the knife sliced through the ponytail Sarah only blinked and sighed, as if she wasn't looking forward to growing it back.

When Boss offered her a job, she changed her name to Valeria. She didn't get less shy, but she seemed to open her eyes to the world once she was away from the knives and had a fresh name. She painted her short hair with bootblack and wove her lost locks into a thick braid of hair and ribbons that she tied to what was left of her ponytail.

Boss fashioned Valeria a shoe of brass and copper that fastened at the ankle—it was a pointed foot, so she limped when it was on, but it peeked out from her skirts and she looked like a clockwork coquette. It was a good effect even if, up close, she always smelled faintly of boots.

Not that I ever minded what she smelled like. She was sweet, and I was young—sixteen, by then, I thought. By then, I was the one with something to prove.

(I was not sixteen. The circus was making an enemy of time, but I was young, and blind, and all I saw was Valeria's dark braid swinging as she walked.)

"I love you," I told her. We were piled together in the canvas-haul truck, our feet dangling over the back. We were kissing, and I had one hand crushed against her hair. (It would take days to wash off all the bootblack.)

"All right," she said, and kissed me.

"She loves me," I told Ying.

She brushed the chalk off her hands and stood up from her squat. "Well, there you are," she said.

I grinned. "Let those Grimaldis tease me now," I said, and flexed my arms.

Ying smiled tightly. "Yes," she said, "now they'll just tease Valeria."

I hadn't thought of that. I frowned. "They wouldn't do that to the woman I loved."

"If you say so," said Ying, examining her hands.

"Ying," snapped Elena from up on the trapeze, "if you're done gumming the sweat off your palms, we need to practice."

A moment later Ying had vanished, and all I saw before she reappeared on the rigging were a few flour-white handprints on the support pole where she had pulled herself up into the sky.

Valeria left that year.

The dancing girls all leave; they come in and out like the tide. Sometimes they leave between one performance and another, if they find a cause to fight for or a job to hold down. Nobody blames them—no one is here because the work is easy—but it's hard on Ayar when he steps into the ring and sees only three dancers waiting for him.

When Valeria left the circus, it was to become a baker in a civil-governed city that was still mostly standing. (Nice work if you can get it.) She kissed me goodbye.

She left her name behind. The next girl who joined up with us liked the sound of it when she saw the name taped on the bunk, and this new Valeria slid on the same skirts and strapped on the metal cast and took her place in the ring. She answered to

Valeria for two years, until she went, too. (She found a man and married him; the only one I knew who left for love.)

The Grimaldi brothers said it was bad luck to take the name of the departed to start with.

"You should tell her where to get off," said Altissimo, jerking his thumb at the other Valeria. I looked over. She was practicing with one of the other dancers (Malta, long gone), both laughing at how silly it looked to shake your hip and smile.

"Let it be," I said.

It was the first time I had ever opposed them, and Moto and Barbaro exchanged glances.

"He loves this one, too," Moto said, and Barbaro laughed.

I didn't love her, never did, but I couldn't find it in me to dislike the new Valeria; it was a pretty name for anyone, and she wasn't the same girl. The new Valeria was sharp-witted and had rough hands from years of hauling ropes at one of the port cities. Sometimes she carried canvas with me, and we laughed about the rubes, but it wasn't as though she replaced the Valeria I'd loved. It wasn't as though I would see her silhouette in the window of the women's trailer and mistake her for my Valeria.

"You worry too much about names," I said.

Altissimo said, "You worry too little."

When Bird fell, Ying came running out of the tent, stumbling and choking and calling for Boss to come and help, but she looked so guilty that instead of running inside to help Bird, I grabbed Ying's hand.

"What happened?"

After a little pause Ying said, "She fell."

She wasn't a good liar. I frowned. "Like Alec?"

"No," she said, shuddering, "no, no," and when she started to cry I wrapped her in my arms—more to muffle the sound than anything.

I had never been so close to her before, so close to the chalk smell of her skin and the pulled-tight knot of black hair and the gold makeup that had started to run from her crying.

"It's all right," I said. "Boss will fix her."

"I know," said Ying, and then a fresh storm of tears.

I didn't understand her. I held her closer.

25.

When the group of soldiers clears out, what's left behind is a pair of glass mugs, and the girl.

Her black hair is cut close to her scalp, like all the soldiers, and her golden skin is sallow from hunger, but her dark eyes are sparkling.

She hops nimbly down the back of the scaffold and walks to the edge of the ring.

"I want to join you," she says to the strongman.

She doesn't say she wants to audition. It doesn't occur to her that there can be a question of her merit. She knows she can do anything they ask of her. It's a matter of routine. The thing Tresaulti has that she wants is a home.

(She's an excellent soldier for shimmying through iron grates, but she has a tendency to hang behind when the fighting starts, like she's not sure if the battle is worth it, and nobody has time for a hesitant soldier. She's been passed around assignments more times than she can count, for not wanting to die.)

"I see," says the strongman. "What for?"

"Trapeze," she says.

From his position on the rig, one of the trapeze men grins and flexes his feet. "Want to step up, girly?"

She holds out an arm to the strongman.

He lifts her one-handed and deposits her onto the trapeze ("Name's Big George"), who has laid out flat and made himself into a table again, a knot of immovable muscle; she is standing on his shins, arms behind her, wrists tight around his long brass arms for balance.

She pushes back and forth until she has the speed and height she needs; she is embarrassed at first to be standing on a living thing instead of a bar or a rope, until she looks over her shoulder and sees that George doesn't seem to mind. He looks strangely content, smiling absently like any child on a swing. Then she pushes like she means it, her heels digging in for leverage.

She waits for the apex of the swing, lets go and jumps; she tucks in on herself once (touches her toes, then dives, her feet trailing like a comet's tail), grabbing George's feet just in time, letting her legs swing around and behind her as they soar backwards.

"Again," she says, mostly to herself, already hooking her feet around his ankles so she can swing by her feet for the next jump.

The tent is quiet after that—just the creak of Big George's hands against the rigging and the sound of skin on skin when she catches herself on his feet, and once on his shin, from underestimating the speed of the pendulum swing.

"Sorry," she says.

Big George smiles and says, "I don't even notice."

A woman says, "How old are you?"

Ying looks up—she had been about to jump, but she stops at the last second, wrenching her shoulder to grab at George's arm to steady herself.

"Fourteen," she says. (It sounds old enough to do something like this, anyway.)

"Come down from there," says the woman.

The strongman is standing at the far end of the tent, with the woman, and is making no move to help her. She glances up for a few seconds—then she shimmies up George's arm, across the rigging to the support pole, slides quickly down. (She sees the strongman smiling; she must have done right.)

When Ying's on the ground, the woman says, "I'll take you to the aerialists' trailer. Do you have anything?"

She's wearing all she owns. She shakes her head.

The trailer looks like it's been cobbled together from a dozen other trailers and nailed at the last second to a truck bed. It's painted gold and green, and the windows have cheap shades in them. (That night, she sees the shades are just paper; when they're on the road and they want to look out, they have to peel away the dingy tape first.)

The inside of the trailer has a small open area near the door, studded with tables and a few rickety chairs and some open shelves bolted to the walls. Behind that is the narrow tunnel of bunks stacked three high.

There are three women inside. Two of them are playing cards at one of the tables bolted to the floor. The third is standing in the back, stretching one foot on the topmost bunk, resting her cheek on her knee. Her face is tight, her eyes closed like she's dreaming.

The girl is terrified.

"That's Elena," says the woman in charge. Then, with a small wave that shows in what esteem she holds them, "And these are Nayah and Mina."

Elena opens her eyes deliberately, slowly (they're green and dark and Ying doesn't like them), and fastens her gaze on the girl. "What's your name?"

The girl trembles.

It's the woman in charge who answers, "Ying."

Ying's surprised (she'd had another name), but she decides she doesn't mind. She's better off keeping her secrets while she can (she knows what it's like in close quarters), and besides, there's luck in a new name.

"You're kidding," Elena says at last to the woman, as if Ying isn't there.

(Ying will get used to this feeling.)

"We'll wait until she's older for the bones," says the woman in charge.

The other two have stopped their game and are looking between Ying and Elena, waiting.

After a long time, Elena says, "I don't want her."

The woman says, "That's not your choice."

"Well, then she'd better take the open bed," says Elena at last. She pivots and lowers her leg, looking at Ying as if she'd be a fool to come one step closer. "But she gets the bones. None of us knows how to be that careful any more. We'll just break her trying to catch her."

Ying doesn't know what she means.

"Too young," the woman says. "Wait four years. She'll be thirteen then; she'll have grown enough."

So much for pretending to be older, Ying thinks.

"She could be dead in four years," says Elena, like it's something to look forward to.

The boy who takes her to the costume trailer is named Little George, and he's as young as she is.

"I've been here ages," he says as they walk. "I've already seen three dancing girls come and go, and a juggler. You'll get used to it if you stick around. Just try to keep the names straight. If you need anything, don't ask Elena, she's so cold she could freeze a roach. Come find me. I know everything that happens here."

"What do you do?"

He stops, frowns. "I work for Boss," he says, like that's all the explanation he needs.

She thought everyone here had a special talent. "But I mean— can't you do anything?"

He looks at her, and she knows what a stupid question it must be. Even people who can't do anything need a home.

But all he says is, "Well, you'd better hope so," and when he smiles, she smiles back.

"Tell me about Elena," she says.

He laughs and says, "I wasn't joking about the roach," and after that the stories never really stop.

For four years, Ying trains on the bars alone.

She scurries back and forth along the rigging to set up the trapeze bar or break it down for Big George when it's his turn to grab the supports; she rolls up canvas with Little George and hauls it out to the waiting flatbed, where the crewmen are waiting to drive it out.

("Who are the crew?" she asks.

Little George shrugs. "Who cares? They don't stay.")

When she is thirteen, Boss shows Ying the workshop and explains what will happen to her bones.

The pipe is paper-thin, and the copper warms up in Ying's hand, beating back against her pulse like a living thing.

Boss explains what the bones mean to her, if she takes them. Ying is ashamed that it hasn't struck her before (what is she, a fool?), but as Boss explains what the copper bones mean, Ying goes clammy. She half-listens. She thinks about Little George and the dancing girls and the jugglers who will all come and go, untouched and unremarkable, free and plain.

Ying cries, suddenly overcome. The end of the pipe digs into her palm as she presses the backs of her fists against her eyes.

Boss leaves her alone in the trailer.

It's Alec who comes back inside.

He smiles, his whole being seeming to understand her, and holds out a hand.

"Let's take a walk," he says.

She flushes as if he's courting her, takes his hand. (She loves Alec. They all do. Any one of them would take Alec's hand any time he offered it. He was true magic, everybody knew.)

It's winter. As she walks down the steps beside him, Alec pulls her close with one arm and wraps his wings around them both. The metal warms from the heat of their bodies into a comfortable cocoon, and with every step the wings shake, a little rain of notes.

He doesn't try to convince her of anything; he just walks with her around the yard like they're working off a cramp. They pass Jonah, who's washing the red truck. His head is bent to his work, but his face is stormy.

"Poor Jonah," Alec says, laughing quietly. "He's had a fight with Ayar."

She doesn't say anything. ("He won't listen," Ayar had told her, "he's going to hurt himself if he strains his lungs like that, and what if one of these days Boss's magic doesn't work?"

"Tell him you'll replace him," said Ying, because she knew that was the cruelest thing you could do to anyone, replace them.

Ayar looked at her and said, "I forget you're still a child," and that was how Ying got the first idea that something would happen soon that would make her no longer young.)

They pass the tent, where through the open flaps Ying can see Elena and Nayah and Mina practicing. (Ying looks at them hard, like she can see their copper bones if she tries.) They pass Ayar, who is dragging the trailers into a smaller half-circle where the trucks nearly touch. It will snow soon; they'll want the protection from the wind.

After they have walked nearly around the yard, Alec says, "You don't have to do anything. You can stay with us just as you are."

"On the trapeze?"

There is a little pause before Alec says, "No. That's not safe for you."

What he means is: Elena insists they all have the bones, so they're all mangled alike. Ying understands; sometimes you have to be one of the troupe, and not yourself. (She wanted a home. She found one.)

"And Little George always needs help," Alec is saying, and Ying thinks about Little George strapping on the brass legs that are too big for him, thinks about running errands and barking at the gates, staggering from city to city and pasting the Tresaulti posters on any walls that haven't been blown in.

"I'm frightened of the bones," she says. Her voice shakes, but it can't be the cold, because his wings are so warm.

He stops and kneels in front of her; his wrapped-around wings lock them in together, the bottom feathers sinking into the soft ground.

(Ying will never forgive him for doing this now; not after she sees his wings trying to burrow into the ground after he falls, not after being reminded of the cocoon he made for her, once.)

His feathers are so close to her that if she turns her face she can look into their warm, bright mirror. His eyes are a deep clear blue, like chips of glass, and she sees herself in them—eyes wide, face drawn, looking frail and breakable against the metal cage.

Tenderly, as only monsters are tender, he asks, "Are you afraid to be like us, Ying?"

"No," Ying says. (How can she be afraid of anything, when he is so beautiful?)

She turns her head. Her breath fogs over the copper petals, until nothing is left of her but a dim reflection in his wings.

26.

This is what they understand:

After the audition, Boss takes them to the workshop, sets out her bone saw. She says, "I'll have to operate. You might die."

Some have turned her down at that. The idea of this woman performing surgery is no comfort, and though a lot of people are dying these days, it's one thing to go down in a firefight and another to throw yourself away.

The rest stay.

(These are circus folk; these are the ones who have nothing to lose.)

She sets out the pipes and the wrenches. Then she says, "You'll die."

This is their first measure. Everyone feels something; no one is that resigned.

Ayar cried. It was a horrible thing to tell the friend he'd carried two miles to save.

Elena had said, "Well, that's one thing over with," and stretched out on the table.

After the worst of their terror is over, Boss says, "You can never leave the circus. It will keep you alive after I finish fixing you."

After they have accepted this, they each, eventually, lie down on the table and have their last moments of fear. Then Boss touches them, and they sink into the dark, waiting to be made new, waiting to be woken.

(When her turn came, Bird blinked up at the ceiling for several seconds, fighting the dark without knowing it. "I wonder what you did to get this kind of power," Bird said, just before sleep took her.

She did not live long enough to see Boss's hands shaking.)

It is no secret to the circus who has the bones, who has the lungs or the springs. When they come out of the workshop, when they stagger finally in their new skeletons from the trailers out to the practice yard, they are welcomed back without comment. Even the living, who have not been asked for their bones, can imagine what it takes to lie down on a table and agree to suffer.

But those who have gone into the workshop, those who are dead, look at one another and know.

For some it is worth it. (Ying is allowed to sleep through the night at last; with her copper bones, Elena is satisfied). For some, there is only the knowledge of time sliding past them, a sense of being nailed to the ground.

Those who have gone into the workshop glance from one to another, looking for signs of aging that never appear. None of them wanders far from camp; magic this deep should not be tested, and no one wants to be the first to fall down dead because he wandered too far from Boss's keen eye.

(She says it's the circus, but they know what she means; they know Boss is the thing keeping them from falling to pieces.)

Little George was slated to be fixed, but Boss keeps him out of the workshop even after he asks, and so he keeps moving slowly through time until he's older than Ying, until he's nearly as old as Jonah, who has been twenty-five since the day he came to the circus and was gifted with his clockwork lungs.

Slowly, Little George begins to wake up to the world in a way he cannot name.

He does not know that Ying will never be older; he does not know why he takes such care not to anger the Grimaldi brothers. He is not aware, only awake.

He knows nothing for certain; he only sees that when the government man is gone, the circus gathers in two groups to see what Boss will do: those who are alive, and those who have survived the bones.

27.

The illusionist has no truck of his own. He follows the Tresaulti parade on foot, walking in the tracks of the red-painted trailers after they pull away from the city borders, and out to the top of the hill two miles out from town. He can see them forming a half-circle on the far side of the hilltop; he can see the first tent poles going up against the flat grey sky.

On his back is the heavy bag with his tricks in it, and he carries the hoop around his shoulders. It bangs the backs of his legs with every step, but that's the price you pay for walking. The little cage with the bird in it dangles from his belt. The bird protests at first, but after the first mile it just clings to its perch and waits.

From their position on top of the hill they can see him coming, so the illusionist is not surprised when there's a knot of people waiting for him when he reaches the top.

He sets the hoop down on the ground and slings the bag off his shoulders, crouching to unpack it. Out comes the pack of cards, the scarves, the silver balls that flatten out when they hit his palms so it looks like they disappear. (A lot of his act is about things disappearing. People don't put much faith in a beautiful transformation these days; a disappearance, they believe.)

The crowd is bigger now. There are some acrobats, looks like, a juggler with clubs in each hand, and a couple of haughty girls in pretty rags.

"A magician?" says a woman from the edge of the crowd, and without looking up he says, "Yes, sir," because he knows what authority sounds like.

"Well," she says. "Go on and show us."

He unhooks the birdcage, sets it on the ground at the far end of his tricks, and stands up, taking a step back and throwing his arms wide to introduce the act.

Someone says, "Don't."

It's not the boss, so he shouldn't pay it any mind (there are always hecklers), but he glances over at the woman who spoke and is struck dumb.

She has an iron plate bolted over some peach fuzz on her skull, and one glass eye that's looking blankly at him. The other eye is dark and fixed on the cage at his feet.

"Ladies and gentlemen," he begins.

"He's going to kill it," the woman with the glass eye says, not really to anyone. No one speaks.

"Go on," says the woman in charge.

He nods and clears his throat and starts his act.

The handkerchiefs materialize in his ears, and the hoop makes his legs vanish, and the silver balls slide into invisibility in his hands. All the while, the circus people watch him, neither applauding nor drumming him out.

At last he says, "For my final disappearing act," and fiddles in his sleeve for the bird that's inside his cuff, waiting.

"No," says the strange woman, and in two steps she's reached the cage, stepping between him and it.

He reaches to snatch it out of her grasp, but she catches him by the throat, an iron grip. Her eye burns.

The illusionist knocks her arm away, staggers backwards. A man is already waiting behind him and catches his arm, flipping the illusionist neatly onto his back. (The sky is pale blue and flat, like glass.)

Someone is opening the latch of his cage, and the illusionist watches the small dark silhouette of his bird as it shoots past all of them and sails out of sight.

After a moment there's a scuffle, and his arm is freed. When he stands up he sees a man with a set of brass ribs holding the other man back, shoving him into his place in the circle.

The strange woman is standing a few feet away, gripping the empty cage in her hands, her gaze fixed on the sky where the bird can no longer be seen. The others in the circle seem to have drawn back, as if the cage is poisoned and she's picking victims.

"Bird," says the woman in charge, "give the man back his equipment."

She sets the empty cage on the ground, turns away, walks into the crowd without another look around her.

"Not bad," says the woman in charge, not unkindly. "We'd have to make some changes to the act if you stayed."

He can imagine.

He looks around at the impassive crowd. It's not the quiet that bothers him. It's that they didn't hold back the one-eyed woman, like they felt she had a reason for doing it, like this is just the sort of thing that happens here.

He wants a circus troupe to belong to so he can have a roof and some steady meals; if he wants to be worried about war, he can stay where he is.

"Thank you for your time," he says finally, and no one seems surprised when he kneels and packs up his tricks.

Halfway back, he shakes the dead bird out of his sleeve; the other man crushed it, and there's no point in carrying a dead thing all the way home.

28.

When Bird fell, it was Stenos who Boss called to come carry her out.

It was Stenos who lifted Bird from the ground, who watched the blood oozing in sticky rivulets through the dirt. He looked at her face, what was left of it, and down her body, where her chest had caved in under her shirt. The few ribs that had pierced her skin gleamed in the dark.

He looked away from the human wreckage. He looked up past the empty trapeze to the very top of the rigging. There was a little tear in the ceiling of the tent, and through it there was the night sky, a smattering of stars.

When he glanced down again, Boss was looking at the woman's body, lifting her hair to look at the skull, brushing the blood away from her remaining eye, as if cleaning off a toy that had fallen in the mud.

"Can you help her?"

He didn't know why he asked. It wasn't like he wanted her helped.

After a long time, Boss said, "I don't know what will happen."

Stenos remembers that it was cold that night; he shivered, holding her.

This is what he sees when he looks at her that night:

He sees the empty tunnel of her eye socket. He sees into her; he falls through and through the tunnel until he is swallowed up by the emptiness there, until he sees the night sky.

Even after the ground has crushed her she is gasping for air, her ribs heaving through the skin as she fights the inevitable, though everyone knows Death is following close on her heels.

His only thought is, If she dies, I get the wings. I get the wings.

He feels them already as if they're growing out of his shoulders; he sees himself leading the procession through the cities, his wings a fan of knives on either side. He imagines the ground falling away as he rises over the awed crowd. The air seems to shimmer, anticipating him.

All he has to do is wait this out; as soon as the woman is dead, he will inherit the wings.

He looks down at the woman in his arms and thinks, *Tough luck*, and flexes his fingers against her arm, against her knee, like a consolation prize.

But when she stops breathing, his chest goes tight; he adjusts his hold and pulls her towards him without thinking; he puts his mouth on the blood where he hopes her mouth is and pushes a breath into her lungs. It comes back to him, sick-sweet and dry as dust, and for some reason he can't name he is terrified, too terrified even to lift his mouth from her mouth.

This is how Boss finds them when she opens the door.

"Bring her in," she says, after too long.

He lays her out on the table, and then Boss is filling the workshop, pressing him out without ever touching him, and when he is outside she locks the door against him.

Stenos remembers that the night Bird fell was cold. Her body was cool when he held her; he had walked from the trailer with his arms crossed in front of him; when he passed Elena, she was trembling.

But this is how memories are—always true, never the truth.

Elena shrank from the blood on his face, and he crossed his arms in front of him to keep them from shaking, and even though he remembers these things, he does not know the truth of the night when he woke Bird.

This is the truth:

The night was warm; Bird had gone cold.

29.

The government man came back, good as his word, our last night in the city.

I forced a smile as I handed him his ticket, and when he looked at me I winked and rapped my knuckles once on my right leg, the brass in tune with Panadrome.

"Welcome, sir," I said, "to the Mechanical Circus Tresaulti. Jugglers and tumblers and girls in the air, the finest spectacle anywhere!"

"I'm sure," he said, and I thought he'd be annoyed, but when he looked down at me his eyes were shining.

I went cold all over, and didn't really recover until he had disappeared into the tent and I was sure he couldn't see me any more.

One of the nice things about so many governments, I guess, is that people don't recognize you from the others who have murdered their way to power. His car was nowhere to be seen, and only one bodyguard followed him in.

I handed out tickets until the last rube was inside, and then I skidded around to the back flap of the tent, close to the trailers, where some of the acts filed in to wait behind the bleachers for their turn.

The government man took a seat at the edge of one of the benches, with a clear shot to the main entrance of the tent, like any man would if he wasn't a fool.

I ran for Boss so fast I slipped in the mud, reached her as a sopping mess.

She was waiting outside the main entrance of the tent for Panadrome to finish his welcome march. Jonah was holding a wide yellow umbrella over her, to keep off the last of the rain, and when she saw me coming she held out one hand, palm out, to stop me from coming closer.

"Watch the dress," she said. "I'm on."

"He's here," I said. "The government man."

Her hand curled into a fist. She dropped her arm to her side, looked at the entrance to the tent. The griffin tattoo peered into the twilight.

"What do we change?" I asked, my mind racing. "I can get Ayar back from the bleachers, no one's seen him yet, and if Jonah—"

"Nothing," she said. Her gaze was fixed on the tent ahead of her. Jonah's hand was shaking a little; the yellow umbrella trembled.

"But he'll see us," I said. I felt like I was sinking into the ground, pulled into the mud by my own terror.

She shook her head, her face set. "Being afraid wastes time," she said, as if to herself.

Jonah said, "The jugglers are ready and waiting for your word, Boss."

Boss stepped out from under the yellow umbrella and opened the tent flaps with both hands; for a moment she was a dark shape against a flare of lights and noise, and then the flaps fell shut and it was just Jonah and me left in the yard, ankle-deep in the mud and looking at each other like a couple of frightened kids.

"Ladies and gentlemen, welcome to the Circus Tresaulti!"

Boss's greeting filled the tent, rolled out past the canvas, over the both of us and out into the darkness, and for a moment I was brave again; Boss's voice does that to you.

Still, after her voice had faded I pulled a stool up to the tent and waited, slowly sinking into the mud, for Boss to come safely back out again.

30.

After Alec died, we drove for two days without stopping. Nobody knew where we were going but Boss, who drove the lead truck alone.

I had meant to go the first leg with the tumblers, and then switch to the other mens' trailer when we stopped for the night, but we ended up trapped in there for two days together.

The first night we got drunk, so drunk that Molto and Brio wept into their sleeves about Alec, and the rest of us blinked at the ceiling. The second night we tried to dry out, so that if we ever stopped we'd be good for something besides the guillotine.

The morning of the third day, our truck stopped. After a moment, Barbaro said, "Well, fuck," and opened the door as if it didn't matter to him whether he died or not.

We were all pulled over; the crewmen who had driven the trucks were already asleep in the bunks above their cabs, and the rest of us staggered out into the morning like a pile of cave rats.

"We'll stop here tonight," Boss said. "He can be buried here as well as anywhere."

We were on a grassy flat outside the ruins of a town that had been long abandoned. Good place for a final rest, I supposed, though I didn't see why we had taken two days to get there instead of any other place.

(It reminded me of the city where Boss had found him, though this place was grown over with weeds, empty for a hundred years, so it couldn't have been.)

"Rest here," Boss said, and then, "except Ayar and Little George. Let's get the body out of the workshop and dig a grave before day's gone."

As I passed the women's trailer I looked at Ying, who was like a wraith after two days locked up with Elena and the rest of the women. She couldn't even manage a smile when she saw me; she looked across the grassy plain at a little grove of trees and shoved her hands in the pockets of a jacket five sizes too big.

(It was one of Elena's things. I would have pegged Elena as the last person to notice someone else was cold, but I guess you never know.)

The coffin was strapped where we had left it, and we dragged it out to the trees for the protection from the sleet and wind, and Ayar broke ground on the grave.

"I want it proper deep," Boss said. "God knows what people do out here when they're desperate. I don't want him to be easy to find."

Ayar and I looked at one another, wondering what sort of people she was expecting. Finally Ayar said, "Sure thing, Boss."

He dug that whole grave himself, of course—he could dig a hundred graves without getting tired. I was there to get him water and bring lamps for a little warmth and to tell him jokes, just to keep him working.

It still took until nightfall, and when he was finished and had hauled himself out of the grave he said, "I don't have it in me to cover him tonight."

"I'll tell Boss," I said.

Turned out there was no need (Boss knows the lay of the land). When I found her and told her the grave was dug, she picked up a lamp and went out before I could tell her a thing, but as soon as she reached Ayar she said, "We'll leave it for now. Thank you, Ayar, for your work. In the morning we'll bury him."

It was winter, so the coffin stayed out. Boss acted like it hardly mattered, and stayed in her trailer, lights on and the sounds of sharpening tools, until everyone else had gone to sleep.

Then she opened the door and looked for me.

When she saw me, I ran to her (old habit), and she took my arm and knelt so we were eye to eye. I was still a boy, and hated being reminded how small I was, but she only took my shoulders like she was the queen and I was the questing knight, and I felt how it really was—that she had come down to me.

"Watch him," she said, her face pinched and blue in the moonlight. "I don't want him to be alone his last night. Bad enough to have been locked away for so long."

It was winter, I wanted to say. I could freeze. He's dead now, I wanted to say, I don't know why it matters.

I nodded.

"Good," she said, with the worst attempt at a smile I'd ever seen from her. Then she cleared her throat and went inside, where she wound up the little radio Jonah had found for her in a junk heap a dozen cities back. The crackle of a broadcast cut through the camp; a government station, it sounded like, from the casualty reports.

I took up a seat on one of the flatbeds, cradled between two rolls of canvas. I could see the coffin from where I was, and at least in the canvas I wouldn't freeze to death overnight.

For a while I dozed amid the comfortable smells of wax and oak and old beer.

At some point I woke. The camp was silent except for the crackle of the radio, and for a while I looked at the far-off lumps that in the daylight had been a city, and now looked like a snoring beast. Funny how things change depending on the light.

Later, when it was full dark except for the moon, Elena came to the coffin.

I thought about scaring her off (what does a sour bitch like that care for anything?), but she had given Ying her jacket to ward off the cold. I let her be.

I watched her for a long time as she stood still beside the wooden box. Her shabby coat hung off her thin shoulders; when the wind blew, the coat flapped against her, showing flashes of white that had rubbed off on the lining from running to the tent in the winter with her coat wrapped over her powdered legs.

I couldn't see her face, so I didn't know if she was crying, or praying, or spitting on the grave.

No. That last thought wasn't fair, I knew it even as I thought it. Out of all of them, Elena wouldn't do that to Alec. Elena was the one who had almost caught him.

She bent to the coffin; her head was a warm silhouette against the mountain of black earth Ayar had dug up. For a moment her lips moved—prayer, then, after all.

At last she kissed the rough wood, as if waking him, as if she was the prince in a fairy tale.

Then she stood and turned back, her feet crunching gently in the frost all the way back to the trailer where the women lived. She didn't look around her, didn't see me at all.

I sat up all the rest of that night, wide awake without knowing why.

31.

This is what Elena said to Alec, before she pressed her lips to the coffin to wish him good journey:

"Coward."

32.

According to Elena, the aerialists are sexless.

They say it's because of the bones. You get sewn up again and something isn't quite right. Some pieces don't work like they should. The girls end up light and strong, and utterly without the sort of thing a man can enjoy.

The rubes don't know, of course. It's for the crew and the jugglers, who flicker in and out of their lives; even when the worst of them are three sheets to the wind, the aerialists still get the sort of treatment that men give little girls or old women.

It's not true, of course—Alto, who's sleeping with Nayah, and Altissimo, who's sleeping with Mina, know differently, but they keep their peace; they can guess what Elena would do if they spoke out of turn.

Elena is fond of the lie. She knows that in times like these a troupe leader must look out for her own, and she does what she can with what she has. You can't trust anyone to be clever or kind; you can trust them almost to the last to be gullible and afraid.

(Almost. Elena thinks differently about Bird. That glass eye goes right through you.)

The first time Elena sees Stenos, she thinks (to her surprise), *He's for me.*

God knows why—she's always preferred handsome men— but when he says, "It was the circus or prison for me," she doesn't tell him to piss off to prison, like she should.

Instead she looks past him as if he isn't there.

"You must be Elena," he says.

She tries not to smile. Boss told him, then. Boss will try any dirty trick just to get a rise out of her. Elena knows better than to bite; it's not worth it. If he doesn't have the bones, he'll be gone before she can bother to remember his name.

Still, she watches him go. On his way to wherever it is outsiders sleep, he passes the strange woman; they look at one another, take a wide step apart like two dogs facing off. Then the strange woman keeps walking into the tent, and after a moment of looking after her, he shrugs it off and turns away, the sharp lines of his face visible for a moment as he disappears into the maze of trucks.

Elena learns his name.

She waits for him to get his new bones.

For fifteen cities she locks the trapeze in place, watches the girls flying back and forth, and keeps one eye on the trailer where Boss molds them into survivors. For fifteen cities she waits, for nothing. Stenos hauls canvas and lumber and dredges beer glasses out of wash barrels for Joe the cook to dry, and is so ordinary it makes her ill.

"Doesn't he *want* anything?" she asks one night as they walk back from the fire, as if it's funny and it doesn't matter what the answer is.

"Food and sleep," says Nayah, "that's all he ever asks for." She knows from Alto; it's probably true.

"Too bad that's all he wants," says Penna with a wink at Ying, who's smart enough to get interested in taking off her makeup, burying her face in a towel.

Elena looks at Penna, who has managed to stay stupid all these years, and says, "No fucking the crew, Penna. What are you, an animal?"

Penna flushes and skitters into the trailer.

Elena finds herself walking beside the strange woman as they approach the trailer. (The strange woman has a name, but Elena's never used it. The woman answers to anything—"Hey," "You there," a snap of the fingers. She's answered to anything for so long that Elena has swung past contempt and is starting to be impressed.)

The woman says, "He wants the wings."

Elena stops walking. "Liar."

The woman shrugs, and Elena realizes with a start that she has misjudged the strange woman, thinking she was beaten and locked onto the bars of the trapeze.

She is docile only because she does not care, because she does not intend to stay where she has been placed.

She's after the wings.

Elena wants to say something, but her throat is dry.

The woman eventually closes the trailer door. Inside come the sounds of laughter and shushing and the creaking of the girls slipping into their bunks.

Long after the lights have gone out, Elena is standing outside, trembling.

When she knocks at Boss's trailer, Boss opens right away. (Boss doesn't sleep much.)

"You wouldn't," Elena accuses. "You wouldn't do that. Not after what happened to him."

Boss is quick to catch up. "They're not Alec's. They're mine. I made them. I'll give them to whoever I want, and if you dare to question me again I'll pull out your bones for a crown on my head."

"Which one will get the wings? Him or her?" The tears are two hot streaks on Elena's face; she digs her fists into the tops of her legs.

"I haven't decided," Boss says at last. Her voice is kinder now, which is worse, Elena knows. "Something will make up my mind."

Elena feels smaller, feeble, as if Boss is pressing against her from across the room; she stumbles out without farewell and staggers back toward the green trailer where a madwoman is waiting.

Stenos is coming back from the tent (has he been practicing? Is he preparing to be one of them? Oh, God, the wings), and he looks up and sees her.

He smiles.

"Lost?" he says, and his eyes are two dark insects.

She turns into the trailer without a word, sets the latch like she can lock out what she knows is coming next.

In the dark, she listens to the madwoman breathing and thinks, You fool, you fool, don't you know?

33.

The city where they buried Alec had, for a long time, fared better than most. It wasn't important enough to be bombed out at the beginning, and then the long line of governments stayed in it as they traveled, rather than rolling over it. It had a series of names that meant as little as any name Boss had given a dancing girl: New Umbra, Zenith, Praxiteles, Johnsonia (only for a year—he was quickly deposed), Haven.

The Tresaulti people don't know the names, for this city or for any other. Boss discourages it. "Our circuit is wide enough," she says. "We might not come back to a city in your lifetime."

The crew scoff.

The ones with copper bones get very quiet.

They buried Alec outside the city where Boss had first found him, the city he left behind as soon as he heard Boss's voice.

Boss would never have come back, would have left it alone until the world cracked to ash, except that he died, and she didn't know where else to bury him. Some unmarked grave along the road was not for him. For him mausoleums were made; for him they carved angels from stone.

(She had tried to carve what she could for him, always. She would not shirk now just because he was dead.)

The city had fallen in, but it was still itself. Thankfully the ones with the bones knew better than to say, and the others were too tired from two days' drive to look around them and recognize anything.

Boss worried when Little George looked at the city and frowned, rubbing the back of his neck, tilting his head at the skyline like a listening dog.

"Come along," she said, and like a listening dog, he came. "Rest here," she said to everyone, and then, "except Ayar and Little George."

Ayar would dig the grave; George would have something to do besides wonder.

She cannot bring herself to change George. She means to; he wants to be a tumbler so badly she can hear him dreaming. Someday she will. He's still young. He can get a little older before she fixes him.

(He isn't broken. She does not know what to do.)

But when she thinks about changing him—when she catches his shoulder to turn him the right way to a task, and he goes away laughing and batting her hand off him—her hand goes cold.

Before Alec fell, she would have already done it. Before Alec fell, she thought this was the kindest thing you could do for anyone.

It is. It is the kindest thing.

But she sends George to the gravedigging, away from the shadows of the city, so he does not have time to think about where they are, and how long it's been since they were there last.

Once, she looks back at the center of the camp to see Elena watching her, her eyes flat and merciless in the milky winter light.

Boss looks at her until Elena drops her gaze.

"Ying," Elena snaps, "you may be able to freeze to death, but the rest of us are useful enough to be missed. Get some wood, or throw yourself on the fire to give us something to burn."

It doesn't carry the venom it used to (now Ying has the bones, and she's in as much danger of cracking and freezing as any of the rest of them), but it's comforting for some people to hear cradle stories told again, Boss thinks.

(Ying was too young, Boss thinks, stops.)

As Ayar digs, Boss watches the ruins.

She's not much impressed by cities, these days. The ancient cities lasted a thousand years. Alec's fell in a hundred, with only some bombs to blame. He'd be ashamed of it, too, she thinks, if he had lived. He understood weakness, but he liked things that were sturdy or strong. He liked Ayar, and cities, and Elena, and the wind.

Boss can see that the tall buildings had fallen first; their iron girders had groaned and bent and sent their towers crashing onto the low roofs, bringing the whole city to the ground.

That's what happens, she thinks, if no one cares for the bones of a thing.

34.

Most government men are not an accident.

Every so often, there's a soldier in the ranks who happens to be standing after all the rest have fallen; there's a rich young man maneuvered into place by those who have plans for him; there's a bureaucrat who happens to keep out of the pit of vipers long enough to grow befuddled and white-haired and become a minister of something without really trying. But most true government men are hungry for it; most government men make plans; most government men are born, not made.

When a particular young boy goes to the circus, and forgets to clap at the tumblers or the strongman because he is wondering if they could be of any use to him, he is a government man.

(While he watches them, he thinks of an agile militia; a way to prepare convicts before he puts them to labor; a body for himself. Government men are never too young to worry about dying before their work is finished.)

Later, his mother will ask him why he didn't enjoy himself. He will lie that he did. She will believe him; he is an excellent liar.

Later, after battle, he will lie awake inside the rubble of a bombed-out building, staring at the sky and waiting for rescue, and think how he could leap over the walls if only he had a skeleton of springs.

Later, he forgets the circus. The war swallows everything at regular intervals, and makes the world start again from nothing; even a clever young man has to pay attention if he's going to scrabble out of the wreckage and keep his head through the next government.

(There are ways to do this. He finds them all.)

Later, he will rise. He will grind peace out of the ashes of little battles, and make alliances with the ones he cannot defeat.

He resurrects factories whenever he can spare the men to guard them. He fences off land for the prisoners to farm. He collects books and singed half-books in his capital city; he thinks that someday there would be merit in a school. He steals enough gasoline to travel, and wherever he goes he brushes off the ruins to make use of them however he can. He listens, and plans, and works in increments to make a world in his image.

People let him build it. It's tyranny, they know, but it's no more than they would do, if they could.

He comes back to the circus.

He watches without seeing; he makes plans. The circus goes on around him, without him. If you asked him what their faces looked like, he wouldn't know.

(The little boy at the circus didn't notice Panadrome's music, the pinkish lanterns, the spangled costumes. Government men aren't carried away with any spectacle but their own.)

A man and a woman step into the ring. She has one eye; he lifts her into the air with one hand. She grips his wrists and fights him, touching her head to the backs of her knees, wrapping her legs around him like a disease.

Once, she fixes her eyes on the government man. The glass one is unnerving; the real one burns.

He does not remember this. This thing was not here before.

Without knowing why, he sits back in his seat as if the tent is plunged into darkness and he cannot remember the way out; as if someone has held a mirror up to him.

(Those with great hunger are born, not made.)

35.

The night the strange woman crashes, Elena finally utters a name that fits—"Poor bird," she says, and they get gooseflesh, knowing they've heard Bird's real name for the first time.

Ying goes first, shouting (Ying always did worry), and the others slide down one by one. None of them look at Elena, except Fatima, who goes down just before Elena and who glances at her every few feet down the rigging, as if she's waiting for the strike and the drop.

Elena goes to a flatbed to stretch, alone; the last thing she needs is a pile of stupid questions on top of everything.

She's walking back across the camp when Stenos comes out of Boss's workshop.

His shirt is black with blood, his face smeared and clotted red like he's been at a carcass.

Something inside Elena turns over, dark and consuming; he has the bones, she thinks. He's one of us, finally.

Desire hits her so suddenly that she recoils, presses away as he passes, in case he can see it on her.

But he's not looking at her—his eyes are empty and glassed over (she feels sick and wild), and he walks past her without stopping. The blood runs off his arms like stage paint.

She knows whose blood it is. She knows what has happened to her copper bones and the fragile skin.

Why this moment should horrify her, she doesn't know. It's not as if this is the first night she's had to live through after someone has fallen to the ground.

At last, she thinks that winter, when she sees Stenos coming for her. On its heels comes the thought, *He's not one of us*, but it's a truth that gets swallowed in her hunger.

They have no time—they'll be missed—and he drags his kisses against her open mouth so hard she can feel his teeth.

After all this time lifting Bird, he's stronger than he looks.

("How could you do that to her?" he breathes into her neck, pressing her against the wall. "How could you do it?"

She makes fists in his hair, wonders if she's doomed to be surrounded by fools.)

Afterwards, he steps back from her, watches with dark eyes as she smoothes her skirt down, pulls back her hair.

"You have powder on your leg," she says.

He brushes his pants with his palms until the white is gone.

When he says, "Don't tell anyone," she makes herself wait a moment before she shrugs and says, "Of course," as if she's doing him a favor, as if it's his privacy she wants to protect.

(What is she, an animal?)

36.

I thought the government man would come out at the end with Boss in hand, barking his orders to have us all taken away. Jonah thought so, too, so much that he and the crew were quietly packing the trucks, and after every act the dancing girls and the jugglers were shuttled off to their trailers, to prepare for flight. By then the rain was pounding down, and I calculated who was safe by how many yellow umbrellas had floated from the back of the tent to the yard and back.

Ayar put up a fight the moment Jonah told him, standing at the back door of the tent.

"What, so we should run like dogs?" He grabbed an umbrella from the waiting crewman and marched across the muddy yard under a little pool of yellow. "Don't be stupid. We do as Boss says."

Jonah matched him step for step, despite Ayar being more than a head taller. "Ayar, we have to think about ourselves."

"Ourselves without Boss?" Ayar snapped. "Easier said than done, Jonah."

Jonah flinched, and Ayar tried again. "She said there's nothing to fear. We'll look like fools if we run."

"Just because someone says there's nothing to fear doesn't mean you shouldn't run," said Jonah.

That stopped Ayar in his tracks, and for a second the two of them stood in the middle of the yard under the yellow toadstool of the umbrella, with the rain coming down around them like it was going to wash them away.

"I hope you're right," Ayar said, and went into the trailer, where I knew he would change into his regular clothes and come out to save anyone he could.

Jonah looked calmer after that, though even from where I was sitting Ayar's words had sounded mournful, as if he was convinced that they would be dead without Boss. Seemed foolish to me; who would challenge Ayar and live?

I thought about Ayar's clockwork spine. Would Boss have made him imperfect, so he would have to come to her for repairs? Did little breakdowns happen no matter what she meant to do?

(I was closer than before, by accident; only because I was waking up. I was no closer to understanding anything about what Boss had done. You can never know someone else's reasons. You barely know your own.)

When Bird and Stenos went into the tent, a single umbrella hovering over them (he carried her), I couldn't take it any more. I left my post and slid my way around the camp to the trailer where the aerialists lived.

I knocked on the door. "Ying? Is Ying in there?"

Fatima opened the door and stepped aside. I thought it was to invite me in, but then I saw Elena and knew Fatima had moved just so Elena could get a look at me.

"What's happened?" she asked.

It was the least rude she had ever been to me, so I must have managed to look important despite myself.

I had wanted to talk only to Ying (tell her to forget the troupe and get in the cook truck with Joe and drive out already, keep going, hide and wait until there was a new government that didn't know her), but looking at Elena I said, "The government man is here. Boss is putting on the full show. He's seen everything."

Penna gasped. Nayah and Ying stood up, like there was something to be done.

Elena said, "Sit down and be quiet."

They obeyed.

Elena crossed the trailer in five long steps, and a moment later she and I were outside on the rickety stair that hovered just above the ground, half-covered by the roof. I wobbled and was sure I would fall any moment. She stood with one foot on top of the other, arms folded, looking out over the camp like she didn't even notice the narrowness of the ledge we were standing on.

"What did Boss say?"

"That there was nothing to fear."

Her lips were a thin line, and, suddenly brave, I took a guess and asked her, "Is this the first government man who's done this to us?"

She looked at me, surprised, like I was an infant who had suddenly mastered human speech.

"No," she said.

"What happened, before?"

Elena pressed her crossed arms into her chest until the metal groaned.

"I have to get ready," she said. "Some people don't have the luxury of running around banging on doors and worrying people for nothing."

"So something happened," I said, but she was gone and the door was closed behind her. Inside, she was snapping at the others to either powder their legs properly or join the dancing girls, who didn't care if you looked sloppy.

I met the government man on my way back from the aerialists' trailer.

He and his bodyguard (who held a black umbrella over the gentleman's head) were coming out the front entrance. I was surprised—we were only half-finished—but too relieved to see him leaving to wonder at it.

"Did you enjoy the show, sir?" I called. "You're going too soon! You haven't even seen the Grimaldi brothers yet, and the aerialists—"

"Does your master always look for lunatics?" the government man asked, too sharply. His steps were careful over the mud, but he was in a hurry to be gone.

I realized suddenly that he meant Bird. He had seen Stenos and Bird; their act had run him right out.

Bold and stupid with glee, I said quite seriously, "That's what happens to some, sir. No predicting how the madness will come upon you."

He shot me a look Elena would have been proud of, and then he was gone, down the crest of the hill where (I saw as I followed) the black car was waiting for him.

I ran, slipping, to the back of the tent, where Stenos was walking out toward the camp, Bird tangled against him.

"He's gone," I said, my relief as overwhelming as my panic had been. I embraced them, my arms circling Bird and just reaching Stenos. Bird accepted it like a statue accepts it; after a moment, Stenos patted my shoulder.

I pulled back and explained what had happened. I stopped short of telling them Bird's madness had driven him away. (I wasn't a fool; if she didn't kill me for saying it, he would.)

Bird said, finally, "How soon do you think he'll be back?"

I blinked. "He's gone," I said, as if to a child.

The pair of them looked at me so pitying that I took a step back, excused myself, and went to the main entrance, where I could thank the rubes as they left, where I couldn't see Bird if I tried.

37.

You're quick to leave the tent when the aerialists have finished.

What is there to keep you? After the last applause, the magic is already over, the tent shrinking around you until you can see the bare bulbs again, the worn-through canvas, the bits of mirror glinting like sharp glass eyes. You leave your beer glass under the bench (or smuggle it out under your coat), and you gather the people you came with, and you wander out through the mostly-empty yard on your way home.

Now the boy in his brass legs seems sad, waving goodbye as if he'd like to follow you. Sometimes there are a couple of dancing girls, swaying halfheartedly to imaginary music. But most likely you are alone in the dark, and your shadows walk ahead of you like they're anxious to be gone, until you're far away from the circus.

It unnerves you, and you don't know why.

By the time you get home you are tired, and on your way you have passed the shabby walls around your city and the sharp-smelling lemongrass growing through the cracks, and just ahead your house is locked up tight waiting for you—things that remind you of the real world, things that annoy and welcome and shake away the creeping unease of some dark circus yard.

By the time the door is shut behind you, you are thinking again of how joyful the tumblers seemed, how fast the jugglers tossed the torches back and forth. You talk about the aerialists—some of them, under the makeup, seemed even pretty. You joke at dinner, tossing rolls back and forth over the table.

Everyone will laugh and pass the rolls high in the air and clap along, until someone starts whistling the sharp-note tune from the circus act.

Then someone (you) will say, "Stop it, I'm hungry, pass me one," and the trick will suddenly settle down, and the meal will take up again. The joke never lasts after someone reminds you of the music.

It's one thing to see a mechanical man, but the Panadrome ruins the meal for everyone if you think about him long enough.

38.

Panadrome was an accident.

Boss had been an opera singer.

There was already a war, of course; there was always war. But a good war was like a good spice, and flavored everything. That season the ticket sales of the opera had soared, as the government men named it one of the things the barbarian enemy did not respect. Their people had not thought to respect it either, before, but it's amazing what a government man can do.

The opera managers made the season a dark, lush one, the sort of thing to stir the deep pride of a nation at war; they lined up *Three Soldiers of the Green*, *The Sorcerer*, *Queen Tresaulta*, *Haynan and Bello*.

Boss was an alto; she sang the nurses, the witches, the kitchen cook. Her closest claim to greatness that season was as the handmaiden of Queen Tresaulta.

Annika Sorenson, the Queen, sang the final aria on the wide staircase of the palace set, descending slowly as her emotions built, until it would be time for her handmaiden to rush forward from behind the great pillar and press a knife into her lady's hands, so that the queen might stab herself and thwart the captors who had sought to use her.

Their *Queen Tresaulta* was a powerful production; it had been advertised as the performance of Annika Sorenson's career, and Boss was beyond disputing it, as much as they all disliked Annika.

Annika was the sort of visiting soprano who demanded that air conditioning be turned off backstage to preserve her throat, as if she'd never been a chorus member shoving herself into a costume in a muggy basement room. (She never had been; a voice like hers spent no time in the chorus.)

The conductor, a stout gentleman just beginning to age, took to drinking after rehearsals. A few weeks before the opening, Boss had come across him in the prop room before rehearsal, sneaking drinks out of a bottle. When he saw her, he gave her a half-defiant, half-sheepish smile.

"My family's vineyard. Early spring, red. Only two years old." He sighed. "I should have stayed there. I don't have the heart for making music no one appreciates until a war breaks out."

She took the bottle and drank.

"It's not a good year," he apologized.

"Tell me about it," she said, and he laughed.

That night, Annika Sorenson was spectacular.

She exceeded even the audition that had gotten her the contract, exceeded the performance tape the opera managers had passed to various governments as part of the invitation to the Summit. That night she sang as if only the notes held her together. By the last aria, the audience was entranced down to the last man, warding off goose-flesh, leaning forward so as not to miss a note.

Her voice echoed off the chandeliers, rolled through the domed ceiling and out the doors. When she fell quiet (after "for this stone hall I lived," as wavering Tresaulta recovers the bravery to kill herself and spare her kingdom from disgrace), the entire hall was silent, rapt.

It was so quiet that the whirring whistle of the bomb was audible for a moment before it reached them.

There was just enough time for Annika to glance up and fix Boss an annoyed look, as if Boss had timed some fireworks on the roof to ruin Annika's evening.

Then it struck.

There are some things Boss knows.

Boss knows that great events have a spirit of their own. Government men speak of it when they hold rallies in beautiful places lined with their soldiers, but they do not think it is true. Greatness seldom reveals itself to government men.

Boss knows the reason some cities fall after the Circus Tresaulti has passed through is because the life of a city flickers and trembles when they are near. Then Tresaulti departs, and the life of the city tries to follow and cannot; even the buildings stumble and fall, become lost. When a city has no greatness, its will is gone; then a city is nothing but a maze of shells that are only stone and steel and—soon enough—dust.

She does not know why it is that some cities have a greatness that allows them to stand, and others crumble less than a hundred years after the circus has passed there. (She tries to save those cities when she can by putting Tresaulti out of reach, as if the spirit of the city might not be offended if it can't see them. "Might not be a good crowd," she says. "We'll camp farther out."

No one suspects another reason; by then, each of them has been driven away from things often enough.)

Boss woke inside a cylinder.

She didn't know what had happened (the bomb—she ached when she remembered) or where she was (trapped inside the pillar). She struck out. The pillar crumbled and peeled under her hands, and she choked on the fine, sour powder as she dragged herself out of her prison as if she was hatching from an egg.

There was no room for her to stand; the stairs had blown apart and the ceiling had caved in. The building was nothing now but a maze of painted wood and marble, deep purple velvet and chips of glass from the chandelier, groaning and swaying and doomed for the ground.

MECHANIQUE: A TALE OF THE CIRCUS TRESAULTI

She called out, absently, for Annika. (It was just the shock talking; she had already seen the fragmented stairs.) The air was so close that with every breath, a layer of powder coated her lungs.

Panic struck and she shouted for anyone, shoving past metal pipes and chairs and the limp arms of the dead.

(More than the bodies, though, more than the air that was already running thin, Boss trembled because the aria had gone unfinished; because the great moment had died.)

She slid carefully through the wreckage, looking for a place with some light or air, some place that indicated there was a way out. She tried to hum, for company, but gave it up—it took up the air.

She found the conductor on her crawl out from the stage, hoping for a pocket of air in the orchestra pit amid the splinters of instruments. He had been separated neatly from his head and hands by a falling beam; his right hand still clutched the baton.

Absently, Boss tied them into her skirt, kept climbing.

It took her three days to crawl out onto the top of the wreckage.

By the time she emerged, she was dragging pounds of detritus with her; springs she'd picked up without meaning to, gears that fell into her outstretched hands, twists of wire that peeled away from the wreckage as she climbed. She had tied a string of ten piano keys to her belt; she had pulled them free of the balcony wall.

The dome at the apex of the Opera House had been blasted sideways and embedded into what was left of the ceiling. She climbed inside the brass-lined curve and lay back, sucking in ragged breaths. When her panic had faded enough for her to move, she unknotted her skirts and arranged her collection at her feet in a little honor guard of metal bits and body parts. The conductor's head rested near her left hand, gazing out mournfully at their city, where war had come.

From where she was curled against the cool metal, she could see burning roofs dotting the sky. Occasionally the sharp report of gunfire would float up from the streets, but it was rare. The fight here was over. Now it was just a matter of the new government grinding the old one to death underfoot, and beginning again with the next city in line. The men who would burn through the city would never even look up and think, What a beautiful building that was, with the brass dome and the music; they would never look up and think, *What a pity*.

"For this stone hall I lived," she sang softly. Her lungs, stretching with the notes, felt like hers again after so many days of struggle. She finished the aria, an octave and a half below Annika's rendition, so quietly that only the walls of the dome caught the sound. They rolled the notes back to her, tinny but true.

She rested the conductor's head in her lap and smoothed its hair. "It was beautiful music," she said. "My compliments."

She watched the sky go from black to grey; slowly the fires burned themselves out, and the gunfire settled, and finally it was that long hour between night and dawn, and she was alone in the world.

She built Panadrome before she ever climbed down from the roof of the opera house.

There was no sign that she had gained some new power. There was just the worm's knowledge that if you push long enough, the corpse will give way. She knew only that if you pull up the brass sheeting with the twisted bar you carry, it will curl into a barrel in your hands and you can fasten it tight; that if you find a home for every gear and coil, for every piano key, you can build a home.

(She did not know, yet, how to do any of it the right way—Panadrome's first set of hands would wither and have to be replaced with ones she fashioned out of silver—but if she had not tried from exhaustion and loneliness and terror, she might never have tried.)

She strapped him to her back for the descent from the heap of rubble that was once the opera house. It took longer than it should have—she stopped, now and then, to pick up wires and joints and the flat backs of the opera chairs, which were useful once the char was scraped off.

When she was on the ground, she put together what remained. She took refuge in the pockets of the outer walls that had been blasted out, and no one with a gun ever looked around enough to see her, working quietly in the grave of the opera house.

At last, she passed her hands over what she had made; and the Panadrome rattled to life. He blinked and flexed his fingers. Tentatively, he touched the piano keys that lay along his right side like ribs. She watched horror and joy and resignation and despair fly over his face.

After a long quiet, he said, "Madam, the piano is not in tune."

"I can fix that," she said, and set to work.

(The dead give way before the worm.)

39.

These are the songs that Panadrome plays:

For the jugglers he plays a march in four-four time, so fast he can hardly keep up with the notes. He changes the song whenever the jugglers change; it gives him a chance to compose something new, and the jugglers will hardly notice.

For the dancing girls, it's a song in a minor key, rolling and swaying. The melody snakes slowly through the tent and, on the right night, can make everyone there think the dancing girls are better than they are.

The strongman gets "The King Enters the Hall," from *Haynan and Bello*. The music suits Ayar, and Panadrome likes the song itself. He's been playing it so long he should hate it, but how can he? This is the music he was born to play, and it's easier to have music sound the way you want it to if you play all the instruments.

For Bird and Stenos, Panadrome plays what he likes; watching them meet and part is a comfort that reminds him of singers falling silent before the knife is handed to them in the final act. Every so often he wishes he could play Tresaulta's theme, but every time he starts, the song bends into something else, and he lets the new notes happen, follows the melody where it leads him.

Some parts of the past cannot be reclaimed, he knows. Better not to raise ghosts.

The tumblers get no song at all, merely a play-along of sounds and scales, where he slides out this note or that one to emphasize how far they're jumping, how fast they flip backwards, to heighten the tension as they crouch and wait.

The aerialists perform to an intricate waltz, a majestic one-two-three one-two-three, timed to the length of the pendulum swing. ("Don't play us the halfpenny oompah those other horrors get," Elena said.)

He plays it the same every night, without thinking. He never has to adjust the tempo of this song; Elena's girls are better trained than most musicians. They do not falter; Elena's girls do not fall.

When Alec had his wings and swooped from the ceiling at the end of the circus, Panadrome fell silent. Alec's wings sang as he flew, each feather a note, and the chord always carried over the gasps and the cheers of the crowd. Every night was a triumph.

Panadrome was forgotten, and when he looked across the tent at Boss, her face upturned to see her lover spiraling down over the adoring audience closer and closer to reaching her, no one thought to look at Panadrome, to see why he was watching his maker.

Maybe it's just that she had been on the road with him for a long time, so long that only the two of them knew, so long that she had gone from treating him like a conductor to treating him like a brother to treating him like one of her own limbs. He looked at her in those invisible moments because he was used to looking at her; because out of them all, she was the only thing that really lasted. That was his reason; that was all.

Better not to raise ghosts.

40.

After Little George has dropped the news about the government man and clanged away, casting resentful glances over his shoulder, the camp seems quieter, as if the worst is already over. The sound of Panadrome playing for the tumblers is muffled by the canvas and applause.

In the distance, Stenos can hear little bell-sounds of the cooking cart being packed away. Mistake; they'll just have to unpack it all again, if they stay.

Stenos carries Bird to one of the trucks, where they can sit alone. She prefers to be away from the others when she can. He has never stopped hating her, but still, better to be alone with her than with the rest of them.

(By now he knows her well enough that hating her is the same as knowing how tall she is; it's a true thing about her; it just exists. He lives around it.)

They sit side by side at the edge of a truck bed, their backs pressed up against the wooden crates where the light bulbs are packed. She's overworked herself; he can see three angry marks on her tunic where the blood has seeped through the scars on her ribs, the black stains on the fabric like bullet holes.

(When he holds on to her he can feel the raised skin where she had been sewn back together, a mountain range sliding under his thumbs.)

One of the crew men passes them and spares Stenos a disapproving look. Stenos ignores it. He used to be one of them, but as soon as Boss saddled him with Bird the crew began to turn their shoulders to him, as if he has the bones by association.

(Boss hasn't said anything about the bones, as if she's waiting for him to prove himself. He hopes she's not going to be too much longer in offering; he hopes she's only waiting until he's earned the wings. No point in suffering more than once.)

The rain has plastered down the dirt, and while she looks at the tent he watches the moon, a white sliver out of his reach.

"What do you think the government man will do with us, when he has us?"

He looks at her. "Soldiers, I suppose," he says, once the terror of her question has faded.

She nods. "Anyone without the bones will be lucky, then," she says. Her feet are hooked on the rigging under the truck, and her legs make two pale crescents against the dark.

He thinks about the last city he hid in, before the circus came, and says, "Or we'll all be shot."

"Same thing," she says, drops her eyes to him. "None of us have any heart left for war."

Us, she says; the ones with the bones.

"If you have any heart left at all," he says.

She smiles like he made a joke; then her mouth becomes a thin line.

He feels like she's always on the verge of telling him something important, but she chokes on it whenever they're alone. Nothing she's said so far worries him at all; nobody in the circus gives a damn about the war, that's something Stenos knows for sure, so he doesn't know what she's getting at.

"We'll see what the government men say when I have the wings," he says.

Her face is suddenly serious, the glass eye gleaming. "Don't get the bones before the government man comes back for us."

She's only saying it because she wants the wings. He can't trust a word of it, he knows.

Still, when she looks at him he can see hunger and fear and hopelessness, but not cunning. He closes his eyes a moment.

"I need a smoke," he says.

"Talk to the dancing girls. Moonlight sells them cheap. She's fair."

"You just want me to die from the smoke," he says.

She glances at him; then she stands and goes. He follows a step or two behind her.

It's strange, always, to watch her walking. Her spine is perfectly straight, her head tilted like her namesake, keeping the tent in the peripheral vision of her good eye. There is a small mark near the small of her back, too, where she's torn the skin and bled.

(He thinks about holding her in his arms that first night, how he had cradled her and felt the cool ridges pressing against his hands. He had thought she was frail; he hadn't realized right away how bad it was, that it was metal against his palm.)

She's light enough that she leaves no footprint in the trampled-down grass.

At the door to the women's wagon she pauses with her hand on the latch, and says without looking at him, "Shall I tell Elena you're waiting?"

It's the first time she's said Elena's name to him. He doesn't know how she knew. There's no way Elena told her. (What else does Bird see when no one knows?)

"No," he manages, listens to the click of the closing door before he leans back against the wagon.

He can still hear her as she steps through the noisy wagon full of girls, the splash of water he knows only her hands make.

It terrifies him to know her.

He sees no way out of this, until one of them has the wings. Stenos knows he's the better choice—he would make a better picture walking at the front of the parade then poor Bird with her one eye. He would know how to make the crowd love him. (He misses applause.)

Looking at Bird, though, he worries; he wonders if she would hesitate to dig the wings out of his shoulders as he slept.

Inside the wagon she has slid into her bed, has turned her face to the wall.

She cuts through him just by breathing.

41.

These are the things Jonah fears:

He fears the government man, who leaves early without explanation. "Bird frightened him off," Little George says, laughing too much, but Jonah has had some experience with government men. He knows they are hard to frighten, because they do so little fighting of their own; Jonah knows the circus will never be safe from him.

He fears the rain. The others come to terms with it; their bones are under the skin, and the rain is a terror that fades. But Jonah's workings are exposed, and it would take so little for him to rust from the inside out. He doesn't know what Boss would do if it happened; maybe she would save him, or maybe she would hold him in between life and death, if she wanted something from Ayar.

(He fears Boss.)

He fears the cold. It makes their bones brittle, and just because they can be repaired doesn't mean it's painless to go under Boss's knife. Jonah knows that more than anyone; she scooped him hollow while he was dead, and when he woke up he was locked for life in a suit that didn't fit and cracked when the winter wind blew.

He has forgiven Ayar, mostly.

He fears for Ayar. Ayar is the kind of man who does any work that's put before him without asking questions, but sometimes he forms an attachment to a lost cause, and each time it drags Ayar through the mud as if Ayar has never had his heart broken. (Jonah knows that for certain; he had been half-awake the whole long walk to the circus yard, Ayar bearing Jonah in his arms like a sacrifice.) If the government man comes back for them, Jonah and Ayar might be separated.

(He fears this most.)

And when he moves through the camp, telling this crewman and that one to pack up the trucks, he realizes he doesn't know their names. He tried to learn everyone's names, and argued with Elena that the crew and the dancers were worth knowing even if they would leave someday.

But now he's worried, and he is thinking only of saving Elena's girls and the tumblers and Ayar and Bird. He has stopped caring about any of the ones who come in and out and grow old and die. He has become like Barbaro or Alto or Elena, who don't even bother to look at someone until they have the bones.

If there was ever a reason to be afraid, becoming like Elena is one.

42.

On the night the government man came, as soon as Jonah had signaled that the tent was empty and the crew had set first watch, I unlocked myself from my metal casts and ran to Boss's trailer.

She was sitting at her dressing table. The last flickering bulbs that hadn't burned out cast her in a sickly light, but I could still tell she had gone pale. The griffin tattoo stood out like ink on paper, she was so white, and she was so distracted that she hadn't even taken off her fancy dress. She was staring unblinking into the mirror, as if she could see past it.

I knocked on the wall (I was too far inside to pretend I hadn't let myself in).

"Come in, George," she said without turning.

I took a few steps closer and locked my hands behind my back like a soldier.

"Some of us want to pack up and go," I said. "You should hold a vote, at least, and see who's for staying and who's for going."

In the mirror, she cut her eyes to mine. Her gaze hit me like a punch, and for a second I felt like Stenos must when Bird trained that glass eye on him.

"I'm going to guess that no one with the bones cares to leave," she said.

(I didn't know what she meant, and I was too angry to examine what she said.)

"Jonah is frightened," I said. "I don't know about the others yet. Elena is scared for sure. Bird doesn't want to leave, but—" I made a face that showed what I thought of Bird's opinion.

Boss smiled into the mirror. "I'm not surprised Bird doesn't want to leave her wings behind," she said. Then, after a moment with me pinned under her stare, she seemed to come to a decision.

She pointed to the stool beside hers. "Come and sit."

I lifted a box of her old circus advertisements off the stool and took a seat. I waited, nervous and glowering at her, feeling like she had brought me low by asking me to sit where I would have to look up at her.

(Now I think she asked me to sit because my legs were trembling from the strain of fighting those false brass knees all night, and she wanted to offer me a little relief before she took my measure.)

Finally she looked away from her reflection and down to me, and she wore that expression I loved most on her, where she was planning something and would need me. If there was sorrow there (and there must have been) it was too dark, and I was too foolish to see it.

"George," she said, "have you decided on the circus?"

I blinked. "How do you mean?"

"Is it what you want, for the rest of your life?"

"Never considered anything else," I said, proud of myself for having an answer ready. "I want to be a tumbler, if I can." Or an aerialist, if Elena wouldn't try to kill me, I thought, but didn't say. I didn't want Boss to laugh me right out of the trailer.

She wasn't laughing. She looked at me, level, like I was her reflection.

"What if you couldn't be an act? Would you still stay?"

"Yes," I said, which sounded less brave, but was just as true. Where else would I go? Join Valeria and be a baker in some town that went dark at sundown, until war started again and I was gunned down in the street?

Her eyes wouldn't let me go. After a long time, she said, "I never wanted you to be like the others. I think that's why I've waited. But now I have something I need to give you, if you'll take it."

It was the most confidence in me I'd ever heard from her. It was the first moment I had ever thought she cared for me. I was overwhelmed; I could hardly breathe.

(I should have known the government man was closing in.)

"Yes," I said.

When she picked up the needle and the little pot of ink, the griffin on her arm leaned forward and shrank back again, trembling, the gears of its metal wings flickering in the guttering light.

"Roll up your sleeve."

I tore it, I was shaking so hard, but I rolled my sleeve up to the shoulder and laid my arm on her desk without having to be told.

"I hope you never need it," she said, and then she began to draw.

43.

The wolf tamer drove the beast up to camp ahead of him, snapping his whip above its head, calling out orders if the wolf strayed from the straight path. The whip-sound carried, and he was half a mile away when the circus started to gather and watch him approach. He whistled shrilly, let the whip sing. The beast cringed with ears back and moved faster.

When he reached the camp, there were nearly two dozen costumed performers waiting for him, and another dozen crew in drab colors. The wolf tamer was pleased; if the circus could sustain this many, it could sustain two more.

"Is the beast yours?"

The woman who had spoken was built like a tower of stone, and had her two lieutenants—one with brass ribs, the other with a brass hunchback—flanking her. So this circus had an order; another good sign.

"Yes, ma'am," he said, picking his next words carefully. This circus was more refined than the bickering cesspool he had expected, and words might matter. "I caught it myself in the woods outside the city. I trained it alone, and it obeys my commands and mine only. Heel!"

The wolf set back its ears and slid at once to his side, half-crouched, waiting for its next order.

"What can it do?" she asked.

"It can jump, and dance, and count to ten."

The woman nodded. Then she half-smiled. "And is the whip for show?"

He had impressed them, then. He bowed and smiled.

"Oh no," he said. "An animal learns best at the end of the whip."

She nodded once, and the wolf tamer thought she was agreeing with him until he heard the whistle, a split second before the whip came down across his face.

(Jonah wielded the thin coil of wire—Boss knew he had the steadier hand, and the advantage of being dismissed when he stood beside Ayar.

Elena admired his aim.)

The wolf tamer thought for a moment that there must have been some mistake, but when he wiped the blood from his brow, he saw thirty stony faces turned on him.

Then Jonah struck again, just below his knee, and he went down screaming.

The wolf tamer stumbled away from the onslaught of the whip, first in shock, then mindless with pain and fear. He tripped and rolled down the hill, banging over rocks and hard ground, until he lay choking on the flat ground below. He staggered up and ran until the terror left him, and then he sank against the city wall and peered back up the way he had come.

He had left his whip behind; the animal had not followed.

The grey wolf lived with the circus for almost a year.

It was largely Jonah's, padding a few feet behind him when Jonah crossed the camp, taking up a satellite position when Jonah was resting. It would not enter Ayar and Jonah's trailer, but it slept on the ground just under the stairs.

As it came to realize that no harm would come to it, it became bolder and harsh, slinking around the edges of the trucks, baring its teeth at anyone it disliked.

It disliked Ayar most; Ayar was the one who had to lock it up at night when they were performing. Animals of its quality were in short supply, and it was too tempting a thing to leave unguarded. Ayar was the only one strong enough to hold the fighting wolf, and the claws seemed not to bother him, even when the wolf drew blood.

Sometimes, as if it missed cruelty, the wolf would follow Elena. It would last a day or two under her icy stares, and then bound away, skulking in the shadows for a week before appearing again under Jonah's trailer.

One day the wolf was wild enough to run into the forest near their camp, hunting something only it could sense. A week later when they pulled down the tent, the wolf had not come back.

"Call it, if you want," Boss told Jonah. "We'll wait."

That night Jonah stood for an hour at the edge of camp, looking into the darkness of the woods.

He came back empty-handed.

Ayar frowned. "It didn't come?"

Jonah said, "I didn't call."

Jonah still thinks of the wolf sometimes when he sees Stenos.

Stenos goes to Elena when he misses cruelty, too.

Jonah wonders if Stenos, too, will grow too hungry to hold; if he will disappear into the dark woods some night and never come out again.

44.

The first city we came to, after we left the city where the government man had seen us, had a name carved in stone above the wall (Phyrra). It had a magistrate, and close-paved walkways, and the only people who carried guns on the streets were the town militia.

When I came through the city with my posters, the magistrate asked me to make sure we kept our camp well clear of the city garden. There were children lining the streets when the parade came through. I'd never seen anything like it; even the peaceful cities and the standing cities weren't like this.

"This is magic," I said to Boss, swinging up into the truck as we drove away from the city up the hill where the crew was setting up camp.

It was the first I had seen of her since she had given me the ink. I had traveled with the dancing girls in their little trailer; we had lost one in the last city (the city needed a stonemason), and I could sleep in a real bunk.

She glanced at me and half-smiled, looking older than I had ever seen her look. She must have had a hard journey. "Most cities were, before the war," she said.

The new griffin on my shoulder ached. (The blood was still drying, over the eyes and along the joints. Boss had tattooed my griffin with metal legs to match his wings, legs that looked like mine.)

"When was that?" I asked. "Before the war. How long ago was that?"

It was the first time I had ever asked her a question like that, and my voice shook.

She looked over. "Farther back than you think."

We passed under the shadow of an oak tree, and in the moments of shade she looked hundreds of years old, like a statue battered by the rain and cracked here and there by a cold winter.

I had never seen her this way before, and I wondered why until I realized it was the tattoo; I saw, finally, there was magic at work here that was darker and deeper than I had imagined, that the tattoo was like putting a pair of spectacles on a child with poor vision.

I stared up at the camp hill, my heart in my throat, and wondered what everything would look like, now that I could see.

The government man came the next day, as the sun was going down, and we were setting up for the show.

His three cars climbed up the hill and slid into our camp, three black dogs come to feast. I feared him, suddenly, as I hadn't thought I could fear anything. How could he have found us, unless he had followed us? How could he follow us and we not have known?

(The magistrate must have sent word when he saw us coming. One government man looks after another, and the magistrate had worked hard for his city's peace.)

I was at the edge of camp in an instant, watching the cars. Boss came behind me. She glanced at their approach, then walked across camp, so that when the cars came over the hill, she would be framed by the tent. (Ringmaster habits; Boss believed in a good show, no matter what.) Then she folded her arms and waited.

The government man had brought more men with him this time—six of them, with jackets that seemed strained under the arms, where a holster would go.

I took a step towards Boss. "What should we do?"

"You'll do what I tell you," Boss said, lightly, and motioned me back with her left arm. Her griffin tattoo seemed to shrink back from the approaching men.

Around us, the performers were gathering.

"Madam," said the government man when he was close enough not to have to shout. He smiled and inclined his head, as if they were alone and he was pleased to see her. "You left so soon."

"We like to hit as many cities as we can before the frost," she says. "The trucks run slow on the ice."

His smile got wider. "Interesting. I would love to hear more about your operations. I'm always interested in examples of order. Would you mind coming with me? I'm always more comfortable having long chats when I'm safe at home."

The two men nearest her shifted and slid their hands inside their jackets.

Boss looked from the government man to his backups. Then she shrugged, as if he had asked for the last glass of beer, and glanced coolly at me over her shoulder. "I'm going with the Prime Minister to discuss the circus. I'll be back soon."

She slid the workshop key off her neck and handed it to me, right in front of him, like it was worth no more than a bottlecap.

I thought, so it's Prime Ministers these days. I thought, It's a lie. You don't come back when a government man takes you away to answer a few questions about your business.

"Yes, sir," I said.

As soon as their backs were turned, I looped the chain over my neck and shoved the key out of sight.

Boss moved placidly through the camp alongside the government man. She walked slowly, though, as if the bulk of her body dragged on her (it was the first time I'd seen it, but a good scam for a rube), and by the time she had reached the cars, there was enough of a crowd that the Prime Minister frowned at us all. Gently, he took Boss's arm and made her turn to face them.

"So they don't worry," he invited her.

She smiled and looked over at us. "I'll be back in a day or two," she said. "The Prime Minister has some questions about mechanics."

Her voice shook on the last word.

No one spoke. From where I stood, I could see Ying, her face chalk-white, her hands balled into trembling fists at her sides. Nothing else moved.

Then, from the center of the knotted performers, Bird leapt out.

The jump was so high and fast that I thought someone must have launched her, but Stenos was too far away.

She spread her arms and curled up her legs as she jumped, her knees tight to her chest and her feet as hooked as a hawk's talons, and I saw that she would land on the government man's throat with her feet and knock his head clean off his shoulders—then we'd have to fight, kill them all before they could call for help.

She hung in the air for ages. Someone in our crowd started to call out.

Then came the gunshot.

Bird cried out and fell; I saw the blood pouring from her right ankle where the bullet had struck her. She landed in a heap, turned away from us, one arm extended and the fingers curled in.

I saw Alec, suddenly, in the crumpled body—as sharp as if I was back in the tent all those years ago, listening to the last trembling notes from his wings.

Mina screamed. The government man shouted an order, and his men converged on Bird, dragging her limp body to one of the three dark cars. Someone in the crowd shouted for the men to stop, and a few of the crew moved forward—they were answered with a volley of shots in the air. The crowd froze, but the murmur swelled.

"Don't wait for me," Boss said under the noise—she was looking right at me, my arm burned—and then she was being dragged after the Prime Minister to the black sedan that was standing open and waiting for them.

Stenos was already running after them when Ayar caught him.

He lifted and swung Stenos around in a single motion, so that when the government men turned, they saw only Ayar's back.

The car's engines roared to life.

"We've lost enough!" Ayar was hissing, over Stenos' struggles. "What can you do?"

Boss's dark head was silhouetted in the window of the black sedan as the three cars snaked away down the hill to the main road, headed east to the capital city.

The camp was shocked into silence, so quiet that I heard Elena's labored breathing as the cars disappeared down the hill.

Stenos pulled at Ayar even after the cars were gone, kicking Ayar's chest, shoving at Ayar's face, aiming for his ribs—a man possessed, trying get some leverage to break out. The only sound in the frozen camp was the creak and bang of Ayar's skeleton as Stenos threw himself against it.

Ayar shouldn't have been concerned about stopping him (Stenos was strong, but Ayar was unstoppable), but I remember Ayar holding on for dear life, as if the moment he let go Stenos would be out of his grasp and flying after the car to murder them all.

(I wish he had let go.)

45.

This is why Elena is breathing hard:

She and Bird reach the gathering crowd at the same time. Boss has not yet turned back to them and spoken—it looks like everything is already settled for Boss, that Boss is already gone.

Elena knows what comes now, and trembles.

Bird asks, quietly, "Will they kill her?"

Elena has gone off with a government man before (perhaps Bird knows—Bird listens when you hope she isn't), but that was a different government. That man felt stupid not knowing how the trick was done, and after Boss showed him he couldn't get rid of her fast enough.

This man, she knows, is a different breed. She looks at his impassive face, the anticipation in his eyes.

"Yes," Elena says.

They watch as the government man pulls Boss around to face them, and invites her to lie about where she's going, as if she's coming back.

Bird says without looking, "Can you throw me?"

Elena glances over at Bird, sizing her up. No reason to go on without the woman who can give her the wings, Elena guesses. Or maybe Bird has the most experience killing people. Some people find themselves very good at killing, once they get start-ed. You do strange things out in the world before you join the Circus.

"You'll die too," she says.

Bird never looks away from the government man. She says, "All right."

Elena doesn't think any more about it. She crouches and laces her fingers, to give Bird a place to step.

The crew knows something is wrong, and the ripple of discontent distracts the government men, who don't know where to look. Elena keeps her eyes fixed on where Bird will fly and knots her muscles around the copper bones; dimly she feels the solid weight of Bird's foot in the sling of her hands (perfect balance), and then in a single motion so smooth that no one sees, Elena uncoils, stands up, lets go.

Bird flies five feet over the heads of the crowd, arms like a falcon's wings, ready to strike, and Elena can't hear anything but the blood pounding in her ears.

It's not fear that makes breathing so difficult. She's just unused to so much liftoff, is all. Elena has nothing to be afraid of. She's not the one who jumped.

(She lowers her hands, so no one sees what happened.)

When the shot comes, Elena's the only one who doesn't jump at the sound.

Then Mina is screaming, and shots are going off, and Ying has cried out, and Elena has to step forward and grab Ying's arm to keep her from running to Bird and getting dragged off, too.

(The problem with softhearted people is that they can't control themselves in bad circumstances. She doesn't know why Boss keeps letting them in.)

Elena watches Bird get shoved into one of the black cars and hopes that Bird is better at planning revenge than she looks, because right now Elena has her doubts.

(It isn't true. Bird was born to plan revenge. It's why Elena offered Bird her hands. Elena doesn't believe in lost causes.)

As the crowd begins to disperse, Elena stands where she is, watching the cars as if Bird will fly through one of the windows and wreak havoc on them. Even after the cars are gone, she watches the horizon. It's the closest she's come to goodwill for Bird, to hope Bird kills them all.

Dimly, she hears Stenos and Ayar struggling, but she doesn't turn to look. If Stenos is hoping to save his chance for the wings, he's too late, and if he's racing after his partner, it's not the sort of display Elena would care to see.

Why make a fool out of yourself for someone you're supposed to hate?

(That's the problem with softhearted people. No control.)

47.

The first government man who asks Boss to follow him comes seventy years before the second one.

That first one comes for a visit, and even though one of the dancing girls shows him that her copper hand is only a glove, he is suspicious. (He was a fool, but not as stupid as some.)

He demands that Boss come with him at once to the capital city over the hill. (They're closer to the capital city than they will ever camp again; after this, Boss loses her taste for capital barter.)

"And bring someone," he says, waves an arm to indicate that all her freaks are the same.

The camp is small back then—maybe ten performers if the dancing girl hasn't run away, and no crew. Still, Boss doesn't even look behind her when the order comes.

"Elena," says Boss.

In the audience hall with windows like prison bars (must have been a factory once), he asks how Boss does it. Boss explains politely that she has no idea, that sometimes these things just come upon one.

"Show me," he says.

Elena watches Boss with narrowed eyes, but she stays where she is, at Boss's side.

Boss passes her hand over Elena and kills her.

The body slumps to the floor. Someone runs from the shadows to see if Elena is really dead (someone smarter and less afraid than his master, whose upper lip is sweating).

"It's a trick," he says.

The man touches Elena's neck, holds her wrist, puts his hand to her open mouth. He shakes his head.

At the end of a long quiet, the government man says, "Bring her back."

Boss passes her hand over Elena. Nothing happens.

The government man is sweating now, wiping his hands on his pants. "But—you can bring her back."

Boss shrugs. "It comes and goes," she says, with the air of the long-suffering.

Twice more she passes her hands over Elena's body. Then she steps back, clears her throat.

"Very sorry," she says, solemn. "I can't revive her."

The government man balks at the words, stares down at Elena's dead body. (The hollow bones are more flexible than bones that are real; splayed on the concrete of the capitol building, her corpse looks like a flattened spider.)

He is a government man by accident, anointed for having survived longer than his fellows. He has been told the circus is a source of income, if he can only convince the woman that it's more than her life is worth to refuse. He is new to war; seeing someone stripped of life is still novel enough to frighten.

"Go," he chokes. He feels ill. "Get out."

"The body—"

"I'll bury it," he says, as if it's an apology.

"Will you dispose of it promptly?" Boss asks. "It's my religion."

The government man has sunk a little towards the floor as his knees give; he looks up at her, blinks.

There is no car waiting for her at the gate, so she walks the four miles back to camp. (Never again does she let the circus get this close to the capital city; important people have no manners.)

She holds on to Elena as much as she can, thinks the name with every step, to tie Elena down to her until they can find her again.

At the top of the hill Boss passes Star the dancing girl, two jugglers, Nayah and Mina on the practice trapeze. Nayah and

Mina freeze when they see her walking alone, but they don't climb off the trapeze or call out to ask what's happened to Elena. In days like these, it's no surprise when someone goes out and doesn't come back.

Alec sees her and comes running, the wings humming behind him.

Boss holds up her hand, stops him in his tracks, keeps walking alone.

She closes herself in her trailer and pulls the shades. It's not the same as being thrown in a grave, but it's close enough.

Boss closes her eyes and listens, tries to grab hold of Elena. She can't wake up still buried in the ground (too cruel even for Elena), but if Boss can't hold on to her until dark, there might be nothing left of Elena to bring back.

(Boss had done it without thinking; she had only done what she knew would frighten him the most. No government man liked to see that kind of power over something he owned. The whole point of ruling was to not be subject to the same death as the common people.

Elena, though, had known what was coming. That narrow-eyed accusation hadn't been for nothing.

Hold on, Boss thinks. Hold on.)

Boss ignores the tinny wheeze at the door that means that Panadrome is outside clearing his throat. She ignores, later, the glissando that begins the aerialist number, which he plays over and over, as if Elena might come looking for the sound.

Boss keeps her eyes closed and her mind fixed on the memory of Elena's audition: swinging on the makeshift trapeze with her eyes closed, sliding and spinning in the moment of weightlessness, dropping and reaching out to grab hold without looking, as if the trapeze is a magnet, as if she knows the bar will never fail her.

Elena was the first person who ever auditioned; back before there was even a proper circus, Elena was the one who knocked on Boss's door and asked, "Do you have an aerialist? I'm trained."

(The first performers who found Boss, that first generation of circus folk, were trained. The ones who came after were only talented—lifetimes of scaling walls and finding things to take hold of to keep from falling.

It makes no difference to Boss how they come by the skill, so long as they perform. Some of them fight like dogs about it when they're alone, but people will always find something to fight about.)

It wasn't Elena's audition that impressed Boss, though it was the best audition Boss would ever see for the trapeze. It was that after Elena had made the trapeze (out of a length of old pipe and two ropes that she slung from a tree), she stood on top of the branch and took off her coat, her boots, her socks, her scavenged sweaters, the belt with her knife strapped to it. By the time she slid down the rope to the bar, she was wearing nothing but a thin shirt and her underwear.

In days like those, the first fever of war, still Elena had left her knife and boots behind for better balance on a homemade trapeze. That's what impressed.

Boss had seen immediately that lighter, stronger bones would be the only things that lasted for the aerialists. Left alone, their bodies would crumble and break. The whole time Elena was auditioning, Boss was deciding how to ask Elena if she was willing to die for it. Though, watching her unfold on the trapeze, looking safer and stronger than she had with her boots and her knife, Boss would have taken Elena even if she had refused the bones.

(In the end it was better to be practical. "You'll die if I give you a metal skeleton," Boss said. She indicated Panadrome, who watched from the corner of the trailer. She said, "But then afterwards you might wake."

There was a quiet as the "might" filled the room.

Then Elena said, "Well, that's one thing over with," and stretched out on the table.)

Boss lets Elena sit in the ground until nightfall.

As soon as it's dark, she opens the door. Alec is standing by the steps, waiting. There is a long, straight groove in the ground where he has paced back and forth.

Boss says, "Bring her home."

Before she's finished, Alec has spread his wings, and he disappears into the night sky in a gust of air and a hush of notes.

Boss doesn't worry if he'll find her in the graveyard beyond the city. He'll know where she is. Something about the wings brings him whatever luck he needs.

Boss brings Elena back as soon as her body is laid out on the table; no point in wasting time.

When Elena takes her first gasping breath, she chokes up a wet cough of mud, claws at the dirt over her eyes. Boss lets Elena struggle back to life without interfering, trying not to notice the tears drawing clean lines on Elena's filthy face.

Eventually Elena is herself again. She sits up, her legs dangling.

Boss doesn't say, I'm sorry. She doesn't say, If I had to choose again it would still be you, because you would work hardest to return.

"Welcome back," Boss says instead.

Elena's face is pale from a day without blood, and her arms, propping her up, are trembling. She flexes her fingers against the edge of the table, fixes her eyes on Boss. There's a leaf knotted in her hair, green against the dirt, and Boss wonders how deep they buried her.

(Years from now, a man will drive a wolf to the top of a hill, and Boss will see this same gaze. Years from now, Boss will rescue the wolf, for old time's sake.)

At last, Elena slides off the table and walks outside without a word.

Outside, Elena's silhouette walks to one of the rain barrels, and after a moment Boss can see beads of water flickering in the dark, falling into nothing.

47.

Elena washed off the worst of the grave, and then she went into the circus tent.

The bulbs were all out for the night, and the canvas was like a cape thrown over the stars, but Elena sat and waited for Alec to come. She was patient; it was no different from waiting in the ground.

(Alec's wings had half-woken her; she remembered being wet and cold, remembered opening her mouth to call for him. That was when the dirt got in.

Then there was nothing but darkness until she heard Boss welcoming her home again. It was her third time being born. She had hoped it got easier. It had been a disappointment.)

She knew Alec was coming before she heard his wings, before he pushed the tent flap aside and let the moon flood the space with light.

When she ran to him, he embraced her so tightly that she cut her hands on his feathers.

"I felt it," he said into her hair. "It was like someone had cut off my wings. It must have been terrible. Oh, Elena."

Underneath the stink of earth that had invaded her, there was the smell of copper bowls in summer that she knew was his.

"It's all right, brother," she said, and felt him smiling into her neck at the word.

Brother was the closest name she had for him. Boss gave everyone a name when they woke again, but she really needed to make new names for everything, Elena thought, names that would fit what happened when you were tied together this way without escape.

"Welcome home," he said, and she could feel his happiness and worry. (His hands were scraped raw from digging her out.)

"Let me see," she said.

He turned carefully (the edges of his wings could slice through to the bone if he was careless), and even in the pitch-black tent the wings shone, folded tight against his body like dragon scales.

When she touched the top of each wing, the arch was warm, and it felt like home. Her bones were inside the sculpted brass there, and the heat from his body bled through the marrow. Under her hands, Alec trembled.

("She made them from whatever she could find," he had told her. It meant that Boss had used strangers' ribs to build her masterpiece, that now Alec carried folded on his back an endless cacophony of the dead.)

She knew which bones were hers (touching there was like waking up from a dream), and sometimes she touched the petals, to straighten one out where the wind had bent the tip, but she never touched anything else of the frame, where the bones were wrapped. She was afraid what might happen if one dead thing seeped into another.

(It was already taking its toll on Alec. He couldn't sleep; he looked around for conversations no one was having, and he folded his wings tighter and tighter along his back as if to cover their mouths.

"Tell her," Elena said, and Alec shook his head, said, "How could she understand?")

"I'm all right," she said, and to prove it she smiled, though he couldn't see. He'd feel it; he was her brother.

Alec sighed, and the wings moved with him, a single note that seemed to close the space between them and bring her home again.

Elena rested her forehead on the warm skin below his neck and closed her eyes. Of all of them, Alec seemed to be the only one who brought all his life with him; Alec was the one who never grew cold.

48.

This is what Elena sees the first time she meets Bird:

Hunger.

Elena sees the darkness of the tent; the darkness of the grave; the shiver of the wings as Alec trembled under her hands, his feathers an armor that would not hold.

"She won't last," Elena says.

Alec didn't.

49.

I stared after the cars for a long time, as if it had all been a joke and any moment they would turn around and apologize. I felt sick, and once my legs shook like they were going to buckle, but I couldn't tear my eyes away from the brown ribbon of road where the cars had disappeared.

(Part of me was waiting for the sound of a gun, as if there was a thread attaching me to Boss, and that one sharp crack would sever it.)

At last I managed to turn my head away and look around me. The crowd had vanished. In all that expanse of trampled grass where they had stood there was only Elena left, and she was watching me.

I had a terrifying moment of imagining we were the only two people left in the world.

"She might want us to get to someplace safer," I said. I didn't sound like I believed it—I couldn't even think it might be true. I wrapped my left hand around my throbbing right arm. I didn't have to listen to Boss. It must have been for the benefit of the government man. How would Boss let one day of this circus happen without her?

"If we're safe, then once she and Bird are out she can look for us," I said. I tried to make it sound like the kind of plan a sane person would come up with. "I bet that Boss could find us in a week flat once she comes out of that city."

Elena's mouth went into a thin line.

"Little idiot," she said too sweetly, "there's no coming back from where she's gone, unless Bird throws you a miracle you don't deserve."

Through my shirt, I could feel the raised scars of the griffin under my fingers. Its mouth was open, as if it was keening for something it had lost.

I walked back through camp out of habit, making the rounds as always. If it seemed like all the color had been seeped from the circus folk, it was only because my eyes were dry from the dust. If it felt like I was locking them in, then it was only because I had changed, not because they had.

(Of course they had changed; their ringmaster was gone. They weren't a circus any more.)

I passed Jonah and the crew and the dancing girls, who were packing up, rolling canvas and strapping down anything that might break if we had to make a break for it. Moonlight and Minette were crying as they lifted, but they worked in time with the rest. There was a show to move; no one slacked.

Ayar was leaning against the door of the trailer he shared with Jonah and Stenos, and I wondered why until I heard the thud of something against the wall. Ayar caught my eye and spread his hands.

"What could I do?" Ayar asked me. "He can't get hold of himself, and I can't strike him."

If Ayar struck someone, they didn't get up again.

"Let him fight until he tires," I said. "If you can wait that long. Then let Elena in—she'll talk some sense into him."

He half-smiled, nodded, and as I walked away I wondered why he had sought my council. I was the person who relayed orders, not the one who gave them.

Panadrome was inside the workshop (he didn't need a key), picking up nails and bolts from the floor with his nimble fingers and sorting them into their jars and cans, his face a mask. He could have been feeling anything, or nothing. Panadrome was barely human; he was hard to read.

My stomach turned sour watching him. I felt more alone now than I had standing at the edge of camp watching Boss disappear, and I didn't know why.

I circled the camp twice before I realized why I was restless: I hadn't seen Ying. Ying, whose friendship had faded every year I hadn't gotten the bones—and thinking about Boss's face in the shadows, I felt like a fool for never seeing. I should have guessed; I should have known.

It was important, suddenly, for me to know that she was within the camp and accounted for, safe from the grip of whatever horror was planning to visit us next.

Ying was inside the tent, under the bleachers, and though she was quiet, I knew before I saw her that she had been crying. (Over the years Ying had found strange places to grieve, because no one cried in the aerialists' trailer; Elena didn't allow it.)

The secret she had been keeping all this time was a fence between us. Even now I kept my distance, waiting to speak until she sensed me there.

"Ying," I said, softly.

She looked up. Her face, too, was different now that I had the griffin on my shoulder. She was no older, but I saw at once how she had changed, how the years had settled into the hollows under her cheeks and the line between her brows, like she had been drawn in ink a hundred years ago and the detail had faded away.

How much time had passed outside the circus since I came along, in all those years when I was only half-awake?

"Is Elena looking for me?"

Were we so distant now that she thought I wouldn't seek her out if something was wrong?

"No," I said, "I am."

Her face grew still, and she watched me with bottomless eyes. I looked at her secret face, wondered if I had changed for her the way she had for me. Maybe there was something different because of the griffin; maybe there was something she could take as a sign of what I understood.

There must have been, because when I held out my hand to her she leapt up and embraced me, her arms locked around my shoulders, her tears warm on my face.

It was the only part of her that was warm. The rest of her was cold as the grave.

Gently I wrapped my arms around her to pull her closer, rested my cheek on her hair. I felt her warming under my touch, watched my hands move up and down on her spine as she breathed.

(There were things about the circus I was just beginning to understand.)

50.

This is what happens when you enter the capital city in a government sedan:

You have been driving since before dark. (It's a miracle he found you in the first place; you make it a point to stay as far from this city as you can.)

You wait in the shadow of the city walls—mostly intact, filled in with shrapnel wherever bombs have carved holes in the rock. The soldiers at the gates glance inside at you, then turn their attention to making way for this year's master.

The city gates are wood, covered with metal sheets, and when they open it looks like the inside of your performers, who each seem awake and alive until you hit the center and realize that this is no real person—this is an armor skeleton with a human wrapped around it.

You wonder if anyone in the other car is tending to Bird's ankle.

The guards don't look at you as you drive through them, which means they don't expect to see you again on your way out.

The city is locked-down and quiet in the dark, tidy avenues and tidy businesses building a monument to the competence of the government man who keeps them safe from the screaming hordes.

(By now the circus will be packing—maybe by now they have already gone. You fold your hands in your lap, slowly, so the government man does not see them shaking.)

The capitol is a beautiful building, the most beautiful thing you've seen inside the gates. As the guards walk you through the front doors (funny, you thought prisoners usually went in some other way), you recognize the architecture of the audience chamber, the rings of seats, the domed ceiling, like a dream someone explained to you a long time ago.

Bird's broken ankle creaks. When you glance behind you to see how badly she's been shot, one of the guards politely presses a pistol to your shoulder blades, in case you were thinking of stopping.

It takes you too long to remember (it has been a long time between your beginning and now), but all at once the memory strikes you: this was a theatre, before.

(Annika looked at you over her shoulder, because the sound of the falling bomb was just within your pitch.)

This is when you are closest to weeping.

"It was a theatre," you say.

The government man says, "Yes," mournfully.

Then he draws himself up, says, "And will be again. Any decent world needs art."

(Here you are closest to loving him.)

They walk you across, and as you step backstage you know that no prisoner ever comes this way if they expect to let her out again.

You hope George listened when you told him not to wait. You hope all of them are miles away, that they never come back to this country. There are other, safer places. A circus always finds a home; everyone wants a show.

The warren of backstage hallways gives way to a door that locks only from the outside, another staircase. When the two soldiers try to negotiate Bird down the stairs, they stumble and argue.

"It only takes one," you say.

"Shut up," says someone, but the sound of shifting bodies behind you means they've listened.

(It's good if they think it only takes one man to handle Bird. Let them underestimate.)

The stairs go down and down and down, until the walls are stone slippery with mold. The only light is from the lines of bare bulbs studded in the walls between metal doors. The bulbs reflect off the doors, throwing light as far as they can before the inky black sucks it up.

The guards have forgotten you, and they keep their pistol hands close to their sides. Darkness is always frightening if you've never really seen it.

(It took you three days to climb out of the wreckage. You know your way in the dark.)

Bird is closer behind you now. The man is beginning to struggle with her. (Boss forgets that it's hard to carry someone when you don't do it every night.) The open wound smells like a penny.

"She needs to be tended," you say.

You don't know if you can do to Bird what you did to Elena. You don't know if Bird would even give in to you enough to die.

"Then you had better answer some questions for me so I'm inclined to let you help her," says the Prime Minister. He stops, knocks absently on one of the doors. The sound echoes down the hall. (F sharp.)

"Here," he says.

The pistol presses at your back and guides you inside—you have to stoop to clear the doorway—and then you are locked in.

There is a slit in the door like in a knight's helmet, and when you press yourself against the door and look out into the soggy dank, you catch the last glimpse of the soldier carrying Bird; when they pass, there is the gleam of one glass eye fixed on you, bright as a lantern in the dark, until they turn a corner and vanish.

Then you are alone in the cell, and at last, fear closes in.

51.

She has not been alone in years; not once, since she made Panadrome.

Panadrome requires the most work—he falls easily into disrepair. (He was made when she was not quite herself.)

Every few months he wanders into the workshop or her trailer, knocking gently on his casing.

"I've gone a little sharp in the upper register," he'll say, making an abashed face. She chalks it up to a conductor's habits. It's tricky to be betrayed by your instruments.

Today he knocks on her trailer, and when she opens the door he's already pulling a face. (He never outright complains about how he's been made, but he finds any other way he can.)

"D-flat," he says, and she says, "Let's have a look."

The workshop is Panadrome's second home, he's in it so often, and when they come in he looks at the bits of metal scattered over the table and gives Boss a baleful look.

She grins, pats the table. "Lie back."

She doesn't put him under—he's so much metal that there's hardly anything left to fix a life to. There's no point putting him to sleep and finding he can't wake up again. Good musicians are hard enough to find.

They don't talk—it's just the soft clinking of his workings, and once in a while the thrum of a string as she tests the tone. But after a while he says, as if he just thought of it, "I think Ying is still struggling with losing Alec, even after all this time."

She can get in line, Boss thinks.

She drops the wrench on the table, closes Panadrome's casing with a careful click. She says, "She'll live."

He is tactfully silent.

("You should have waited," he said, when he saw that Ying had gotten the bones, but when she said, "No point in waiting any longer," he didn't argue. A moment later he ran a scale with one hand and said quietly, "Poor girl."

By then they had seen enough children raised up on roots and scrounge-meat to know that there was no bloom of youth worth waiting for. Now children grew like hard little scrub-trees, short and wiry, and skin thicker than bark if they wanted to survive. Ying would have a better childhood on the bars under Elena's iron hand than she would have anywhere outside.)

Boss and Panadrome step outside into the late afternoon light, and for a moment Boss feels that the circus is a true home. Sometimes, by accident, they become a family.

The crew is resting, playing cards in the truck beds with the dancing girls. Elena is drilling her girls in the newly unfurled tent. Jonah and Ayar are sitting side by side against their trailer, passing a badly rolled cigarette back and forth. The Grimaldis are doing whatever counts as practice when they spend most of the time leaping over one another and laughing.

They can't find a decent hill in this wasteland, so she can see Stenos and Bird (still a new act) coming back to camp long before they want to be seen.

It doesn't look like things went well; from this far away Boss can still see the two red marks on Bird's thin shirt where the blood has turned tacky. Bird is draped across his shoulders chest-up, like a corpse or the bent wood of a bow.

"I worry," says Panadrome.

Boss knows he worries (she knows every part of him, she made him fresh from nothing), but what can she tell him to do—stop?

"Too late now," she says.

He doesn't argue with her , but when he opens his mouth a moment later, it comes out a sigh in D flat.

(Bird stared up at the ceiling as Boss cleaned out her bad eye in preparation for the glass.

"My lungs are full of smoke," she said, and Boss didn't know if it was better or worse to tell her that Stenos had been afraid to see her die, had given her air she didn't need.

"Close your other eye," Boss said. "This will hurt.")

Boss holds up her hand against the angling sun and watches the perpendiculars of their joined backs disappearing.

Maybe the wings aren't worth this, she thinks. She should take them apart. That would settle the question. With nothing to fight over, maybe their dread would bleed out of them.

"You should dismantle the wings," Panadrome says, after a while. (They've known each other too long.)

"I should," she says.

(She never will. They were Alec's.)

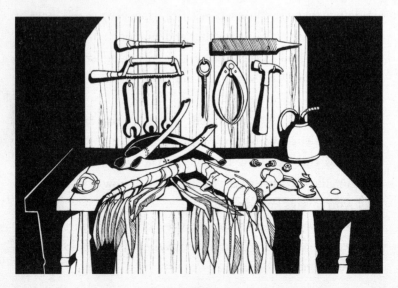

52.

Elena never thought of Alec before he got the wings.

By then the circus was growing. They had Alto and Altissimo (the Grimaldi Brothers, as if they needed another reason to feel smug—Boss got carried away sometimes with the names), and Nayah and Mina with her on the trapeze, and a dancing girl who was just a dolled-up refugee, letting the circus bring her home by degrees as she draped herself in tattered veils and enticed soldiers into the tent every night.

Elena hadn't wanted her ("What's next, a brothel under the benches?"), but Boss had a soft heart for lost causes.

Sometimes Boss knocked on her door and asked her to take a look at someone, if it was hard for Boss to get a read through the performer's desperation to please. (One thing Boss never questioned about Elena was her ability to tell who had the heart for something and who didn't.)

But Elena ignored when Boss scooped some kid out of the dirt and raised him as a lap dog, and she ignored when Boss saw a handsome face in the crowd one night and pulled him out to be her favorite.

He came through the camp every day of their engagement outside that city, with Little George running after him whenever he passed close enough to catch, and the dancing girl setting down her sewing to wave properly at him. After ten days, Elena couldn't ignore him any more. Boss had kept them near this city twice as long as they'd ever stayed in one place—he was no camp follower.

He was beautiful (she gave Boss credit for good taste, at least): golden hair and a smile as if he had never seen war. But Elena couldn't imagine what Boss's plans would be.

"Will she give him the bones or not?" Elena asked Pana-drome. (There was no point asking Boss anything.)

Panadrome watched Alec crossing the camp, and spread his human hands on their metal stems. "Could you cut out the bones of someone you loved?"

Elena thought about the table that had served as a workbench back before Boss had a circus, the little glimpse of the blade before the knife came down, and knowing that whatever came next would have to be better than living.

"He'll be better off than any of the rest of us," she said. "Wait and see."

And that was the last she thought of him. Even when they were back on the road, and he had somehow come with them instead of being left behind in the city like any other visitor would be, Elena thought no more about it than that Boss was a fool to be so loving, knowing how the circus ground everything to powder in its teeth.

Big George came to them with one working arm, asking for work in the crew, and ended up under the knife as a living trapeze.

"I don't like it," Elena said.

Boss said, "I don't care. When I wake him up, take him to the rig."

"You can't keep taking everyone," Elena said.

Boss looked over. "There's only one so far that I regret," she said, and Elena rolled her eyes.

(Boss had listened, though; after that she was more careful about who she chose.)

"You'll get used to me," George said as they crossed the yard. He kept his arms out in front of him like two battering rams, never quite looking at them, and it sounded like he was trying to convince himself. "It's no different than a trapeze partner."

Elena said, "I wouldn't know."

The next time Alec came to her notice, she was rehearsing Nayah and Mina and Big George, deciding the best way to arrange jumps now that their trapeze was alive.

"It would help us to think of you as alive if you actually put power into the swing," she said to George. "We usually leave the corpse impressions for the dancing girl. We'll send you over to her, if you like. There has to be some way you can make yourself useful there."

George blinked, frowned. Mina shot him a sympathetic glance. (Mina's heart bled for everyone. Elena was surprised Mina had lasted long enough to find the circus to begin with.)

"It might be easier if I held myself lengthwise," George said, and Mina obligingly took refuge on one of his arms so he could balance himself.

Elena was on the verge of her decision (horizontal was better, George was right, if he could hold it), but she felt a sudden tug, as if someone had tied a thread around her ribs and pulled it taut.

When she turned to look for what had happened, Alec was stepping down from Boss's workshop, spreading his wings for the first time.

He shook them out in a hail of notes, stretching them wide. Elena couldn't breathe; the thread around her ribs was painfully tight.

Alec frowned for a moment and glanced at Elena, but then Boss was saying something, and Alec turned his laugh to her, and Elena was left looking at the dorsal of the wings. They were beautiful—she'd known he'd have it better than the rest of them—but something about them pained her.

It had pained him, too. Elena had seen Alec's face when he looked over at her, confused and frightened, as if someone had given him more information about her than he'd cared to know.

At first she thought what she felt was desire. He was beautiful, that was no secret, and everyone in the circus got lonely enough to find someone attractive, sooner or later. But it wasn't; she hadn't thought much of him that way before, and she didn't now.

Then she thought it was envy that he merited the last act because of his wings, when she did all the training to make her act remarkable. (Even before the war, their aerial act would have been something to see. She trained them as if there were still an intact world to impress; she refused to let everything go to seed just because some people settled for less.)

But Alec watched her as much as she watched him, and she knew at heart what it was; she knew what the trouble was the first time he stepped outside and shot her that one glance.

It was the first time he had ever looked Elena in the eye, and there was only one reason he would have turned away from Boss for even a moment.

Something was wrong with the wings.

Elena waited nearly a year to see Alec alone.

Before the show began he had to climb to his place in the rigging, where he would wait during the entire performance for the lamps at the top of the tent to turn on and reveal him. The rest of the time he spent with Boss, who was the only person who didn't seem diminished standing beside Alec. (Against Boss, everything gave way.)

But one night, when Elena was alone in the tent practicing on the trapeze, Alec found her.

She was upside down when she sensed him, and it worried her that she knew it was him before she saw him. The sound of the wings must have told her, she thought at the time.

(It wasn't true.)

She wrapped one leg around the rope, curled into herself, grabbed hold, slid upright. When she was sure the rope would hold, she looked down at him.

"If you're going to stare, you should pay your way like the rest of them," she said.

He said, "Elena, would you please come down for a moment?"

She hadn't thought he had manners. (She'd never listened.) She'd assumed people loved him because he was beautiful. Manners were a different thing—rarer than beauty, and more lasting.

She came down.

It was the middle of the night, and the tent was pitch dark, since Elena never wasted oil on a lamp just to practice by, but as she stepped off the rigging she knew already where he was.

It was just that the wings gave off some light, she thought. (It wasn't true.)

When she reached him, his face looked more serious than she'd ever seen it, and for a moment her heart seized like it used to when she was a child and imaginary sounds were enough to frighten her.

He asked her, "Have you felt anything?"

She thought about growing up during the war, dying, living through the circus.

"Not for a long time," she said.

His face was suffused with sympathy, as if he really did think it was sad, as if he wanted to understand her. She wondered what his game was.

"Have you felt . . . " he frowned, made a vague motion between them with his hands. "To me? With me?"

She went cold.

"Why?"

Alec glanced away. The wings shivered. "She made the wings with human bone," he said.

Elena thought about detailing her lack of interest in Boss's procedures, but the way he said it sank into her, and after a moment she understood.

"Who else's bones are there?" she asked, when she had a voice again.

He shrugged, tried to smile. "They must be dead. I don't recognize them."

She wondered what connection the wings gave him to those from whom it was made; for someone constructed from the dead, he was taking it well.

(It wasn't true.)

"She should remake them," Elena said. "Bad luck to have those on your back."

He didn't answer, but she knew all at once, as clearly if he had spoken, that he would never tell Boss she had made a mistake; he would live with the demons rather than seem so weak that he would ask her to take back the gift she had made him. Better to die proud.

That she understood. She might as well have been the one who said it. It might be the first thing she had really understood in someone else since she'd joined the circus.

There was a twinge in her ribcage.

"There. There! Do you feel that little thread?" He watched her face with eyes bright as a fever.

She said, too late, "I don't feel a thing."

He looked ready to argue; she crossed her arms and waited where she was. She wasn't about to be chased out of her own circus because some man imagined he could read the hearts of the dead.

At last, at last, he turned and left. When he opened the tent the moonlight fell on the wings.

Well, she thought when she was alone, now that little feeling has a name, and that's the last time I'll have to think of it.

(It wasn't true.)

53.

It was well into the night when I walked Ying back to the aerialists' trailer. Twice she leaned into me and I stopped, resting there with her and letting her steal some of my body heat.

"You got taller," she said once, as if it surprised her. I probably had—the last time we had touched was after Bird fell, years back.

Mina pulled Ying inside. "Why can't you ever stay with us when it matters? Quick, pack up your things and then be helpful, we might have to move out."

Outside, I saw Elena still standing at the edge of camp, her gaze still fixed on the horizon, her arms crossed like she was daring them to come back for her.

(Elena always did have more fight in her than the war could provide.)

After a moment I went back to Ayar's trailer, where I could at least pretend to be useful.

Ayar was gone, which was a good sign. I knocked, counted to three, opened the door.

Stenos was alone inside, sitting at the edge of the bunks with his elbows on his knees. Scattered around him on the floor was the wreckage of tin plates and broken chairs. It looked like the scene of a murder, like a man had fought for his life.

Stenos didn't move. The dim light that filtered through the torn paper shades highlighted the fresh bruises against his pallor—his forearms, his knuckles, and an enormous one at the base of his neck down into his collarbone, where Ayar might have held him back from the government cars. It was so purple that his face seemed almost grey beside it. I wondered if it was broken.

Without thinking, I said, "What on earth were you fighting for?"

Stenos didn't look up. He took a breath (carefully, around the bruises), said, "I wanted the wings."

I let it pass without challenge. The wings had a way of ruining someone's peace of mind.

"Clean up," I said, "and get ready to move out."

He frowned and stood up—too fast, he buckled and grabbed at the upper bunk for balance. "We're leaving? They're back?"

When I didn't answer, he frowned. His bruised knuckles went white around the edge of the bunk. "We can't go without them. We'd be leaving them to die."

My throat went dry. That was how I felt, down to the bone.

"Pack up," I said, and left.

I couldn't bring myself to go inside Boss's trailer, even to look through her things, even to get a moment alone. I didn't want to think about why. (I had never opened the door without seeing her inside, feeling like I had come home.)

Jonah found me there, standing outside Boss's trailer like I was waiting for orders.

"Who's the ringmaster now?" he asked. His voice was low and even, as if Boss had just died of old age instead of being ripped from us.

Jonah only ever wanted to be of use, I knew, and he was better at heart than most of us, but I looked at him and hated him. How could he stand there? Didn't he know everything was over?

"You looking to fill the position?" I snapped.

He blinked. "No. I thought she'd named you. When she spoke to you before—before she went."

The griffin burned.

I wrenched the door open, jumped inside, slammed it shut. The bolt slid into place, and then I was alone in the dim, close quarters.

(When I was a boy, I would come in for my morning orders and see Alec still sleeping with his wings draped around him like a blanket, Boss sitting at her dressing table tucking her curly hair into a bun, and without looking away from the mirror she would say, "Almost on time today," even though I was never late, and when I smiled she would smile, too, without ever looking.)

I sat at the dressing table, in her seat, and felt as cold as if her ghost was there. I shook it off—it was my imagination. There was no way they could have killed her so soon. They might not have even reached the city yet, and once they were inside, whatever questions the government man would ask, he would take his time getting the answers he wanted.

(Poor Boss. Poor Boss.)

When I looked into the hinged mirror, I saw that it faced the long window opposite. From my seat I could look in the mirrors and see the yard, from the tent on one side to the aerialists' trailer on the other.

I wondered where she was; what the government man was trying to get her to do.

(I wondered if she would eventually give in and make him some soldiers. She was practical; sometimes she made what she could of whatever was at hand.)

Behind me, the camp looked empty as a grave, and on my arm it felt as though the griffin was stretching and pulling, coming to life under the skin.

Boss's trailer was warm and dark, and the dressing table smelled faintly of her greasepaint, and I might have stayed there all night without moving, if Stenos and Elena hadn't gone to war.

54.

Alto comes to the circus when they set up outside a city without smoke on the horizon. (It's early days for the war; good signs are relative. A lack of smoke is the best indication Boss has that a bomb won't strike them as they drag the poles off the back of the truck.)

The little canvas tent has stopped being a sideshow; now it has one act. Now Boss announces The Amazing Elena, who performs to Panadrome's music on a trapeze suspended from the crossbar. By the end of the act, the whole tent sways back and forth, and those on the edge of the crowd have to lean with it so the canvas doesn't hit them. Alto approaches in the middle of the afternoon, so they can see him coming. (People who come in peace do so when the sun is out.) He still waits outside the trailer for half an hour before Boss opens the door in answer to his knock. Panadrome is behind her; Elena appears like a ghost from inside the tent.

"I'm an acrobat," he says.

Boss says, "Congratulations."

"I want to join you."

Boss says, "I'm sure," but she looks him up and down for a moment, and then she says, "What can you do?"

"I can juggle," he says. "I can be a porter. I can balance. I can do partner trapeze."

"The hell you will," says Elena.

"Show me the balance," Boss says. She looks at Elena and gestures once, sharply.

Elena rolls her eyes and goes to the truck for a spare tent pole. She shoves it deep into the ground into the middle of the yard, where he will crash clear to the ground without breaking his fall with the trailer or the tent.

He grins at her, jumps up to grab hold for the climb.

Ten minutes later, he's a part of the circus.

"You'll sleep in the truck until we can find you something," Boss says. "Bring what you can carry, except weapons."

Alto's heart turns over, thinking about being so naked.

"No offense, boss," he says (he assumes another name is coming), "but what if we're shot in our beds?"

Boss waves Panadrome out of the trailer. In the daylight, away from the lanterns of the tent, Alto sees the little welds and screws holding the barrel closed, all the mismatched bits of pipe that are lashed together for his arms. The human head, with its little brass collar holding it in place, seems like a cruel joke to play on a perfectly useful machine.

"Here, being shot is only temporary," Boss says, and Alto looks back and forth, realizes how Panadrome got this way, that the head isn't a joke, it's a man.

He blinks, takes a step back.

"Relax," says Elena, from the top of the trailer. She looks down at Alto, her legs swinging gently back and forth. "It's not like she can make you look any worse."

He grits his teeth. "No weapons," he agrees.

Boss says, "Step inside."

(People Alto has killed: 47.)

Altissimo was a dancer. When war broke he was recruited to the makeshift gate, a rickety pile of doors and tractors and rusted-out barrels. Anyone who was nimble got sent there; they could scramble over the mess without being crushed.

During his night watch, one of his friends who had snuck out through the gate came back. After Altissimo lowered his gun (his friend just stared at it, half-smiling, like it was a puppy), his friend introduced himself as Alto.

Altissimo snorted and wiped the nervous sweat off his brow

with the back of his hand. "You think a new name is going to get you out of here?"

Alto grinned. "Come with me. See what I've found."

"I won't like it," Altissimo said.

(People Altissimo has killed: 30.)

They get chased out of a town.

It's early enough in the war that they're run out for deep, cold reasons—suspicion of witchcraft, suspicion of spying. (Later they will be run out because of greed or boredom, which are easier to understand and to run from.) When the performers race for the trucks, the bullets spray into the ground at their feet.

When they've leapt onto the trucks and are racing to outpace those chasing them out, Boss sees they have three more men than they started with; they jump onto the last trailer, and lay down some cover fire during their escape.

"What are you doing?" Panadrome shouts, leaning out the window on his side of the truck.

"Like we were going to stay in that shithole?" one of them calls back. He turns back to the road, lifts the gun to his shoulder, fires.

Two of them are already bleeding as they swing up into the truck, and by the time the town soldiers have given up and they can pull over and take stock, all three have been shot. One of them is already dead. Another one follows a minute later, pressing his hands into his dead comrade's, grimacing his way into the next life.

Boss steps around the truck, looks over the two dead men. The last man is still alive, though blood is pooling out through the slats of the truck (the stain remains for years) and his time is running out.

She asks the dying man, "Are you agile?"

He frowns at her through his tears, nods yes.

Boss sits back and rubs at her eyebrows with her thumb. "Bring them into the workshop, if they're still warm," Boss says. "Then we'll see."

(People Spinto has killed: 22.)

(People Focoso has killed: 26.)

(People Brio has killed: 13.)

When Brio wakes up, he's already laughing, gasping for breath, reaching for anything he can get his hands on. He was happy to be anything, in any shape, so long as he was alive.

He is the one who tricks Alto into becoming friends; he is the one who makes them all brothers.

Moto was with a local militia that came to the camp on their last day to demand a tithe from Boss (as soon as they decided Ayar wouldn't kill anyone on his way out, they got bold enough to shoulder guns and march over).

When the others started the walk back to the city, Moto stayed where he was, standing in mud up to his ankles.

"You need anyone?" he asked.

Boss looked him up and down, raised an eyebrow. "You trained?"

It was a trick question—by then the only training anyone got was for soldiering—but Moto just shrugged and smiled. "I'm trainable."

"How will your employer take you leaving his service?"

Moto smiled wider.

(People Moto has killed: 19. The last four of them he killed on the night he left the city to join the Circus Tresaulti.)

Years after, a man auditions for them in the normal way, which Boss thinks is a nice departure from the way her last four acrobats have entered her scope.

Barbaro looks like the first Grimaldis on her poster, dark hair and high cheekbones and skin like an oak tree. He flips and grins at the audience just as an acrobat should, and when Moto and Focoso lock hands underneath him to give him a place to stand, he steps up without hesitating and lets them launch him, flipping three times before he comes down again. Boss hasn't seen acrobatics like this since the early days, when her applicants were trained. Even Elena looks a little impressed.

"If you join us, you give up your gun," she says. "There are no guns in the Circus."

"Oh, I'm done with weapons," he says.

(People Barbaro has killed: 88.)

Sometimes, a member of the crew is devoted enough to the circus to want to stay. It's rare; the traveling life is hard enough on people who are guaranteed to live through it, and life is too precious to spend ten years hauling canvas off trucks. Crew come and go. Most crewmen never bother to give names; they know they'll be forgotten.

But sometimes, Boss is having a softhearted morning, and when a crewman asks, "May I audition, Boss? I've been practicing," she sits back in bench on the truck bed and looks him up and down, and says, "By all means."

At her side, Little George looks as though she's sliced his heart open. The whole audition happens with Little George's eyes fixed on the crewman, as if George can knock him over with the depth of this injustice.

(People Pizzicato has killed: 0.)

He's proud of the number, though when Barbaro asks him "How many?" he says, "Six," just to have something to say.

Barbaro laughs once and claps him on the back and says, "Welcome, brother!" and they all pour out fingersful of the gin Joe makes in the barrel that hangs from the back of the cooking cart. It's worse than gasoline, but Pizzicato is used to it. He drinks it in a single swallow.

He never admits to the real number, though they might not be cruel about it. The Grimaldi brothers don't argue amongst themselves, not badly.

This rule does not apply to everyone else, of course. With everyone else in the circus, the Grimaldi brothers are more than happy to put up a fight.

55.

The shouting reached me even inside Boss's trailer, and as soon as I open the door I could tell this wasn't the usual disagreement, because the rest of the camp had gone totally quiet, everyone pausing with one hand still on their work as if waiting for the outcome before they bothered taking up their burdens again.

As I closed in on the tent, I passed Ying and Mina, Jonah and Ayar, and Barbaro and Brio, taking bets.

"Ten says he hauls off first," said Brio.

Barbaro smiled. "I'll take that bet," he said, and snatched the little bag from Brio, who looked suddenly nervous at the bet he'd made.

(Brio had never been the cleverest. You didn't bet against Elena.)

I slipped inside the tent and tried to look invisible as I got my bearings.

Stenos and Elena were the only others inside. Stenos was pacing. Elena was standing still, arms crossed; she might as well have been picked up from the edge of camp and carried here in the dark, she looked so little changed from the way she had stood and watched the government cars drive away. Underneath the sound of Stenos's feet, I could hear the high thin groan of the copper pipes as she pulled the skin tighter across her shoulders.

"We can't just leave them there," he shouted. "What are we, animals?"

"Boss wouldn't want us to wait," Elena said. She wasn't shouting, but her voice was pitched to carry—she wanted everyone outside to hear. "The government men have her now, they've had her for nearly twelve hours, and any minute they'll figure out what Boss does one way or another. How long do you think they'll be satisfied with just dissecting Bird?"

Stenos spat, "Don't talk about her," just as Barbaro threw the door flap aside and stalked in. Brio was behind him (looking for black eyes, probably), and as the flap dropped I saw that the others were closing in.

"You're one icy bitch," Barbaro said, half a compliment.

Brio cut him off. "He doesn't mean it," he said, "we're just— Elena, we don't know if our bodies will fail us if we leave. If we go too far from Boss, who knows what could happen to us?"

"The same thing that happens if we stay," she said, looking at Barbaro.

Brio was looking back and forth, pushing for a truce. "But if we could only wait a little while for Boss—"

Elena cut him off and told Barbaro, "Then if the government men don't get you, you grow two hundred years old and get so brittle your bones snap in a cold wind, and when you finally fall to pieces I'll dance on your grave."

Stenos was looking at her the way the wolf had looked at her, a long time ago—narrowed eyes, shoulders down, betrayed.

It was nice to see that someone else hadn't known about everything the bones did to you.

("We are the circus that survives," Boss had told me, and I had been young and blind. Only now was I standing on solid ground. At least Stenos hadn't waited long for his revelations.)

I wondered if Stenos was going to ask her anything about how she knew what she knew—of all of us, he was maybe the only one who could get a real answer out of Elena—but all he said was, "We're not moving."

Elena turned and walked out. We followed her outside. I already had a knot in my stomach, guessing what was coming. (What would Boss say? I knew her orders, but how could I go? How could I go?)

"Just a day or two," Mina said to Elena as she came out of the tent. Ying stood beside Mina, nodding, and a few of the other aerialists were gathering closer, silently agreeing.

"They might come back," Mina added.

Elena shot Mina a look. Mina took a step backwards.

"There's no use in waiting," Elena said. Her voice carried. The crewmen were leaving their packing behind and wandering over one by one, trying to get a better view of what was happening. The Grimaldi brothers had gathered off to one side, and the aerialists were converging on the other, like two militias about to face off.

My arm burned. I felt the ground tilting under us, but part of me was still at the edge of camp watching Boss disappearing into the black sedan, and I couldn't think long enough to stop the disaster I knew was coming.

"There's no use in running!" Stenos said. "You think that government man can't find us again if he wants to? We're of more use here in case they come back. We can protect them here."

Elena's face was incredulous. "You keep dreaming that somehow they're coming back," she said. "They're marked for dead. We can only hope that if we run, they'll last long enough for him to get bored with it all and not come after us one by one."

Fatima swayed like she was on the verge of blacking out. I sympathized.

"Boss knew what was coming," Elena said to the crowd. "So did Bird. They made their choice. We need to make ours. We shouldn't wait."

I said, "We waited for you."

The old-timers froze like the words had stupefied them; even Fatima and Ying looked at me as if they guessed what kind of trouble I was in for.

Slowly, Elena turned to face me. We weren't far apart—I had been close on her heels coming out of the tent, and had only moved to the side to watch the crowd—and I knew she could cover the space between us with one jump (not even trying) and snap my neck like Bird would have snapped the Prime

Minister's. I could hear Ayar's spine creaking as he moved into place behind me, where he could reach over my head to catch her before she did anything.

But the anger coiled in her didn't seem like it was for me. We stood in silence for a while; she looked at me as if she pitied my stupidity.

Finally, she cocked her head to the side and said, as if we were alone, "Little idiot, who ever said I wanted to be woken?"

Her voice slid over everyone like the first shovelful of dirt in a grave. Most of the crew shoved their hands in their pockets. Ying shuddered.

Stenos stayed where he was. He seemed to have relaxed now that the fight was in earnest, his hands loose at his sides and his eyes fixed on her, and I thought suddenly (strangely) what a good thief he must have been before Boss caught him.

"What do the rest of you say?" he called, glancing from group to group of the performers with the bones. His voice was light, as if this was a call for drinking songs and not a battle. "I can't imagine the rest of you are willing to risk your lives by putting yourselves too far from Boss."

The performers looked at each other, nervous and torn. Behind me, Ayar let out a heavy breath.

Elena looked around and snorted. "You can't be serious."

"There's no way I went through all this just to drop dead because I ran scared," put in Spinto.

"But it's foolish to sit here and wait to be taken," said Fatima.

Moto said, "So what are we going to do, drive up there and get them back?"

"Sure," said Ayar, "because the first thing we should do is declare war on ourselves."

Ying said, "But we can't go far from her, not with what's happened to us—"

"No," Elena snapped. She looked around the camp at each of the performers. "The war happened to us. This—" she swept a hand down her body "—is a choice you made. Don't for one moment pretend Boss never told each of you what the dangers were."

Ying dropped her gaze. I wondered what Boss could have told her, to make such a case that Ying had agreed to the bones, and where I had been that Ying hadn't told me—I had been blind for so long it was hard to tell when we had grown apart.

(It didn't matter; sooner or later, you agreed to anything Boss asked of you. My arm still ached where she had tattooed the griffin.)

Stenos had the crowd's attention now; they were waiting to be convinced.

But Stenos wasn't shouting. He stood with his hands in his pockets like the crewmen, like he hadn't just been arguing for everyone to be brave enough to wait for Boss.

He had to argue for it, I thought, my muscles aching. He had to. My hand was tight against my arm.

"I'll stay myself, then," he said. "Give me a truck, and I'll go as close as I can to the city. I'll wait for them to come out, or . . ." He faltered. "Or. I'll find them."

He'd find their heads on sticks and he knew it, I thought, going cold all over. Maybe Elena knew what she was doing; maybe Boss had been right.

"No," I said, too loud. "We're all moving on."

The Grimaldi brothers stopped their arguing and blinked at me, shocked and pleased. The crewmen seemed surprised I had spoken. Fatima looked at me like I had finally screwed my head on straight.

Ayar said, "We know you loved her, but who are you to lead us, Little George?"

"Boss gave me her last order before she was taken away," I said, taking advantage of the momentary hush, trying to sound certain. "She said we shouldn't wait for her. I think, as orders go, that one's pretty clear. Does anyone feel like arguing her last words?"

Elena looked at Stenos; Stenos looked away from us, down the hill and out toward the road.

From his place at the back fringes of the crowd, Panadrome turned away from us and walked toward Boss's trailer.

I swallowed hard, once, but the circus and the crew were looking at me, and I couldn't back down or I'd lose them all.

"Load up," I called. "We leave as soon as the camp is packed, and we drive straight through until nightfall, no stopping."

(Sooner or later, you agreed to anything Boss asked of you.)

56.

Bird's ankle burns long after the bleeding has stopped, which means that the bullet has sliced through the bone, and there are little metal splinters grinding into the muscle. The first dark hours she sits alone in the cell, she thinks that when she gets out, she'll have to have Boss take everything out of the joint, scrape it clean, start again.

The government man comes back shortly after, and adds to the list of things Bird will need repaired.

First are the two ribs, which he pushes until the pipe groans and buckles. He slices her forearm open down to the bone. He dislocates a finger and makes a careful cut to see how the joint is constructed.

He digs out her false eye and rolls it between two fingers, peering like a man who's never seen anything made of glass. He holds it up to his own eye, as if there's a mirror in the cell that can tell him how he looks with a milky iris.

"Lovely," she says. The word comes out a little higher than she means—the way she's tied down leaves hardly any room to breathe—and she sounds like she's trilling, like she's on the verge of laughter.

He looks away, tosses the glass eye to the medic he's brought into the cell. The medic turns and fixes the eye back into the socket without quite looking at her. The glass slides into place with a wet suck, as though her flesh is reaching out for it.

She doesn't think about it. It's not the time. She can worry when she's home again, in her top bunk in the aerialists' trailer, the winter wind leaking through the nail holes near the ceiling and Stenos' heartbeat strong and even through the wall.

Now she has to pay attention; she has to be focused when she escapes.

When he slices down to the bone, she sees where he keeps his knife (inside his belt, in a thin sheath that lays nearly flat against his waist). She tilts the blind side of her head to the ground and listens to the clink of tools in the medic's bag, to see if there's anything inside that she can use. (She knows, because of her fingers, that he has pliers. Bird hopes it won't come to that. Once she starts pulling him apart, she might not be able to stop, and time is important. She has to get them out; she can't get lost in revenge.)

At some point she stops listening—you can't keep listening to things like they're saying, it's what drives you over the edge—and she drifts.

The ceilings look too slippery to find purchase; the mold is nearly yellow in the light the government man has brought with him. It's just enough to see by, but not enough to really examine (the medic he brought grumbles the whole time he's putting her back together. She doesn't know why; of course he's less interested in exploring than in confirming what he thinks already, like most government men. He's a boy with a bug).

Bugs have wings, she thinks, and smiles up at the yellow slime that fans out above her like feathers on the wall. In the right light, the metal wings would be yellow, or red in the light of the circus lanterns, or blue, if you spread them wide just before dawn and caught the last of the deep night.

("Stop her smiling," says the government man, sounding afraid, and she feels a needle in her jaw.)

She dreams that Boss gave her the wings already.

She dreams that as soon as they went into the workshop and Bird saw them, Boss smiled at her and said, "They're not bad, if you can handle them," and unbuckled them, fanning out one wing for inspection.

"I want them," said Dream-Bird, and Boss said, "Of course. Come sit on the table while I kill you, and then we'll get started."

As Bird turned over on the table, Boss was pulling the goggles down over her eyes, was reaching for the bone saw and the wrench; Boss looked like the kindest mother there ever was.

The knob-joints of the wings moved into place under Bird's skin as if Bird had been made for them, and when she breathed the air coursed through the ribbing.

Boss said, "That should do it. How do you feel?"

"Whole," Bird said, and sighed, and rested her smiling face against the cool metal of the workbench.

Boss smiled and fixed the joints in place with the sound of a door closing tight, with the sound of a lock sliding home at last.

When Bird wakes up, she's alone, and it takes her too long to remember she doesn't have the wings, that her shoulders are flexing around nothing.

Then she remembers where she is, and what's happened. Then the pain comes.

She wraps her sleeve around her arm to stanch the bleeding, and uses a piece of the canvas wrapped around her feet to hold the wound on her finger shut. It will get infected; Boss will have work to do.

The dark cell smells of copper.

She listens for any signs from Boss. She hears the hush of feet on stone, but the hall echoes so much it could come from anywhere.

Still, it's company. She closes her eyes, tries to ferret it out.

Boss is in the cell to the right of the door, three or four doors down—that incredulous, through-the-nose breathing of someone who has spent time under interrogation and has almost broken. (Bird knows that sound. She was a soldier once.)

The guard is farther away in the hall, and not moving except to re-shoulder his gun, which scrapes against the stone wall behind him every time he shifts his weight. The sounds come farther apart; he's falling asleep, starting awake at intervals. Otherwise, Bird and Boss are alone.

Now, she thinks. Now.

At the end of the hallway is a door with a lock. The door leads to the stairs (eighty-two, she thinks, or eighty-four—once they jostled her ankle and she blanked out, lost count), and then comes the labyrinth of the halls, the empty stage and the rows of seats and the long, long run from the front door through the city streets to the wall, where Boss will learn to climb if she wants to live long. Then, it's home to the circus.

Beyond that Bird doesn't think. Boss handles the circus like an egg; whatever Boss does then will be the right thing, the safest thing. Still, Bird hopes they make their way east to a port town where they can catch a boat to some other country. She's always wanted to fly over open water.

(She'll get the wings. This is not in question; this cannot be in question, if she is to rescue Boss. Boss has her reasons for holding back on what people want, and she plays one thing against another if it buys her time, but even Boss knows what's fair. Even Boss has to know that the wings are not meant for Stenos.)

The scraping sound has not come for several minutes. The guard's asleep.

There's a ragged edge of metal she can just reach if she digs through the hole in her ankle that the gunshot made; she bites back nausea, twists it off. It cuts her fingers as she unscrews the frame of the narrow window set into the door.

(The buckled ribs help her slide through the tiny space, but the groan of copper echoes through her skull as she drags her hips through and wrenches herself free.)

She walks on the balls of her feet down the hallway. The pain is like a spike being driven into her ankle, straight up her back. She ignores it. She's sweating cold; she doesn't have much time left before infection sets in.

She can't stand in front of Boss's door; without the momentum of walking, her ankle buckles. She grips the ledge above her, pulls herself up until she can look through the window into the cell.

Boss looks whole, but Bird knows that doesn't mean the government man has been any kinder to Boss. Boss had probably had a worse time of it; at least Bird hadn't been expected to answer any questions.

"Boss."

From the dark, Boss's eyes gleam.

Bird pulls her mouth tight. Did they break Boss's jaw? "I can pick the lock," Bird says, "I have a key."

"Be quick," Boss says, so quietly the walls swallow most of the words.

Bird drops to one knee, starts picking the lock.

There's the scrape of the gun against the stone as the soldier jerks awake.

Boss hisses, "Go."

No. No. Bird's throat goes dry. She can't have done all this to leave Boss alone in this dank grave. She tries with sweaty fingers to hold the sliver of metal steady inside the lock.

"It's you he's going to kill," Boss says through the door, "not me. He's coming back any minute, and that's the end for you."

Boss has always had a sense of when trouble was coming; she always knew when one of her own was broken. She can probably smell the copper, too, and Bird suffers a moment of shame that her maker has seen her this way. The ankle she suffered as a wound of war, but to have lain on the ground, to have been slammed against the wall to make the cutting easier—she should have fought, she should have wrenched the knife right from his hand and slid it through his ribs instead of being weak.

She works faster on the lock; her face burns.

Boss rises up behind the door, and faster than Bird can blink Boss is at the window, stretching her fingers to the open space.

MECHANIQUE: A TALE OF THE CIRCUS TRESAULTI

Bird lurches to her feet and lifts her hand to Boss's fingers, feels the pain ebbing out of her as her body heals around the wounds the government man has made—one finger, two fingers. A moment later the stabbing pain in her ribs eases enough for her to see straight.

Boss says, "Go, he'll come back any second," and Bird knows it's true, but still she drops out of the window and bends to the lock. There's time, she thinks wildly, there's time if she can only get the door open—

The soldier's boots scrape on the floor as he stands.

"The catwalk will have a ladder," Boss whispers through the lock, but Bird is already moving.

It would be clever to go back to her room, almost-close the door, wait until he's asleep, but there's too much terror in turning back, too much danger that the government man will come again before there is another chance, and Bird's first instinct has always been up, up, up.

When the soldier walks down the corridor and peers into Boss's cell, Bird is clinging to the curved ceiling, shadow-soaked and silent, her bare feet slipping against the yellow slime.

Bird knows there's nowhere in the cell she could be out of sight. She has a few seconds, maybe, before the guard walks farther down the hall and realizes the room is empty.

When the soldier passes underneath her, she drops soundlessly onto his shoulders.

After all this time, she knows where to land so that her partner is unharmed, and where to land so that he's caged and her impact is twice as heavy as his bones can bear, so that he lurches forward and crashes to the floor, landing against the stone with a sickening, wet sound.

Bird hops off the body, slides her hands inside the jacket. When she feels the hilt of his knife (carried where his master carries it), she sticks it between her teeth. There's no time to look for anything else; nothing else she can carry, if she stands a chance of living.

Bird moves for Boss's door. There's time, there's got to be enough time—

From the soldier's jacket is a burst of radio static. "Come in. Come in?"

From behind the wooden door Boss says, like it's a blessing; "Find George."

Bird runs.

57.

This is what happened to Boss:

She was in a room alone with him. He sat opposite her, and looked at her very seriously, so seriously she might have liked him except for the blood in the beds of his nails. His hair was grey, like he was her father.

"I want you to understand something," he said, and there was no trace of the false gentleman; it was the voice of an honest man.

He watched her, and when she stayed silent he went on, "I'm not some petty tyrant out to nag you for a share of the winnings. I don't want to kill anyone in your circus, unless you give me a reason to use them against you. What I want," and here he sat forward a little, his eyes as eager as a boy's, "is to make this city like the old world."

(Boss didn't breathe; couldn't.)

"I want to make every city like the old world," he said, "one by one. For that I need lieutenants who won't die from gunshots. I need soldiers who can leap over the city walls and drag everyone into a world that isn't just animal colonies snapping at one another."

His eyes were blue and steady, as if he had swallowed the sky.

"I need," he said, "to live as long as this takes."

When Boss had a voice again, she said, "Good luck."

He frowned, sat back. "I know you're against me," he said. "I know you don't want to give up your little show. But you have a great gift, and I'll make use of it one way or another. There's no point in fighting me."

"You can't make someone do this against their will," she said. "What's to keep an immortal soldier from turning on you?"

Here he smiled. "What's kept yours so close to you?" he asked. "There must be something they're afraid of that's greater than you. Everyone's afraid of something."

Boss didn't give him an answer; there was none to give.

He stood up, adjusted his jacket absently. "You can decide how far I have to take this," he said. "The one in the other cell should last a few more days, and then I'll send for the others, if we're both still waiting."

At the door he paused. "It was a mistake to leave them human," he said, looking back at her. "I was disappointed to see they can bleed."

She sat alone all that night, thinking about the last night of her real life, when she had stood in front of hundreds and waited for her chance to sing.

She was terrified, terrified beyond sleep, beyond tears, and when Bird came to rescue her, Boss stood up from the chair for the first time and found that the fear had knocked her legs out from under her. (She crawled the last few feet to the door of her cell.)

This is what happened to Boss:

She began to understand the government man.

58.

I made it through the crowd with my head up, as if I knew what I was doing, until I got to the trailer.

Then I sank down in Boss's chair, shaking. My face in the mirror was gaunt; I had gotten ten years older.

I had never had illusions about what it took to manage any kind of hold on a group of people who scrabbled and squabbled as much as we did, but Boss had always seemed equal to it, as if her body had grown tall and wide just to make room for her authority. Even Elena, who was a tyrant in her trailer, gave in when Boss said the word. Boss was someone people followed.

And I was the barker who had received her last order. That was all.

How soon before the circus became just another war? What would I do when they were shouting me down instead of waiting for me to explain? What if Elena rose against me and mutinied? She wasn't liked, but she was clever and hard to oppose. Stenos, out in the yard just now, was the first one who had ever put up a fight against her for that long, and even then . . . well, the circus was leaving, even after all of his fighting, wasn't it.

I knew when the knock came that it would be him on the other side. Some people never knew when to give up. Bird, now Stenos. (Acrobats were mad.)

"I'm staying behind," he said.

"Sorry, no," I said, like it was someone else giving the order. "The whole circus goes."

Stenos' face pulled tight. "No one's named you the ringmaster yet," he said. "I'm telling you as a courtesy, not asking you for permission."

"Stenos, if you go, what's to stop others from staying behind?"

"Why stop them?" Stenos shrugged. "If you try to be a tyrant they'll plot against you. If you let people feel they can come and go, you have a better chance at being ringmaster for the ones who stay."

Stenos had it wrong, all of it. I didn't want to be ringmaster. I wanted to be plastering posters on city walls. I wanted to be handing out tickets, pointing rubes toward the beer, sneaking into the tent the back way under the parade of yellow umbrellas that guided the performers back and forth to the camp. And the others who stayed were doomed—Elena was rarely wrong about how vicious people could be, and I had seen the gleam in the eye of the government man as he shoved Bird's body into his car. I didn't want anyone left behind. I couldn't be half-leading a fractured circus in fits and starts, trapped between two dangers, suffering either way.

I said, "If you go near that city they'll kill you." I already sounded older, too. Tired.

Stenos shrugged. "They'll still need someone to bring them back to the circus."

He was looking at me like he could read my mind, and I scowled, shoved my hands in my pockets. No matter how good he was at reading people, he couldn't read the future. He didn't know what could happen any more than I did.

Except I knew some things Stenos didn't know; I had a crisping tattoo burned into my shoulder, and a last order that was feeling more and more like a weight dropped into my arms by someone who was about to die.

"You can have Ayar hold me prisoner if you don't want me going," Stenos went on, "but it's the only way you'll keep me with you, and I imagine Ayar will eventually start to feel a little sympathetic."

I had forgotten how convincing Stenos could be when he had his wits about him—he must have been persuasive to get a place in the circus after Boss had caught him red-handed—but now he was half-smiling like he was sympathizing with me, like he was here on behalf of the person who was really the trouble, and I found myself thinking just the way he wanted me to before I got the better of it. I couldn't believe him; I couldn't understand him at all.

"What are you staying for?" I asked, marveling.

Stenos flinched like I'd struck home, and too quickly, too sharply, he said, "Boss owes me a pair of wings."

I thought about Boss dealing for years with Stenos's wolfish glare on one side of her and Bird's glassy eye watching her from the other. Boss must have had a stone heart just to get to sleep at night.

When I didn't answer, he frowned, snorted, said, "What other reason would I have?"

It hadn't occurred to me before that moment that he would be thinking of Bird. I had imagined they were cut apart, once Bird was shot. (I had been quick to imagine Bird a goner, quicker even than Elena.) But looking at Stenos scowling at me in the middle of the yard, asking to leave the circus and stay where the government men could find him, I had my doubts about Stenos letting go of Bird.

"Stay if you want," I said. "Take your trailer. Ayar and Jonah can stay with the brothers."

That meant I would stay in Boss's trailer, where the ringmaster slept. I felt sick. How could I sleep in her bed knowing she was probably dying behind the city walls?

"What if others want to stay?"

I blanched. "Who else would be as stupid as you?"

If Stenos was offended he didn't show it. He only said, "You never know," watching me for my answer.

"Look, I'm not the ringmaster," I said, bristling under his gaze. "Don't try to turn me into a tyrant just to drive people to your useless cause. I'm here just until Boss gets back or we can elect someone for the job. Just—take anyone. Anyone who wants to stay here and get killed, that's fine with me. What do I care?"

(I believed it when I said it; I didn't care about anyone who didn't care enough to stay, because that was simple enough.

I didn't know yet who would ask to go with him.)

"If you want the trailer, start moving Ayar and Jonah out," I said. "We're leaving as soon as the crew is finished. Get whatever food you can from Joe before he's tied everything down."

"Where are you heading?"

To Death, more slowly than you, I thought. Then I realized I hadn't thought about it. I tried to remember the circuit we'd made the last time we'd been here—it felt like a hundred years ago, suddenly. (Had it been?)

I said, "Straight north for two days. Then we'll catch a vein east if we can, but if we can't I don't know where we'll go. You might never find us."

"Boss will know where you are," Stenos said, and when he smiled I smiled back, only because it was nice to pretend Boss was still alive.

Across the camp, Elena was standing next to the aerialists' trailer, watching us with the expression of someone resigned to knowing every strange and terrible thing they had foreseen would come true at last.

59.

This is what the fruit seller sees when she comes in the early morning light to set up her stall in the square outside the capitol building:

The empty square stretches out in front of her, the towers and dome of the capitol building casting shadows on the ground. Everything is quiet. No feet but hers have touched the ground since curfew.

She sets up her tables with the ease of long practice. The produce truck is on its way in from the government farm an hour south, so she works slowly; she has time. (She thinks this whole thing is an act, an appearance of some quaint life no one even remembers, but at least here there are no gunshots, and almost half the people who come can pay with coin money instead of barter. She had it a lot worse before she came to this city, so she just shuts up and sells whatever they tell her to sell.)

She's attaching the last awning to the support poles when she sees a flicker of grey in the corner of her vision, like a scrap of material caught in the wind. She turns—one of her awnings has come loose again—

Someone is moving along the edge of the capitol roof.

The figure is thin and pale, running unevenly, and where the mouth should be there is only the glint of metal. There's not enough space left to turn—she wonders what this person is going to do at the edge of the roof.

Don't jump, she thinks. It's a waste.

Then she thinks about the prisoners who walk into the capitol for trial and don't come out again. She decides maybe it's just as well for the poor man to jump.

The runner on the roof speeds up.

There's nowhere for the runner to go—no roofs close enough, it's just the open square and a few bombed-out trees, and rows of squat houses much too far away. The woman's lungs seize up. She doesn't want to clean up any blood today.

The figure takes three pumping steps as it reaches the edge of the roof. Then the figure disappears for a moment (crouching? fallen?), bursts back into sight as it jumps.

The woman covers her mouth, steps back so the blood doesn't hit her when the poor soul lands.

But the figure is flying, legs together, arms out, hands pointed towards the great black tree.

Impossible, the woman thinks, it's too far, but the figure's reaching out, catching the branch out of thin air. The figure twists, folds, seems to float from that branch to the next even though the woman hears the crack of wood when the figure catches hold, the groaning protest at receiving so much momentum at once.

Something bangs open inside the vestibule of the capitol building; there's the sound of a man calling out, of boots on the marble floor.

The figure has leapt to a second tree, farther off; she's swinging around once, twice, to gather speed; she lets go blind (impossible, impossible) and twists in midair, arms already out to catch whatever she can. She grabs the awning of the nearest building (the woman hears the canvas tear), scuttles up to the roof. The woman sees a glimpse of a silhouette with a pointed mouth before the figure disappears.

The woman stands in the middle of the square, her heart pounding, until she hears the doors opening and drops to her knees, lashing the awning cords tight around the supports, pulling the knots tight, keeping her head down.

She sees a pair of soldiers' boots stop next to her and looks up. Behind the soldier, the sky is moving from grey to blue; it's almost morning.

"Did you see a woman come this way?"

She shakes her head. "No, sir."

"She's a prisoner," he says. "Escaped acrobat. Dangerous. You don't want to be caught hiding her."

She sits back on her heels and gives him half a smile. "I don't think I'd want to try hiding anything from anyone in this city."

The soldier's grim face softens a little. They've seen each other before; he's bought fruit from her (everyone does), and once when she had to examine apple blight he was the soldier who checked her out of the city, reminded her to have her papers ready at the gate. ("Some of the guys get antsy when you reach into a bag," he said as he shouldered his weapon, stepped back, waved the truck out into the road.)

"Be careful if you see her," he says. "She tried to kill the Prime Minister."

He sounds less than outraged—admiring, if she didn't know better. She doesn't know if she should smile, or if it's a trap. She doesn't want to risk it.

"I'll be careful," she says sincerely, and after a moment the soldier seems satisfied and moves down the street. Others join him—they come out of every alley at once, they're worse than the rats. They confer quickly, spread out again, and then she's alone on the street.

An acrobat tried to kill the Prime Minister. The world is strange.

When she hears a roar she looks up, but it's only the morning truck, and the farmer gets out to help the farm-soldiers unload the truck. She carries flats of peaches and green beans, arranges the stacks of corn, points where the last of the apples should go.

"Has something happened?" the farmer asks, when they're close. There must be more guards outside.

"Looking for someone," she says. "Someone tried to kill the Prime Minister."

He raises an eyebrow, turns back to the truck, never answers her.

All day as she sells the fruit to the same people who always come asking, as she nods to the soldiers and watches pairs of them skulking in and out of the alleyways, the woman keeps one eye on the black tree.

She imagines the acrobat dropping out of a tree on the side of the road, folding and spinning and striking the Prime Minister like an arrow with her pointed hands, driving him straight into the ground.

She hopes the soldiers never find her.

60.

As soon as he was free of George, the little ringmaster apparent, Stenos ran to Ayar and Jonah's trailer.

It was his trailer too—he lived in it when they were on the road, he slept in the bunk opposite Jonah—but it was their home, not his. He slept there only because the crew didn't want him after Boss made him an act, and the Grimaldi brothers hadn't wanted any strangers, period.

The trailer was clean and spare, three fresh-made bunks and three bare ones. The only thing Ayar and Jonah really possessed was a haphazard collection of books and half-books they had scavenged. Those would have to be boxed and handled carefully. Even in his rage, Stenos had left the books untouched.

Stenos had come into the circus with nothing, and he had collected nothing. (He didn't live in the circus yet; all these years he had only been waiting.)

Ayar found him while he was packing the books into a crate lined in canvas. Stenos thought about apologizing for the trouble, but he couldn't be sorry, so he only nodded and kept working. Ayar would forgive him for taking the trailer if he understood.

"Don't do that," Ayar said, looking at the books.

Stenos said, "Don't try to stop me. I've had enough trouble today."

"I mean, there's no need to pack my things. I'm not going with the rest of them."

That, Stenos hadn't expected. He stood up, a book still in one hand. "Are you sure?"

Ayar shrugged, his metal ribs squeaking. "I owe Boss a debt. It's time I repaid it."

"And Jonah?"

Ayar's smile slid. "He should know better than anyone how sometimes you have to pick the losing battle."

After a moment, Stenos handed Ayar the book.

"Let's hurry and finish," he said.

Ayar came back with a scowl, a box of supplies from Joe's food truck, and Barbaro and Brio in tow.

Stenos crossed his arms. "You're staying, too? This is turning into a party."

Brio said, "We should all be staying. I'm hoping my brothers realize that before the circus goes."

If all the brothers realized that, the trailer was going to be a tight fit.

As Brio and Ayar took supplies inside, Stenos glanced over at Barbaro, who was smoking the last inch of a flattened cigarette. It was hard to believe Barbaro was going on a softhearted mission; he had been a machine of a soldier, though he'd never said much about it. When you carried yourself the way Barbaro did, no one had to ask.

Barbaro looked over and shrugged like Stenos had asked him a question. "When we run off to die, I'll take a few out for you before you get shot," he said, examining the horizon just over Stenos's shoulder. "At this point, a few more on my head won't matter."

"No one's running off to die," Stenos said.

Barbaro looked at him and raised his eyebrows, took a drag off the cigarette. The smoke snaked through his nostrils, and for a moment Stenos saw what Barbaro's enemies must have seen— his expressionless face, eyes like two pistol sights.

"Sure thing," Barbaro said. "My mistake."

He pinched the cigarette between his fingers, snuffed the fire out.

Stenos snuck last into Boss's workshop. He had guessed right—
no one had come to lock it up yet. (Without Boss, only Panadrome or George would think of the workshop at all; George
was too scattered to think of it, and Panadrome was too grieved
to remind him.)

Stenos scooped up anything that looked like a weapon and
wouldn't be missed: wrenches, a handful of nails, a half-circle of
cog that looked like it had been wrenched out of Ayar's shoulder.
It was so sharp Stenos cut his finger picking it up and had to
wrap it in a curled sheet of tin just to carry it out.

"I figured I'd find you at the scene of the crime," Elena said
from behind him.

He didn't stop packing. "Then I'm slipping in my old age."

"You don't know a thing about old age," she said, but she
stepped inside. The workshop shrank around them; when he
turned to face her he felt like they were standing together in a
coffin.

"You know it's foolish of you to stay here and die," she said.

It was hard to argue.

She stepped closer, so close that her shoulder brushed his.
He looked down without moving; she filled his vision, her cool
skin, the smooth expanse of her hair knotted behind her.

(He wondered how blinded with need for her he had been, to
be this close to her so many times and not to realize something
was wrong, not to realize what was different about anyone who
had the bones.)

"Bring them back," she said low, and it startled him so much
that he looked her in the eye. He must have misheard.

She never blinked, and her voice was steady. "Bring them
back," she said, "if you live."

This close, he could lean in and kiss her.

He bared his teeth. "Even Bird? Why not just let the government men finish your work?"

Elena's face shifted, and for a moment he wondered if he had hurt her. (How? How could you hurt someone who had a knot of metal where a heart should be?)

Then she leaned in and said, too sweetly, "If you can't rescue them both, I suggest admitting defeat. You'd look a fool coming back through the city gates twice."

She was gone as silently as she had snuck up on him, the empty yard spreading ahead of her.

For a moment he felt unsteady, as if he had been pushing her for something without knowing. (Was it Bird? Why did she care if Bird came back?)

Outside the air was crackling with anticipation. The tent was gone, the trucks packed, and even as he knew he wasn't going with them, he checked the trucks as he passed out of old habit, making sure the ropes were lashed tight enough, that all the locks were thrown.

("I don't care who drops it," Boss used to say. "You all pay together for anything that breaks. Look after things or don't, your choice."

Of course they looked after things. They got paid poorly enough as it was without having to pay for the nails to mend the broken benches.)

Someone beside him said, "Take me, too."

It was Ying. Her face was drawn and pale, but she moved beside Stenos without hesitation. He frowned at her; she was a stranger. Had they ever spoken?

"Go back," he said. He knew Ying was older than he was (twice as old? A hundred years older?), but she couldn't have lived very long out in the war before they took her in. Boss would never forgive him for dragging the ones she'd saved back out into the mud.

"No," she said. She looked around, nervous, but never moved. "No. I'm staying."

They were at the trailer now, and Ying seemed surprised to see two of the inseparable Grimaldi brothers making themselves at home in the little trailer.

"How many of us are there?" she asked. She sounded pleased. Comforted.

Stenos shot her a look and wondered how often she must have been left behind, to feel so tied to the strangers who were absent, to be hoping for a new group as soon as she was near one.

Ayar was inside, and at the sound of Ying's voice he stuck his head out the trailer door, frowning.

"No," he said to Stenos, pointing like Stenos had dragged her over. "She's not staying. Elena will kill us."

The government men would probably kill them first, but Stenos only spread his hands. "I'm no one's master. If she wants to stay, she can stay."

Ayar's face seemed to fall in on itself a little, and he fixed sad eyes on Stenos. "How can we let her?"

So Ayar also knew not all of them would come home again. Maybe it was just as well they all suspected the worst. It would make their defeat easier to handle.

"Ying!"

It was George, walking quickly across the lawn. Too quickly for comfort—he wasn't blind, then. He knew that Ying hadn't come to say her goodbyes. He was hoping to head off disaster.

"We're ready to go," George said as soon as he was close. He stopped on Ying's other side, and over her head Stenos could see how weary George looked already, after leading them for less than a day.

"You'd better get in the trailer before Elena misses you," George said. "We're almost ready."

Ying looked at him. "Goodbye," she said.

Under her gaze, George's face slowly drained of color.

"You can't," he said. "You can't—I only just understand, you can't stay here when—"

"George!" Jonah called. "We're ready to roll out."

"One minute!" George snapped over his shoulder, and turned back to Ying, caught both her wrists.

"If they get hold of you, you'll suffer," George said through grit teeth, and again, tight with fear, "You'll *suffer*."

Poor George, Stenos thought; lovesick children always over-sell. Still, he shivered. (Little George had eyes like plates, and his hands were pulling at Ying's like he could grow over her in a tangle of vines and keep her with him, safe and hidden.)

"You can't leave," George whispered.

She slid her wrists from his grip, slowly, and stepped back. "The circus is a troupe," she said. "I made a contract. I'm keeping it."

He looked at her, his eyes pleading. "I can't stay," he said. "We have to get everyone out of here. I can't—"

"Goodbye," Ying said.

"George!" Jonah's voice carried like a bell. "Everyone's ready. If we're going to reach water by nightfall, we have to go *now*."

For a moment George tensed, poised on the edge of a decision. Stenos held his breath. (George had to love Boss, didn't he? This re-treat couldn't be what he wanted—it couldn't be what he'd choose.)

Then George was kissing Ying's forehead; a moment later he was running across the camp, dirt flying under his boots.

There was the roar of engines, the whine of wheels grind-ing on earth, and the trucks were pulling out one by one. Boss's trailer went first, and then the crewmen's trailers, the cooking truck, the supplies, the performers, the entire circus disappear-ing in less than a minute.

Over the rattling bedlam floated one raw sound like a human voice (it might have been Elena calling Ying's name), and then the five of them were alone on the empty field.

Ayar offered a hand to Ying, who took it to walk up the stairs, even though Stenos knew she could have jumped over the truck without breaking a sweat. Brio followed her into the trailer, glancing behind him at Stenos.

"We head east," Stenos said, closed the trailer door.

Barbaro was waiting in the cab, in the passenger's seat, which suited Stenos. He knew the road to the capital, and they would get there faster if he drove. Behind them, the open window to the living quarters was open, and Stenos heard the little sounds of everyone settling in for a long and uncomfortable journey.

"Good luck," said Ayar, disappearing behind the flimsy curtains of his bunk. The wood groaned under his weight.

It was the last thing anyone said until dark, when the great stone wall of the capitol city came into sight on the horizon.

Then Barbaro said, "Fuck, I wish I had a gun."

No one asked for explanations, and they drove straight into the dark, towards the city walls.

Stenos looked at the silhouette, a hulking animal cast in black against black, and wondered where Bird would be.

(He knew she wouldn't still be in a prison cell. Bird had a way of escaping your grasp, no matter how much you tried to hold her.)

61.

One of the cities they find that year is more civilized than most—regular guards, demilitarized city center, even a school—and Boss extends the gig to a three-week run. The crew pitches some extra canvas and poles over one of the flatbeds to serve as a dressing room for the performers, to give them someplace else besides the cramped home trailers to spend their time, now that they have a little space.

The aerialists still get ready in their own trailer ("Hard enough to get these girls to do anything without the rest of you interrupting," Elena says), but everyone else crowds into the flatbed, crouching along under the fabric ceiling, jostling for places at the three scraps of mirror they scrounge up the first night as barter for tickets.

(Ayar can't stoop—his spine doesn't allow it—so he leans against the side, peers in, makes jokes from there.)

The jugglers paint on their childish faces first, bright eyes and smiling mouths, and pile out into the tent. Jonah usually doesn't wear any paint. ("Who's looking at my face?" he asks, laughing, reaching out past the canvas roof as he hands Ayar the charcoal pencil for his eyes.) The brothers tend to stay to themselves, more like the aerialists than any of them would admit, and so for a long time it's just Bird and Stenos alone in the flatbed.

Bird has poached some greasepaint from the others, and she's making up her whole face—white skin, an eyelid the color of iron. There's a pot of red beside her, and Stenos wonders what her mouth would look like if she painted it red. Probably like she was drinking someone's blood just before going on.

"Ladies and gentlemen," Boss is calling, "we invite you to marvel at the strength of Ayar the Terrible and his Skeleton of Steel!"

The applause rolls out through the tent.

"I wonder what they sounded like when the Winged Man flew down," Stenos says, half to himself. (He's only ever wanted applause for his work, and the awed, loaded silences after they perform have begun to grate. He never notices the silence until he's outside, and the relieved applause that greets Boss's return moves toward his back like the tide coming in.

He'll never get anywhere with damaged goods.)

"You'll never find out," Bird says, running her hand down her throat, over her neck, to the collar of her tunic.

He stands up and moves behind her. She doesn't pause; her hands are on her neck, smoothing the greasepaint down and down and down like she's sculpting a new body from white clay.

He says, "You're just telling me that because you want them for yourself."

"Of course," she says. It's the first time they've spoken of it, but she sounds as though they've had this conversation a thousand times.

(They have; every time she twists in his arms, every time he catches her, they're talking about the wings.)

Stenos glances down at her. "When Boss is tired of punishing me with you and gives me the wings, you're going to feel like a fool for being so petty with me."

She pauses, lowers her hand, frowns into the glass.

"Don't you understand?" she asks the mirror, not unkindly. "She's never going to give away the wings. It's just the promise that keeps us from going mad. She wanted an act out of us, and she got one. I'm the wild thing, you're the cage. We're cheaper than keeping a pair of animals, that's all."

Stenos goes white, his gaze fixed on the mirror. She doesn't turn to look up at him; her face in the smoky glass is as still as a corpse. Her lips are dry (it must be winter), and she smears them with stolen greasepaint until they disappear into the sea of white.

Her brown eye gleams in the light from the single lantern. He doesn't see the glass eye, though; he never sees it. He sees only the broken socket from the long-ago night, the film of blood across her face, her one good eye staring up at the stars.

She had gasped shallowly in his arms, her open ribs pressed against his fingers.

He wraps one hand at the back of her neck, pressing down just short of pain.

"I'm not the cage," he gasps at last, like a drowning man.

She looks at him in the mirror, unblinking.

A long time later, from somewhere far behind them, Jonah pulls back the tent flap, says, "You're up."

62.

This is what happens when you are about to die:

You lose, slowly, your muscle control. At first you're only a little sluggish. Then you think the ditch beside the road must be full of rocks that trip you up. But it's your body shutting down, turning off what you don't really need (it remembers more than you do about the practical process of death), and eventually you start to stagger. You stumble. You crash.

Your blood is oxygenated (you're hyperventilating—the panic has set in, that wordless animal fear of death that gets its teeth in you), and it takes all your energy to move from where you have fallen to the copse of trees beside the road. They were bombed out once, but they've started to grow over, thin green branches breaking free of the corpse.

The lethargy comes on the heels of the panic, when your body has burned up the last of the adrenaline, and there's no reserve of strength; now there's nothing left for you to do but drop dead.

Your body temperature sinks. This effect is worse if you're bleeding, and it comes faster; the body can't compensate for the sudden lack of circulation, and if you ever bleed to death, your last real memory is one of pain and cold.

Then the dementia sets in, and things get worse.

You forget where you are. You think it's spring. You have not run from a city full of soldiers and liars and left your ring-master behind. You have never even seen a circus. You are on patrol, resting by this tree until your watch is up. You are a child, hiding in already-bombed buildings where the soldiers will be less likely to look for you. Something cold and metal is resting against your leg—a pipe from the broken building, maybe. Your rifle.

(Your leg, you think, struggling for consciousness, it's just your leg and the metal is inside, but that's worse, that's dementia creeping in; who has metal bones?)

You run along the edge of the opera house roof over and over again, too frightened to jump, knowing it's too far to run, knowing that if you jump you'll fall short, and you need your other eye. You race around the cupola, with the bells strapped into cages so they don't make a sound, enormous birds with their wings folded, and how can you leave Boss here, how can you leave her?

But you jump, and after that, you don't remember what happens to you.

It's night when you open your eyes, so it must have been hours (you're resting), and the cold has set in (is it winter?), and the shadows are rising up to meet you.

(When Boss laid you on the metal table the first time, you felt all the corner shadows sinking lower, pulling greedily at you, and you looked at her, marveling and fiercely certain. Unafraid.

"I wonder what you did to get this kind of power," you said, a compliment, just before all the light in the world was snuffed out.)

You were cold, then, too. You wonder if you have ever been warm since.

This is what happens when you are about to die:

You only dreamed that you were resting.

You are still running, staggering along behind trees and bushes near the road, and if it weren't a moonless night you'd have been spotted by one of the soldiers sent on rounds to find you.

You want to give up—you *want* to rest, you want it to be over—but you can't. Fighting is too old a habit. You drag one foot in front of the other, fumbling, shoving yourself up again with one hand, bloody as the rest of you. (You used to slice through the air.)

You will keep moving forward until your ankle groans and snaps, until the last of your blood is drained, until your lungs give out, until you fall into the dirt and the worms start work.

Then you are in someone's arms—you're taken, the soldiers have found you, after all this you will die a prisoner—and you lash out to slice his neck (you still have the knife in your hand, old habits are hard to break, you can't rest, you keep fighting), but you're being caught up carefully, cradled too close to do harm, and you know how this feels; this is home.

"Bird," he says, and his voice cuts through you, "Bird, stop." (You're surprised you recognize the name.)

You think, He knows my name; you think, I must have had a friend.

(You've been this way before, you remember; this is the second time you've died and he has carried your body home.)

Home is the tent; home is the workshop with the wide table, with your mother's hands sewing her up again.

Your mother. You made a promise.

"Find George," you say. You don't remember what it means; it doesn't matter any more.

He lifts you closer; his skin is burning hot and you close your eyes, press your face to his throat (your eyelid is about to freeze). Your hand is pressed tight between your lungs and his.

He hasn't taken your knife away; your fist is still closed tight around it. If you turned your wrist an inch you could slide the blade into his heart.

Your friend runs carefully, wherever he's taking you; the darkness swallows you whole, and after that you don't feel a thing.

63.

As soon as the truck stopped Ying had the doors open (she was cold all over, she knew something was wrong), and she jumped down to the ground, ran around the back of the truck, and watched Stenos jump from the driver's seat and run into the dark like the wolves were after him.

The truck's working headlight shone out feebly into nothing—Stenos appeared in the light for only a moment before he disappeared—and she couldn't imagine what he had seen. Had he lost his mind? How close were they to the city by now?

(Oh god, she thought, if we're close to the wall, don't let the soldiers see you, Stenos, please.)

It was pitch black and moonless, and he had to have been as blind as the rest of them. There was no telling where on earth he thought he was running to.

"I'll give him one minute before we go on without him," called Barbaro from the front cab. Ying didn't believe he'd give Stenos the full minute, but still she started counting.

After seventy-eight seconds Stenos reappeared in the sputtering light, running with a sack of rags in his arms that Ying realized after too long was Bird.

"Clear off the table," she said, only it came out as a shout, nearly a scream.

She heard Barbaro shoving his way over into the driver's seat, and as soon as Stenos had passed the headlight Barbaro was gunning the engine.

(Where were they going? Where could they go?)

Out of habit Ying followed Stenos when he ran past, jumped up after him, closed the door like the troupe was being run out of town and she was the last aerialist in.

(She never had been; Elena always went last, to make sure the rest of them got inside.)

Ayar was dumping the sacks of tools and the tinned food onto the nearest bunk to make room on the table, shouting something at Barbaro that Ying didn't hear. He had to bend over almost double just to be level with the cab window.

Stenos slid Bird's body onto the table, and Ayar frowned for a moment before recognition hit and he sucked in a hissing, doubting, "No."

Ying would have answered him, but when she opened her mouth her throat was too dry.

In the light of their two oil lamps Bird looked even worse than she must have looked in the dark, because Stenos's face was hard-set, and after he set Bird down he gripped the table on each side of her as if she would fall apart as soon as he took his arms away.

"Where am I going?" called back Barbaro, even though he was already driving forward, closer to the city.

Stenos grit his teeth. "Back to the circus."

"What?" Ayar shook his head. "Boss is still in the city—"

"Back to the circus," Stenos said, as if Ayar hadn't spoken. "She's going to die if we don't help her."

"How can we help her?" Ying stepped closer, peering at the blood-soaked bandages. "These are wounds only Boss can heal." She tried to smooth away some of the worst of the muck. "I can't even tell where she's hurt," she said to Stenos, half a question. "There's blood everywhere."

Ayar moved to Bird's ankle. "She was shot in the leg, we know that much for sure," he said, taking hold of her foot to look for it. Then he saw it and stopped short, stared at the wound.

Brio glanced over, and then looked quickly away. He slid around Ayar in the cramped trailer and dropped to his knees, rummaging through the supplies—for water, Ying hoped. They couldn't even see where to help her with all this dirt on her.

How could Stenos possibly have seen her, camouflaged like this, moving in the dark?

(Bird's glass eye had reflected the light. Ying never guesses.)

Ayar set Bird's foot down, but Ying didn't go any closer. She knew better than to look at an open wound that had been left untreated for that long. (She had been young when she joined the Circus, but she had still been a soldier.)

She stayed where she was and kept her hands on Bird's bandaged arm, squeezing the wet cloth under her fingers, stanching any blood there was left to stanch.

In the silence, Barbaro glanced back through the open window. "Well? Where are we going?"

Stenos said, "We have to find George."

Ying frowned, but she didn't want to ask, because Bird had to get somewhere, anywhere, where they could try to hold off death long enough for someone to help. If it was George and the circus, then let it be George.

But what about Boss? What if Boss was inside the city walls, injured like this, and she came out at last to look for them?

The blood was everywhere, crusted over; it looked like Bird's skin had been painted purple.

Ayar and Stenos and Brio and Barbaro crowded the window, shouting one another down, fighting for the circus, fighting to stay. Ying watched Bird's shallow breaths; she hoped Bird wanted to come back.

(Elena's words still echoed in Ying's stomach; it was what Ying had been most afraid of, when she was young and alive, that death would be comforting, and then she would have to be woken.

George had gripped his arm when Elena was talking about it, jerking back, as if someone had scorched him and he was favoring the wound.)

As if someone had scorched him.

Ying looked down at Bird, who had escaped from the city.

Surely she would have gone to Boss first, to get her out of the city, and Boss would have seen Bird's wounds—if Boss had told her to get to George, then there must have been a reason. What did Boss know that no one else knew?

And where was Boss? How close were they to the city—if Boss was still in the city at all? What if Bird had gotten her out—what if Boss was out here in the dark, bleeding and stumbling along the road, looking for them?

Ying had left people behind, in her other life. It was the worst thing you could do.

"Ying?"

When she looked up, Ayar was looking at her. They were all looking at her, except Stenos, whose gaze kept dropping to Bird. Bird was unconscious now, her lips drawn back with pain, teeth gleaming like an animal's mouth.

The Grimaldis were looking at Ying like she was a nuisance, but Ayar was looking at her the way he had when she first walked into the tent all those years ago and asked to try out—he was willing to be impressed as long as she was willing to fight.

"We're split," Ayar said. "Two of us want to go back. Two want to stay. What's your vote?"

Bird sucked in a ragged breath (wet, like the blood was seeping all through her), and Stenos flinched like she'd hit him.

It was the third time in her life that Ying had had the power to decide. The first time brought her to the circus, and the second time brought her the bones. She never knew if she had chosen right; there was no way to ever really know.

Ying's hands were steady on Bird's arm, and cold blood pooled between her fingers.

She said, "We stay."

She didn't look at Stenos (she couldn't), but she looked at Ayar, went on before she lost her nerve. "We'll take care of Bird here, but we can't leave Boss. We aren't leaving anyone behind."

That was the worst thing you could do.

Ayar said, "All right," in a way that Ying recognized as approval. Then he went on, "Barbaro, park this under those trees for tonight. Brio, Ying, start cleaning Bird up, do what you can for her. Stenos, you and I stand watch. Maybe Boss is out here, too. We'll move on at dawn."

Barbaro threw the truck into gear and started the crawl along the road to shelter.

"I'd rather be here," said Stenos, quietly. He hadn't looked away from Bird.

Ayar looked at him, over at the brothers. "Brio," he said, "you and I take watch."

Brio slid around the table, grabbed a pair of wrenches from one of the bunks, and opened the trailer door.

"Let us know if you find water," Ying said. She didn't add, *So we can find her under the blood-and-dirt coat.* It was too much like something Elena would say.

(All her life Ying had assumed Elena was naturally cruel. She wondered now if cruelty just crept up on you when the world was crashing down and there was nothing else to do but fight.)

Brio looked back at her and smiled thinly, like he'd heard what he wasn't saying. Then Ayar was moving in front of her, and then the door was closing behind them, and she and Stenos were alone in the trailer's cabin.

(The smell of copper was everywhere; it was worse than in the workshop when Ying had been made.)

Stenos yanked the sheet off his bunk and tore it absently into strips, and then he bent to his work, dragging the fabric gently along Bird's arms and legs, wiping away the first layers of grime and exposing the skin underneath. He frowned at Bird like she had tricked him into it, moving along the planes of her body with the ease of long familiarity.

(Ying understood. She hated Elena, but after all this time

with the circus Ying could tell without looking how much longer Elena's middle finger was than her first finger, which set of arches was hers in a long line of the aerialists' pointed feet. It was strange, how much you found you knew.)

Stenos never looked up—he seemed to have forgotten she was even there—but when Ying slid her pocketknife along Bird's shirt, he peeled back one half as she peeled back the other, and when Ying poured water from the canteen over Bird's bare arms, Stenos lifted his hands from Bird's skin for a moment so the water could do its work.

It was worse than Ying had thought, once they got the dirt off. All of the wounds were deeper and more ragged than they had seemed, and the blood still seeping, but Ying tore strips of cloth to bandage Bird up again and never retracted her vote. If Boss was out there in the darkness, they'd have to do the same for her, that was all.

(If Boss would even live through this much. If this much would even bother Boss. No one knew what Boss had done to live so long; whatever it was, Ying hoped it held.

Ying wondered how far the circus had gotten. Maybe it was the circus and not Boss that kept them all alive, and they were all well and strong, and it was Ying and her companions who were doomed.

Or if Boss was really their lifeline, Ying wondered if the circus had gone too far from Boss already and all her fellows had dropped dead, and now they were all waiting for these few of them to bring Boss home and raise them all up again; the dancing girls and the jugglers standing watch, all that was left of the living circus.)

"We can't go," she said. Her voice was startling in the quiet trailer.

"I know," Stenos said, without looking up. "Get me a needle from the kit, and some thread. We need to sew up her arm."

Stenos opened the glass bottle, and the smell of alcohol mingled with the penny stink from the copper and the greasy smell of the smoke. It was one thing too much, and Ying held her nose as Stenos bathed the wounds with cheap drink, and brought the lamp closer, and sewed Bird up like a come-apart doll.

When the stink and the smoke stung her to tears, Stenos said without looking, "Go rest your eyes," which was the kindest thing she'd ever heard from him.

When she curled up in the top bunk it was less cold than she'd feared, from the lamp smoke that had gotten caught in the crannies. The sound of thread through skin (less disgusting once you got used to it) was steady, and as she fell asleep she thought how, if Bird survived, it might still be all right.

When she woke up the sun was rising, and they were gone.

64.

This is what Ayar has forgotten about Stenos:

Stenos can acquiesce to you without giving in.

When Stenos agrees to something, it's because it's the politic thing to do. It's a way to buy time until he can decide what he really believes.

(Boss knew this. It was why she handed Bird to him and gave him his orders, all those years back, without asking him a thing.)

He's seen what happens when he puts up an open fight (locked inside this same trailer like a child, Ayar keeping watch outside). When you put up a fight you risk being outnumbered. It's no way to get anything done.

So when Ayar declares the vote, Stenos nods, acquiesces. When Stenos and Ying are alone, he goes to work on Bird's body, and says nothing against the plan they have to stay and sew Bird up so she looks respectable when she dies in the morning.

His hands are steady as he sews up the wounds, until he reaches her shoulders. The water has pooled between Bird's collarbones. He can see himself in the reflection, trembling whenever she breathes.

He turns her onto her stomach faster than he means to. He's glad Barbaro and Ying are sleeping; there's no one to see him and worry.

When Brio and Ayar come back and Ayar names Barbaro and Stenos as the next watch, Stenos says, "Of course." (It's a way to buy time.)

Stenos goes out with Barbaro until the night has parted them and swallowed them up. Then he comes back, slips into the trailer, carries Bird to the cab of the truck. Ayar is asleep, caught in some nightmare, and doesn't even open his eyes. (Why should he? Everyone in his party has agreed.)

Stenos has wrapped her in his own shirt (it's all they had to dress her in), but she's bandaged in so much sheeting that it might as well be clothes, and she doesn't shiver in the cold.

(He knows why they're all staying—for Boss, if Boss lives. He knows. But for him, now, it doesn't matter. He hates Bird, but he can't let her die on his watch; not twice.

He has, in the last day, thought a lot about that long night holding her, pressing his open lips to her bloody mouth to force air in. He had figured it was a close call to get her into the workshop before she died.

He is guessing, now, that death in the circus is not what he used to think it was. It's the reason he can leave—Boss is too clever to die before they get there, too clever to give away what anyone wants so long as she has any leverage.

Boss sent Bird away so there was one less thing to hold against her, Stenos knows.)

The trailer hitch comes off without a sound, and if you put the truck into an open gear, it rolls a hundred feet before you ever have to turn it on.

This is what Ayar has forgotten about Stenos:

Before he was a circus man, he was a thief.

65.

The truck drivers were terrified enough to floor it all the way down the main road. We made such good time that we hit the river before nightfall, and we followed the current for miles before it was dark enough for us to pull over for the night.

I hadn't wanted to go those last ten, and even though nothing had happened, I still walked the line as soon as the engines were off, like we were dragging a demon that no one else could see.

But I went up and down the rows (we parked like soldiers in rank, so that in case of trouble four trucks could be gone before the misfortune had really set on us), and everything was quiet, and I got all the way to the aerialists' trailer, and still nothing was wrong. It was just a cool night outside, and inside me was the rattling sense of having gone faster than you wanted to from a place you hadn't wanted to leave in the first place.

(Homesickness, Boss calls it. It happens, sometimes. You get used to it.)

Elena had me by the collar before I knew she was even out of the trailer.

"Was that Ying driving away with the other walking dead?"

I mule-kicked behind me and got her shin; when she let go I danced out of the way, twisted to face her.

"I'm not a jailer," I hissed, "and Ying knows her own mind."

Elena snorted. "What little of it there is, apparently."

"Do you think I wanted her to go?" My voice carried. "But I can't keep her prisoner! I'm not a tyrant!"

"Not yet," she said.

It was bait, that was all. She was just looking for a rise. I straightened up, pulled on my clothes to settle them. "Well," I

217

said, "put in your name as ringmaster. Then you can be the big tyrant, and that'll show me."

"I prefer to be a little tyrant," she said. "They get away with more."

It was so true of Elena that I almost smiled before I remembered we were fighting. (Fighting with anyone in the circus got confusing; it was hard to come down cruelly on your brothers and sisters when you knew your turn was coming soon.)

"Something's wrong with the camp," I said instead. "Do you feel it?"

She looked across the trucks and half-closed her eyes, listening like the engines could tell her something.

"We should never have let them stay," she said after a moment. "The place is going to fall apart at the seams now that people have the idea they can leave. It's a house of cards tonight. Try not to make too big a fool of yourself trying to hold us all together, all right, George?"

I rolled my eyes. I didn't know why I bothered asking her anything. "I'll think twice before I pitch the tent and order a command performance for the fish, how's that?"

As I was turning to go she said, "We went an extra leg after we hit the river. We're too far for them to reach us before morning. That's what's wrong."

I walked back to my trailer feeling like my pockets had been stuffed with stones.

I woke up to Stenos with his hand over my mouth.

If I had even thought to fight (and there was no fighting Stenos unless you had metal ribs), I gave it up when I saw his face. He looked like I felt.

When he saw I wouldn't raise the alarm, he sat back on the bed, balanced on the balls of his feet at the edge of the footboard. In the dark (the last of the dark, it was almost morning, we were too far for him to reach us before dawn) he was little more than a silhouette with two gleaming eyes. He seemed to have grown; his shadow on the wall was twice as large as he was, as if his purpose had made him grander than before.

"I've brought Bird," he said quietly. "She's dead. Two hours ago."

My heart seized.

"Boss told her to look for you as she escaped," Stenos said, watching my face. "Can you help her? Is that why Boss told her that?"

The griffin on my arm felt like a second skin.

"I can try," I said. "But I can't—I don't even know what Boss gave me. I don't know what to do."

"Try, then," Stenos said, and I had never heard such a warning.

I knew I couldn't do it. I prayed Stenos wouldn't kill me when I failed.

Stenos stood up and motioned me outside. The camp was quiet, the river louder than any of the noises from inside the trailers, and I wondered how late it must be that everyone was finally asleep.

I looked around for Bird, but when I turned behind me to ask what had happened to her, Stenos was walking down the stairs, and I saw that what I had thought was his shadow behind him was only Bird, draped over his shoulders.

He had folded her legs under one of his arms, and her head was tucked between his shoulder and his neck, as if she had for a moment gotten shy. One arm hung down Stenos's back. She looked like a lash of crooked branches on its way to the fire. But it was the limp fingers (the nails crusted with dirt) that terrified me.

(Poor Bird, I thought, wondering what she must have done to get out from behind the city walls. Then, going cold to the bones, I thought—Poor Boss, who must still be behind them.)

"Follow me," I said, and turned for the workshop.

The inside of the workshop smelled like metal and earth and the patchwork of perfume oils that Boss used whenever we could come by them, and for a moment I was five years old again, skittering along the floor of the workshop between the table legs, plucking up the screws and nails that had rattled loose during the day.

I turned on the little generator and clicked on the nearest table lamp. The light was harsh and hopeless; I wished for a lantern, as if soft light would make any of this easier.

Stenos laid Bird down along the table, and I looked at her face (one closed eye, the blue glass one staring up at nothing), and all the bandages pulled tight around her and stained with red, and felt sick.

"What happened to her?"

"Some of it was from running," Stenos said. Then he fell silent, which meant that the rest of her wounds were from the government man cutting her open to see how she worked.

I close my eyes. The griffin burned. I hoped it was a good sign; did it wake up to help or to warn?

The air got thick, as if there was an electric current just under the table, like Bird's body was made of a million filaments and I had magnets in my hands. I held my palms a few inches above Bird's body, hovering back and forth, trying to follow the feeling, to find whatever I could draw to myself.

I thought about the first time I had seen Bird walking up the hill to the camp, how she had come out of the tent with powdered hands, how her gaze had never wavered.

From under my hands, Bird croaked, "Give me the wings."

I jumped and yanked back my hands. I'd done it. I'd done it, I'd woken the dead, Boss hadn't warned me—I couldn't breathe, I clenched my fists to my chest. I didn't feel any different, I didn't know what I had done.

(Later, I knew what I had done would fix me tighter and tighter to the circus, that by passing my hands over her and using what power Boss had lent me, I had turned the lock but good.

But even if she had told me what it would mean to use the power, even if she had warned me not to act, how could I have held back, looking at Bird laid out on the table, knowing she would go into the ground if I did nothing?)

Stenos startled at the sound of Bird's voice, and for a moment he moved forward, reaching for her like he was going to embrace her. (I didn't understand him.) Then her words must have hit home, because his face clouded over, and he looked at me.

"You're not ringmaster yet," he said. "That's not your call to make. Boss hasn't decided. Don't you try."

"I need them," Bird said. Her voice was dry and cracked, like she'd been dead a week and her lungs were dusty. "He'll put her in the bell cages, there's no other way to reach her, no one can jump that far . . . " She wheezed.

I wanted to believe it was just a fever speaking, but Bird didn't sound hysterical, and by the desperate, cunning look on Stenos's face, he didn't think she was speaking nonsense, either.

"Anyone with the wings could do the same," Stenos pointed out, as if I was going to argue with him, as if he wanted as quickly as possible to seem reasonable.

(He was very good at sounding reasonable. Not a lot of fools lived to his age.)

Most things in the circus were unfair; I wasn't stupid enough to have missed that. Everyone got an equal shot at performing if they passed their auditions and sat quietly for the bones, but more than that was up to luck. If you ended up under Elena then you would never hear a kind word again, and there was nothing you could do about it. Everyone got their chance to perform, sometimes with the person they hated most in the world (even Stenos, especially Stenos).

And some people had stayed human and handsome and still got to star under the circus lights, and meanwhile their partners got mangled this way and that way with nothing to show for it.

Stenos was looking back and forth, from Bird's bone-white face to the wings strapped up and hanging from a butcher's hook just at the edge of the light, like he was gauging the distance, like he was going to beat her to them if she lunged.

(He might have beat her to them, but if she had found the strength to reach for them, I'd have stopped him in his tracks if he followed.)

(Why anyone would want the wings, I never understood. Even Alec must have hated them by the end; he jumped from the trestle just to get away.)

"It's not complete," I said. Stenos wasn't the only one who knew how to spin a convincing lie. "She's only back for a little while. I have to concentrate if I'm going to help her. You'll see her when I've finished."

He took a step closer—looking at her, not at me. "You'll leave us the moment you get them, won't you?"

Bird opened her eye, focused it on him. "How could I leave such pleasant company?"

I stifled a laugh, tried to concentrate on the feeling of pulling her back into her body. I held a hand out over her heart and she twitched.

He said, "You can't give them away. I've been waiting for them."

Bird said, "Don't wake me up again without them. If you're going to give them to him, just let me go. I've had enough of life on the ground."

"Stop that," Stenos said through clenched teeth, but he didn't back down from his claim.

Never had I needed so much to know Boss's mind. Which one was she saving the wings for? Had she ever saved the wings for someone, or were they the memorial of Alec she could carry with her?

(She had probably lied to them both just to keep them in line; it felt the most like what she would do.)

"Bird," I said, "don't make me decide."

She slid her good eye to look at me askance. "Boss told me to find you," she said. "If you won't decide, who will?"

"Boss," I said. "She'll find a way out. She'll meet us here, and then she'll decide."

Slowly, once, Bird shook her head, then sighed like it was too hard, like it didn't matter.

"The wings are not part of this," Stenos insisted.

"Did you bring her all the way back here just to have this little fight?" I asked.

Stenos closed his mouth over his words, paused like he was deciding why he had brought her back. On the table, Bird was looking from one of us to the other, the one dark eye sliding back and forth.

I felt her slipping away from me suddenly, like the tide going out, sliding away from my power and back into the dark.

"She's dying," I said, like Stenos could help me. I grabbed at her leg, at her arm, looking for any connection I could force. I didn't know what to do or how to do it; I hated Boss for putting me here.

The helplessness pressed on my lungs, I was desperate for answers—answers to anything, from anyone—and I said to Bird, "You, you, the wings are yours."

(I meant it, but I would have said anything to bring her back into my care. If I couldn't look out for them all now, who could?)

I felt her again, as if a coat of dust over her was being slowly brushed away—I closed my eyes and tried to grab at anything I could to keep her there.

The door to the workshop burst open.

Elena stood in the doorway, a thin metal poker held like a javelin in one hand, and without hesitating she launched it.

I was the first silhouette, I guess, because that's where she aimed it. She had a steady hand—I wondered wildly if Boss's power worked if I tried it on myself to keep from dying of a javelin wound.

Stenos reached out a hand and plucked the poker casually from the air, so fast I didn't see it—just the glint of the metal, then Stenos standing with his fist closed around it.

Elena looked at Stenos, and after a long moment of pleased surprise at seeing him, she looked at me, and noticed Bird.

She went pale. Then her javelin hand dropped. Then finally she murmured, "Oh my god."

"Quiet," Stenos snapped. "She's alive. George is working on her."

She rested one hand on the doorway. "And what can George do, except clean up afterwards?"

"He brought her back from the dead," said Stenos.

Elena looked at me with wide eyes. I'd seen her surprised more often in the last two minutes than in the last several years—I had thought she had moved beyond caring what other people did.

At last she managed, "You have the griffin? That's what Boss gave you?"

It pressed against the skin like it was trying to break loose and meet her; I clasped my arm and glared at Elena, which was all the proof she needed.

"Nice of you to bring Bird's carcass back just to satisfy your curiosity," she said, looking at Stenos.

He glanced over at her, and for a moment the two of them shared some silent conversation that passed me by. I didn't want to know what it was. I couldn't risk Stenos arguing about the wings again.

Finally I said, "Go outside."

Stenos said, "But the wings—"

"It's not your decision," I said. My voice echoed in the workshop. "They go to the person with the greater need. They're Bird's."

Elena looked from Stenos to me. "No," she said. She stepped closer. Her eyes swallowed the light. "George, you can't give her the wings."

"They're mine to give," I said, "no matter what Stenos might have told you."

"No," she said to me, then paused, looked over her shoulder at Stenos. "No," she said, softer. "You don't want them. You don't know what they do to you."

Stenos crossed his arms, narrowed his eyes at her. "Are you afraid I'll finally equal you?"

The trailer went silent. I looked down at Bird, whose eyes were closed, but there was a shallow rise and fall of her chest, so she was listening, she was holding on.

(I didn't know why I had looked down at her in that moment; I didn't yet know how quickly you became connected to your children; how, whenever they sorrowed, your heart ached.

Poor Boss.)

Finally Elena said to him, more tenderly than I'd ever heard her, "No, you fool. The wings are made of bone; when you get them you're strapping yourself to the dead."

Now she was looking at Bird, looking finally at me. "It drove Alec mad," she said, and it was like I had swallowed a stone, so I knew it was true.

"I've never minded the dead," said Bird. "I only want to be free of the ground."

Elena lunged for her; then she was locked in the cage of Stenos's arms, still reaching for Bird, fingers straining at the air.

GENEVIEVE VALENTINE

"Don't you understand?" she said, her voice rising. "I dropped you to spare you the wings!"

In two steps Stenos had her at the door to the workshop; then he was letting go of her (no, he was throwing her), and she unfurled in the air and landed lightly on the balls of her feet, her face alight. Stenos leapt down the stairs after her. Past the doorway the others were gathering, one at a time wandering into the thin circles of light coming from the open trailer doors.

"How could you?" he was shouting, the words carrying like a bell. He advanced on her. With each step he took she moved, weightless, just out of his reach.

"Boss doesn't give favors she can't control," Elena said.

He lunged, she moved; a moment later, her shadow followed.

"She learned her lesson with Alec," Elena said. "You don't know what the wings do to you, you never saw Alec at the end. Bird would have stayed on that trapeze, until wanting the wings drove her to do what Alec did. At least when I dropped her she survived."

"But she still wants the wings!" Stenos spat. "It's all she wants!"

Elena's face was a mask of grief. "I did what I could. I can't help it if people are fools."

"And what about me?"

Elena flinched, glanced around at the gathering crowd before she turned back to Stenos. She fixed him with a glare she must have summoned from the grave.

"I'd never have looked at you," she said, "if I'd known it would come to this."

I was watching, rapt (the faces I could see were silent, too, and fixed on Elena), and it startled me when Bird said my name, softly. She was struggling to sit up, her legs dangling off the edge of the workshop table; she was watching them argue, too.

"Close the door," she said. "It won't take long."

I did, and when we were alone she said, "You have to decide. Now."

"Or what?" I said. It was supposed to come out bold, but instead it sounded like the truth, which was me scared to death and not knowing what to do.

"No one else will go back for Boss," Bird said. "I will."

"Stenos would."

She smiled thinly. "Stenos left her to bring me back to you. You're so sure he'd go back for her, once he had what he wanted?"

With Stenos there was no telling (he had been a thief first; thieves did as they pleased).

"Elena says they'll make you mad," I tried. "That's why Boss never gave them to anyone after Alec."

Bird shrugged, winced at the exertion. "I don't think I can get any madder," she said.

I bit back a smile.

Outside, Jonah was calling out to Stenos not to be stupid. I wondered what was happening (whatever it was, I was afraid of it), but under Bird's eye I was rooted in place, being dragged into making a choice that would ruin someone. (Only one, if I was lucky. If I wasn't, who knew how bad it would get.)

Bird lay back on the table, turned her head to look at the buckled wings on the butcher's hook. Their edges caught the lamplight, little winks of bronze and gold, and even I had to admit they were beautiful.

"I knew they were here before I ever came to Tresaulti." She closed her eye. "As soon as I saw them, I knew what they were," she said, so quiet I could hardly hear.

My arm ached to help her. I reached out without thinking and rested one hand on her forehead, one on her chest.

I felt like the earth was tilting, that I was being swallowed up, that there was nothing around us but the darkness and the void, and I realized I was being carried with her into death. I resisted, straining, begging her to fight it for my sake.

There was a sickening rush, and then we were back in the workshop. I was sweating from exertion. She was coughing up blood.

In my years at the circus (and by now I knew I'd been here longer than I had thought, that the circus had kept me young and hidden from time), I had only ever wanted a real place; a need—any need—that only I could fill.

Boss had given it to me as a parting gift. Now I had the choice to use it, or stay who I had been, Little George who relayed choices other people made.

(I had made my choice as soon as Bird opened her eyes under my hands and spoke, but sometimes you delay something that has no resolution. Even Boss had delayed this choice, and I had learned all her habits long ago; habits that old were hard to break.)

Finally I said, "Turn over," and reached behind me for the wings.

Outside the trailer in the dark, Elena danced out of the way of Stenos's reach as he closed in on her. His face was grim, and he didn't even seem to notice they weren't alone—his eyes were fixed on her.

"I'll kill you for what you did," he said.

She said, "Go ahead if you want. It doesn't take."

The little assembly around them was still sleep-addled, but one or two of the performers were quicker to wake and realize what was happening, and they were glancing back and forth with sharp eyes.

"Stenos, welcome back," called Jonah, jogging up to the circle. "And where's Ayar? I had no idea you'd be back so soon."

Stenos's face went taut, and he glanced up at Jonah, didn't answer.

Elena knew what that face meant, knew it as sharply as if she had been kicked; Stenos had played two sides against the middle. Ayar and Ying and the others didn't even know he was gone. He had abandoned them all their first night, for Bird's sake.

(That was the problem with softhearted people. No control.)

While Stenos was distracted, she took two running steps and leapt for the trailer. The wings weren't affixed yet, the little silver thread had yet to pull at her, it wasn't too late if she could only reach—

Stenos caught her out of thin air like she was no better than the javelin and locked her in his grip. He wasn't metal, but in his anger he was a cage, and Elena twisted uselessly in his arms.

(She knew these arms so well; it was cruel.)

"Let me go," she said. "She can't have the wings."

"You'll kill her," he said, quietly enough that the people around him couldn't hear.

"I'll kill *you*," Elena said, wondered how hard she could push before she broke his back. "Don't you want them? Won't you help me?"

"I do," he said, but it was like a man speaks in a dream—unsure, resigned.

"They're yours by right," she said, "you can't give them up. Set me down and let's stop this."

For a moment there was hope, his eyes went sharp and narrow; but then came a metallic scrape from inside the workshop like a warning bell, and he looked mournfully at the trailer for a moment, then shook his head at the door, at Elena.

"It's too late," he said, and Elena watched him look around at her as if he was just now realizing the wings would never be his; that his dream was over.

(For a moment Elena's heart betrayed her, and pitied him. Then she came to her senses and tried to use it to advantage. It was too late for anything else; she would use him until it was over.)

"Help me," she said. "Let me go in and talk to George—he doesn't understand what it means to have the bones, he could kill her, surely you don't want her to die?"

(There was a knot in her stomach that she recognized; she must have been this way before, in some other life—desperate and powerless, losing ground against one bully or another, striking at anything she could see and hoping to draw blood.)

"Put me down, Stenos," she said, and her face was hot, tears stinging the backs of her eyes, "you have to let me go, it's my bones in the wings—I get a voice, I get a voice in what happens—George can't just give them away to her like this, he doesn't know what they do to you, Stenos, please, please."

Her voice gave out at last; she gasped for air, pushed against him until his shoulder dislocated, hoping for mercy that never came.

(She didn't say, Alec was a better man than you and even he was a coward at the end. She didn't say, Alec was my brother, because no one else would understand.

She didn't say, I reached for him when he fell, and he pulled his hand away from my hand, and for that I can never forgive him.)

For a moment Stenos was stunned, caught short by the idea of Elena's bones wrapped up in the wings.

Elena felt the infinitesimal slack in his arms and took her moment—she twisted and pulled, doubled and stretched and tried to break out.

(From somewhere far away, Jonah made a quiet sound, like he was just now seeing that something was really the matter.)

She made it far enough out that he had to scrabble after her, drag her back against his chest by her ankle and one wrist to keep her from flying free of him—but Bird was the only thing Stenos couldn't keep hold of if he wanted to, and he held fast against Elena even when her bones began to wail from the stretch.

He had pinned her leg up behind her, clasping the foot and the thigh so she couldn't get leverage against him, and his other arm was around her chest, his hand cradling her neck. It was an impossible hold—she was trapped.

Her body was shaking now; from the strain, from anguish, from the cold and from being half-asleep, from knowing something terrible was happening ten feet away that Elena was powerless to stop.

(She had never promised Alec anything, not once from the first time he spoke to her, but she would have; if he had only asked her, she would have promised anything.

He had pulled his hand away from her reach as he fell beyond her help; in the split second she could see him, he was looking at her with sad eyes, already knowing she would never understand what he had done.

GENEVIEVE VALENTINE

It wasn't true.

When she had let go of Bird, in that long moment before the ground rose up to meet her, Bird had looked at Elena with something like gratitude.

How could you explain the relief of finally falling to anyone who didn't love the air?)

When Elena gave up at last, Stenos sank to his knees with her (he was panting, she must have put up a long fight). When he cradled her head against his neck so the others wouldn't see her tears she cried harder, pressed her fists to his shoulders to protest against this kindness from him, when it was already too late for anything.

When he rested his face against her face his breath warmed her skin; she had gone cold from sleep and from terror.

(She had loved him once, and now it was all over; it was cruel, it was cruel.)

67.

Jonah stood in the pockmarked circle surrounding Stenos and Elena, even after Elena had stopped fighting and the others had begun to wander away, in search of a quick bath or another hour of sleep.

Jonah was watching Stenos, frozen in place by his own frightened guesses about what had happened, and long after he wanted to be gone, he hadn't moved. (He had to know what had happened to them. He would wait as long as it took for Stenos to answer.)

Shortly after the sun rose, so did Stenos, unfolding Elena from his arms and setting her carefully down on the grass. Elena looked grizzled and worn out from her fight, and Jonah wondered why she had been so hysterical about the wings, when there was no danger of anyone getting anything until Boss got back.

If Boss got back.

Elena wobbled as Stenos set her down; when he moved to help her, she knocked his hand away. The move threw her off-balance, and she went down on one knee, crashing onto her weak and bloodless leg, but she turned her back on Stenos and crawled away from him until she could stand enough to stagger, and all the way back to the aerialists' trailer she didn't look back at him.

(Jonah thought: It's the worst thing in the world, to grow as heartless as Elena.)

Finally Jonah and Stenos were alone, and Jonah approached Stenos—carefully, it was never smart to surprise Stenos—and asked, "What happened? Where's Ayar?"

"Alive, when I left him," said Stenos, and with no more answer he walked back to the workshop trailer and posted himself like a guard on the stairs.

Jonah went cold all over; Stenos was hiding something awful

from him. He approached and pressed on, "But is Ayar all right? Are they in danger without you? How did you get here by yourself?"

"Ayar's still alive," Stenos snapped, "which is more than Bird was when I made it here, all right, Jonah? Let me carry one corpse at a time."

Oh, God. Jonah's heart sank. Poor Bird, to have died after all that trouble.

Finally he said, "But you all got Bird out of the city, then?" Even that much would be good news; it would mean the city could be breached, which was more than Jonah believed was possible. (He had seen the capital city once, on a poster announcing the institution of a Chief Governor. The drawing had looked like a prison with a road slicing through it, not like a city at all, and Jonah had looked quickly at something else. It was always a shame to see a standing city used that way.)

"Bird got herself out of the city," said Stenos, as if that would be obvious. "We met her on the road. It was already too late to save her. She died before I found you."

Jonah thought about the extra miles they had driven, beside the river, too far away for Stenos to reach them in time.

Jonah didn't dare ask any more about Boss with Stenos leveling that gaze on him. "I'm so sorry about Bird," he said instead. He couldn't imagine what that drive had been like for Stenos.

(Ayar would know better how Stenos felt. He had made a journey like that himself, once. Jonah was luckier; he didn't remember a thing from the time the fever took him until he woke up on the workshop table with his clockwork bellows easing air into his lungs, and Boss standing over him to welcome him home and tell him not to stand around in the rain.)

Stenos said, "Save your grief for when we need it."

Jonah frowned, wondered about the meaning, and finally turned from Stenos without another word. Stenos had always been odd, and Jonah had bigger problems; the whole camp now needed to reach a consensus about how far they could make it once the sun went down.

As he walked from trailer to trailer, taking the votes, he smiled and shook hands as always, but inwardly he was empty, faltering; behind his eyes flickered the image of Ayar and Ying and the others sitting in the little trailer he used to live in, looking like an old box with broken dolls inside, all of them lifeless and waiting for Stenos to come back.

The consensus in the camp was that they could clear another hundred miles overnight if it didn't rain. Most of the crew seemed to hope for more, like they were making a push for the other side of the world and there was no time to lose.

But this time, he saw, there was a little more doubt that the day before, when they had been in the grip of panic. Now the crew peered at the horizon and snuck a glance at Stenos in front of the workshop trailer before they answered.

Spinto and Alto looked at one another and shrugged and said, "If that's what the others say," and Jonah wondered if the idea of someone bringing back their brothers' corpses had cautioned them against too hasty a retreat.

The aerialists, who looked up in unison when he opened the trailer door, had no answer for him except determined, tight-jawed looks. When he said, "How far could you make it tonight, do you think?" they looked right through him for a long time before Penna finally said, "We'll go as far as we have to."

"Fine," Jonah said, angry at them without knowing why (nothing today was the way it should be). "The crew thinks we can do another hundred miles if we don't blow an engine along the line. We leave at sunset."

Fatima followed him out to the trailer doorway, and she leaned in at the last moment and said, "Would we really go so far, so soon?"

That was a surprise. Jonah said, "Would you have us turn back instead?"

Fatima glanced back down the road. "No," she said finally, and closed the door, but her face had been mournful, as if she had also seen a little box of broken toys. Maybe some of the girls of the trapeze were quietly changing their minds.

Jonah wanted to ask Little George what he thought, but Stenos was still standing guard, and Jonah figured George's answer would not have changed, especially after dealing with Bird's corpse. (What was he doing in there?)

Jonah had an image of George pulling Bird's bones from under her skin to save for later, and lost his appetite for breakfast.

By the time Joe was preparing the afternoon meal, Little George's breakfast had gone untouched for so long that Big George and Big Tom finally took it. (You didn't eat much once you had the bones, but there was still no point in letting a meal go to waste.)

Jonah usually ate with the crew, or with Ayar, but the crew was tense and silent, and Ayar was gone. He found an empty place by eating with the Grimaldi brothers, of all people. They must have been feeling the same loss, too, to make room for him outside their trailer. (A hole in a family circle must be swiftly closed; any open wounds were a weakness in this circus. Jonah knew that was why the crew had never welcomed Stenos back; it was why Stenos carried Bird with him even after she had died.)

"I'd like to know what George plans to do about this," said Altissimo between bites. "I hope the graveman's rites don't turn his heart soft."

"He's not ringmaster," said Alto. "He doesn't get to make any plans."

"So what do we do?" asked Spinto. "Do we just go on without one?"

They looked at one another, and even Jonah thought what a useless question that was. They were like a pack of squabbling dogs at the best of times, and no vote would hold sway for long. And worse, which Jonah didn't dare say, there was no knowing how far they could even go on. He didn't think the leash as short as Elena must think it, but it still worried him that one day they would go too far from Boss at last, and it would be his turn to fall dead to the ground.

"Depends how long we can even go on," said Alto, as if he had read Jonah's mind. (They must all be thinking it, Jonah thought. To anyone with the bones, the whole camp must sound like a ticking clock.)

"We need a ringmaster," said Pizzicato.

"The new ringmaster should be Elena," hooted Altissimo, and he elbowed Moto, who collapsed in laughter. After a moment, Spinto joined them, and after him, Pizzicato pretended to laugh, too.

Jonah noticed that Alto wasn't laughing at all.

Jonah picked at his lunch so long that Moto finally gave up ("It won't turn into something else, all right, Bellowsair? Give it over") and scraped it out evenly in each of their tin plates.

There was nothing to do after the meal but wait until the sun set. Jonah hated being idle; he didn't know what to do with himself when his hands weren't busy setting something up or breaking it down again.

(Some of the crew hated it, and one day they would stand up and say, "I can't unpack this circus one more time," and they would wave him goodbye as they pulled over the crest of the hill down onto the road. Jonah understood. He could afford patience; for them the clock was always moving.)

Fatima found him as the sun was starting to sink behind the edges of the tallest spindles of the forest. Jonah was standing beside the tent truck, watching the door to the workshop; watching Stenos, who hadn't moved from his post in all that time.

"If you want to go back," she said, "some of us are with you."

Jonah glanced over at her, and up (she was so tall, he always forgot; when she jumped from George to Tom she seemed no more than a ribbon in the air).

"Some of us?" he said, and smiled. "Have you changed your mind, Fatima?"

Her face was stony. "I come on behalf of some others," she said, "so Elena will not know there is dissent."

He understood that much. "And you speak only for them?"

She didn't relent. "Ying was one of our best, but I will not walk into danger for anyone's sake."

"What about Boss? She made you."

Fatima shook her head once. "Before I came to the circus," she said, "I was a captive. I wished every moment that I was dead. When I got out—I can never feel that way again. Not for anyone's sake."

Her voice was hard and flat and seemed not her own, and for a moment Jonah could only nod. He had been dead so long that his human life, when he thought of it, felt like an uneasy dream. Jonah's worst fear had been leaving Ayar behind when he succumbed to the fever, and nothing more than that. Jonah hadn't thought that people's first lives would carry over with them, would shape them at all.

(As soon as Fatima spoke, though, he knew it was true; he was still the same as he had been when he caught the fever, no braver and no sharper. Death had not changed him.)

He reached over without thinking and clasped Fatima's hand, let go again before she had enough time even to look down.

"Keep going," he said, "if you have to. As far away as you need."

She watched him, her dark eyes unblinking, her posture guarded. "What will you do?"

He looked back at the workshop, imagined George carefully picking out the little finger bones that Boss rolled in her bare hands, which she pressed into shape against the edge of the table.

It could take George all night to be finished with Bird, if that's what he was doing to her. They couldn't move until then.

"It all depends," Jonah said finally, and shrugged. "We'll have to see what happens when the door opens."

68.

The government man isn't fool enough to leave a prisoner where others can find her. As soon as the report comes in that the man sent to relieve the prison guard found the poor idiot dead and the acrobat's cell empty, the government man gives the order for Boss to be handcuffed and brought to him.

(He doesn't know why he gives the order for her to be handcuffed when she has never been unwilling, and her cell was found as locked as ever, so he knew she hadn't even tried to escape.

He doesn't yet know that quietly, deeply, he is beginning to fear her.)

He meets her on the empty stage. He has brought two guards with him, and the two guards he sent down to the cells are flanking her. Her dress is torn a little at the hem from tripping much on rough stone, and the handcuffs have been shut too tightly.

She is looking out at the empty chairs, a wistful expression on her face as if she's remembering better times (though he can't imagine how). It's a good trick, but he's seen it before, and it can't hide that she's made her trembling hands into fists.

The sight of her this way does the government man a little good, and as he approaches her (not too close, one never knows with her) he gives her a smile, decides to skip the pleasantries.

"I think," he says, "you had better tell me how you make your toys."

She raises her eyebrows. "I'll show you anything you'd like to know, Minister."

The way she says it makes him wonder, but he only says, "You'll have to demonstrate on someone soon, since our living specimen is gone."

It's her turn to smile. "Is she? Good for her."

He ignores it. All prisoners scramble for hope near the end. "I need to know how, exactly, you make them. What do you put inside them that lets them move like they do?"

"You know the answer," she says. "You cut her pretty well open before she flew away."

For a moment his curiosity threatens to take over—he *needs* to know how the copper gets wrapped so tightly around the bones—if there are any bones at all under the metal—how many of these hollow bones there are. (Had there been a metal spine under that acrobat's dull skin? If he had broken her in half to find out, would there have been nothing but a copper casing and a tangle of wires spilling out?)

But a good government man knows the wrong times to be curious, and now is not the situation in which he wants to be asking questions. It's too public; they are too equal.

She needs to be forgotten for a while. She needs to be a little colder; a little closer to the grave. When he asks her again, he wants her unable to stand, blind from days of full sun. He wants her to beg to be allowed to tell him what he needs to know.

Winter is coming, but he can risk this gambit for a while; she can do her work with eight fingers just as well as with ten.

(You must break them utterly. He learned this lesson early; it is why he has survived so long.)

"Take her up to the bells," he says.

The flicker of terror on her face as they take hold of her arms makes him feel as close to happiness as he has been since he went back to the circus, when he had been delighted to see the same performers, just before the acrobat turned that empty glass eye on him and it felt that he would never see a happy time again.

In the flush of his triumph, and wanting to close up a lingering doubt, he says, "When we find your friend, I'll let you know."

She watches him for a moment longer than he likes. Then she says, "Good hunting."

He lets them drag her backstage, listens to the thump and clang as she's shoved up the stairs. After the stairs will come the catwalk, then the ladder, and by the time she's locked among the bells he hopes she'll have been well repaid in bruises for her last answer to him.

He had been too curious, right at the end. It was his worst habit. He should have known by now when it wouldn't pay to be curious.

(He doesn't know that he is beginning to doubt.)

Outside the capitol building he glances up at the tower. The tower was built after the wars began as a lookout and a clarion for the soldiers defending the city, and the government man always imagines that the shadow it casts on the open square is somehow darker, newer than the rest. The bells and cages cut the light into filigree, and he wonders which of the shadows is Boss, trapped like a pigeon in the rafters.

But even as he thinks it, the government man feels a pang of pity. He trades in loyalty, and he would have bet his money that out of so many acrobats of her own making, there would have been more than one willing to come with her to the city gate.

He would not have thought that she would end up so alone.

69.

Four of Boss's performers are in the rickety trailer parked among the trees, just off the road, and they wake up before it's light.

Ying is first to open her eyes and see the empty table. After her first silent panic is over, she wakes Ayar and tells him what's happened.

He's quiet for a long time; then finally he stands (as much as he can stand in the little trailer, it's never been the right size for him), and wakes Barbaro and Brio.

"We're stranded," he says. "Stenos took her in the truck. We need to decide what to do."

He doesn't say that they're stranded until Stenos comes back, and none of them suggest he might; they can see where Stenos's loyalties were, and it's too late to hope for anything better.

"Fuck," says Barbaro, "I wish I had a gun."

"We can't stay here," says Brio. "It's full daylight. We're just asking to be killed."

"We can't go back," Ayar says. "Boss is still prisoner."

Barbaro snorts. "Where out here did you think we would be safe?"

"The city," says Ying.

They look at her.

After a moment, Ayar says, "Go on."

The hardest thing for them is not the wait for someone to drive down the main road (it takes almost until nightfall for a truck to drive past). Nor is it hard to beg for help—they were betrayed by their master, they say, and now only want to see the city (the truth is easy).

The man leans out of the cab, wary, but pulls no weapon. He looks over Ayar and Brio and Ying.

"What do you do?" he says.

"Labor," says Ayar, as if there was anything else he could say, and Brio says, "Carpentry," and when the driver looks at Ying, Ayar drapes his arm around her as if that explains why she's on the road with them.

It does; the man raises an eyebrow, but doesn't ask.

("But you're so young," Ayar had said, and Barbaro said, "What else is a girl that age supposed to be, out on the road with two men?" and for a moment all of them were very quiet, and their human lives crept over them like smoke and filled the little trailer.)

After a long time, the driver shrugs and says, "We'll see what the guards say. No going against them."

They joke with each other as Ying and Brio take places in the back, sitting among the wooden boxes of fruit, and Ayar takes his place near the cab window, and the driver is laughing as he pulls away into the road.

He never sees Barbaro moving around them from behind Ayar's trailer, wedging himself into the gap, eleven inches high, between the bottom of the truck and the top of his wheel bed.

(All of them were soldiers, first, and some habits come easy.)

The soldiers at the gate refuse them point-blank, and wait with their guns half-raised.

"There's nothing in the whole city?" Ayar asks. "We have to find work somewhere. I'm a decent soldier, if you need one—are you looking?"

The soldier scowls and waves them off with the tip of his gun. "No standing around waiting for a ride, either," he says. "Start walking, and keep walking."

For a moment Ying hesitates, bracing to resist, but Ayar rests a hand on her shoulder hard enough to hurt.

"Where's the nearest town?" he asks.

The soldier points west, and Ying and Brio and Ayar start down the path, as the truck driver waves them goodbye and drives past the gates and into the city to deliver his fruit.

"What will we do?" Brio asks.

Ayar says, "We wait until nightfall, find Barbaro, and climb."

Ying walks beside Ayar, and says nothing (what can she say?), but she knows they have made a mistake; the worst thing you can do is leave someone behind.

Barbaro slides from the truck bed under the fruit seller's table and stands up with an apple in his hand, as if he'd just knelt to retrieve it.

When he looks up, he's standing in the shadow of the bell tower. For a moment he stops, the hair on the back of his neck rising, knowing that this is where they will find Boss. (You get a sense, after long enough, which buildings are prisons.)

He wanders the square for twenty minutes, watching soldiers weave in and out. There's a narrow, shaded alley where some of them sneak off for cigarettes.

Barbaro decides that in a city with so many soldiers, there's room for one more to go unnoticed. He'll need a uniform, and then he'll need to be on the gate at night, just in case the other three come looking for him.

(People Barbaro has killed: 89.)

70.

This is what happens when the workshop door opens:

It's nearly sundown, but no one has yet moved for the cabs of the trucks. There are long looks and half-questions throughout the camp, but nothing has really been answered. Everyone is waiting to see what has happened inside.

Stenos, drained of his certainty by the grinding wait, has his head in his hands. A few times he has cast suspicious glances behind him at the workshop; once he ran up and banged on the door, but when there was no answer he didn't break it down (everyone watching seemed surprised), only raked his fingers through his hair, took back his place, stared at the ground. No one knew what to make of it; no one came near.

(What Stenos hears all day is Bird's little hisses of pain as George cuts and drills and makes way for the wings.

She cuts through him just by breathing.)

The sun sinks until it's disappeared under the river with only a smear of orange left on the darkening sky, and even Jonah at last leaves his place, his head bowed. They can't wait any longer for George to finish his work; they must keep going until they are free from the reach of the government man.

For a little while longer the camp is quiet, except for the creaks and rustles of people sitting down inside their trailers to wait, and Stenos feels as though he's holding up the weight of the workshop on his back.

He's lost in thought, and only looks up when Elena runs out from between the trailers and freezes like an animal in the open space, her gaze fixed on the workshop behind him, the heels of her hands pressed against her chest as if she's been stabbed.

Only after Stenos sees Elena, after his heart has leapt into his throat at seeing her so panicked, does he hear the footsteps coming from inside.

He stands up and staggers away from the door. He has never been so afraid; whatever has happened in that workshop has ruined him, and he let it happen, and he feels for a moment like he does not exist, as if the sun has bleached him out and nothing, nothing remains.

The door opens, and Bird steps through the door and onto the top step.

She looks like herself again, Stenos thinks with relief.

(Later he will realize it was a stupid thought, since of course the wings were new and she looked utterly different, but when he is standing on the grass looking at her, he only sees that she seems, at last, as if she has no more troubles.)

He has never seen the wings before, except laced tight in the workshop, and for a moment he can't move. They're more amazing than he dreamed; in the last sunlight they seem to be orange and purple and gold, the edges of the feathers tinted deep blue by the night behind her, and even folded along her back he can hear soft notes as the breeze comes off the river and makes the feathers tremble.

Beside him, Elena makes a small, grieving sound.

But it all happens in a heartbeat, because by the time he sees that Bird has looked at him she has already spread the wings, she's already in flight, and the music is carried on the wind as if from far away.

The camp hears the chord when she takes off, and all the performers who know what those notes mean run out, tripping on the stairs and shoving out the doors to get a look at her; they know better than to be joyful, they know what happens once you have the wings, but still they come, charging into the empty places and staring up at the sky.

Panadrome is the last of them to emerge. He stands on the

stairs of Boss's trailer, gripping the doorway with his mechanical hands, his eyes half-closed, his face turned up to the music.

(He had always hated that song a little, because of the man who played it; now he listens to the clear, sweet notes with a calm heart. The E flat is too shrill, but the rest of it is beautiful, beautiful.)

In the air, even with her shape, she looks more like a bird than Alec ever did, and almost every one of them looking up at her is already thinking of her that way, so deeply they don't know it; she is no longer Bird, but The Bird, and some part of them all is thinking how odd it is that the bird should look nearly human.

Stenos is the only one of them not watching the wings; he's watching Bird's face. He sees that she is afraid of the music, and of the gathering crowd; she had wanted to disappear with the wings, he knows, not draw them all out for a show. He fights the urge to call out to her that it will be all right (what sympathy has he ever offered her, and why bother now with some lie?), and he feels his lungs will pound out of his chest from the pressure of the unsaid words.

(Elena is silent.)

From somewhere on the ground, someone calls, "Bird, come back!"

(It's Little George; his voice is rough from a day of disuse, and he speaks with an authority no one recognizes as his, and he sounds like a stranger.)

Stenos, who has met this new George, only hates that George calls Bird home like she was a wayward child, and when Bird looks down Stenos shakes his head and thinks, Don't, don't, never come down.

She gives no answer; one of the wings glints orange for a moment as she changes direction in midair, so sharp and fast no one really sees it, and then she's gone, the night falling over their vision like a curtain and her shape swallowed up by the black.

(Alec was not an acrobat, and learned the wings as a man learns a machine. She knows the wings as she knows the bars of the trapeze, and she has lived long enough in the air; already she has more mastery of the wings than Alec ever did.)

She seems to take the air with her, and everyone left looks from one to another in the sudden cold, seeking answers.

Finally Jonah says, "Where is she going?"

Elena says sharply, as if the words hurt her, "To find Boss."

(She would know, thinks Stenos, and pities.)

A few of them look unsatisfied with the answer, like they suspect it's a trick, but Stenos's face must be more convincing, because no one argues.

It's Panadrome who says with admiration, "So she's keeping her promise to Boss," and after a moment adds, "We should all be so lucky."

Stenos and Elena look at George, whose eyes are fixed on the sky as if he can will her to come back. He has rolled up his sleeves for work, and the griffin's legs are visible under the grimy cuff.

When he stops looking for Bird, Stenos watches George take in the picture of the camp, the shock at what he's done, the feeling that everything is in the open at last. The crewmen frown and shrug at one another, not really understanding why it should be a worry that Boss had adopted George as one of her clan. But the performers with the bones go very still, as if the griffin has plucked some unknown string inside them.

(They have a ringmaster. They are a circus again. Anything, anything could happen now.)

George, standing in the doorway of the workshop and feeling under their stares like he's the one who's got the grafted bones, looks out over the camp at Big Tom and Big George, at the Grimaldis who are left, at the crew and the human jugglers, at the knot of aerialists who are standing as far from Elena as it's possible to stand. He looks at Panadrome, whose face is empty of hope now that the circus can go as far as it likes without Boss.

Jonah says, "Are you our ringmaster?"

"Yes," says George, though he sounds surprised at his own answer.

(Here, Panadrome closes his eyes.)

Stenos raises an eyebrow, asks, "Then, Ringmaster, where do we go?"

There is a flicker of terror on George's face (which Stenos is happy to see, since it means he still has an ounce of sense), and then he looks at the road ahead of them, and behind them.

"Some of us are missing," he says after a moment. "It can't be up to a few. We all should put that right."

Jonah, looking terrified but more relieved than George has ever seen, turns to the crowd. "We roll out now," he calls, "everyone in the trucks, we are clocking a hundred miles before morning and there won't be any rest when we get there!"

The crew runs for the engines, and the performers for their trailers, and after a moment Stenos and Elena are standing nearly alone on the grass. Elena is still watching the sky, and doesn't seem to notice that everyone is leaving.

"Elena," Stenos says finally, quietly. He steps forward to touch her; the look she gives him stops him in his tracks.

"I didn't think I'd live so long," she says. "The war was taking everyone, and I thought maybe with the bones I'd have a chance at a normal span." She shakes her head.

"You won't die," he says.

"I don't care," she says, as if he's taken his place as the fool now that George has gained some sense. "If we're going, then we're going."

Elena's profile slices the rising moon in his vision. He can't speak.

"I can hear her," Elena says. "She sounds so close; she's so much a part of the wings." A shudder runs down her back. "This is worse than Alec."

"We have to go," says Stenos.

"She won't last," Elena says.

She walks straight for the aerialist's trailer, keeps her eyes on the ground.

Stenos stands on the grass a moment longer, checks the sky one last time.

Bird looked at him, he thinks; in that moment before she turned, she looked at him, and he regrets that he didn't call her back to him. What if she had come? What if she hadn't, and he had shouted her name into the wind for nothing?

He's glad he didn't call.

(The worst thing about Elena's cruelty is knowing it's true; it's knowing Bird's days are numbered.)

71.

Barbaro burned up the daylight hours with rounds of the city. First he walked the city wall (no exits anywhere but through the main gate; this government man took no chances), and then made smaller and smaller circles until he was back in the open market, people parting absently to let him pass.

Barbaro had never seen a market with money exchange; he had never seen a market in the daytime, orderly and relaxed. He had never seen a market where there was enough of anything to be able to choose.

(He had devoured the apple in six bites, standing in an alley out of sight of the crowd; it was the best thing he'd ever eaten.)

It felt good to have a gun in his hand again, and he shouldered the rifle with the ease of long habit, glancing this way and that way as he walked the main streets.

(Even the sewers had grates. This was a government that had the caution to last.)

At dusk, the soldiers flooded the courtyard and gently chased out the last of the market. It was just the fruit seller left, and she smiled through her apology as she packed her tables into the little truck.

Then it was time for the change of the guard. Barbaro watched to see who headed out for the gates, and so he found himself on watch at sunset (perfect), and took his place on the wall with the others.

The other soldiers didn't keep to the line as much as he would have guessed for a city run by someone like the government man. As soon as it was full dark and they couldn't be seen from the capitol, the soldiers wandered this way and that way, passing a single cigarette back and forth along the line. Barbaro held his drag as long as he could. It was real; whatever evil this government man was doing, he had gotten tobacco up and running somewhere, and for Barbaro that was something.

As night set in, the soldiers sniped back and forth about anyone who had scrambled to get the inside watch. Their voices carried on the thin air.

Barbaro didn't join them. He cradled his gun and tried to look sullen. He wanted them to keep their distance, so that when the others came back they could climb over the wall unnoticed, and he couldn't talk all night about how cold it was; he didn't know how to talk without his brothers there.

"I'm freezing," the soldiers muttered back and forth, shivering and grinding their teeth.

(Barbaro really was freezing; he stamped his feet and crossed his arms to keep his bones from frosting over.)

They started to nod off at their posts an hour after that, and five hours after Barbaro had taken the wall, he was alone.

At first he was pleased, all his attention bent on the wall as we waited for his comrades, but as the minutes ticked by with no company but the wind and his own teeth rattling, the hair on his neck began to prickle.

(This is what happens when you have seven brothers all your own, when your nights are filled with applause and your days with the roar of engines; when solitude creeps up on you, it terrifies.)

It was so silent that, when the wind blew across the roof of the capitol building and out to the gates, Barbaro heard someone moving inside the bell tower, and he knew without doubt it was Boss.

("Barbaro," she had whispered, "he knows you're here, get out," but his name was all that reached his ears.)

The road of rooftops stretched out ahead of him almost to the capitol, and even across the open square Barbaro saw some hope; he was no aerialist, but he had strength and power enough to make the jump from the tree, if he tried.

He disappeared from the wall and over the roofs without a sound, his gun strapped tight to his back.

(The problem with a man alone is that time slows down for him in his solitude. Because he is unchecked, he thinks there is time to reach Boss and come back with her; because he is restless, he thinks there is enough time left before the others reach the city walls and start the climb.

When the others reach the top of the wall, the soldiers haul them over the crest and hold them with guns to their temples while they wait for word on where to bring the prisoners.

From the rooftops, between one leap and the next, Barbaro sees the messenger running for the capitol building, and for a long moment before he remembers, he wonders what the matter is.

Then he runs.

He has to catch the messenger before he reaches the building, he has to keep the alarm from being sounded, he has to isolate the soldiers on the wall until he can get there and do something—

But he's too late, too late, and the soldiers spill like ants from the capitol into the streets below, and above him Barbaro sees the glinting of the gun barrels as soldiers emerge one by one onto the roof, taking up places around the bell tower.

Barbaro glances from the capitol rooftop—he's closer to Boss than to the others—and down to the swarm of soldiers below—where he can be anonymous, where maybe he can follow where they're going and wait for a moment to free them. He looks back and forth, but doesn't move from where he stands. There is no road for him now; there's nowhere he can go that doesn't condemn him.

It's easy to trap a man alone.)

72

Panadrome secured everything he could in Boss's trailer; they would be driving over rough road to get to the city, and if Boss came back (when she came back, he corrected) he didn't want her to open the door and find a roomful of broken things.

The knock startled him, and he opened the door to find Elena carrying a handful of pipes as tall as she was.

"If you have any aim left, you can put those arms to some use," she said, shoved them into his hands. Her arms were trembling, and she didn't meet his eye, and he understood what it must be like to meet old ghosts.

He said, "How bad is it?"

She looked on the verge of bolting, but they had known each other a long time, and after a moment she stepped inside, and he closed the door behind her.

(For years it had been the three of them, Boss and Panadrome and Elena. He knew Elena's favorite songs by heart. He knew how she walked when she was tired.

He could never forgive her for turning her back on Boss this way.)

"It's worse," she said, not quite looking at him. "It's her, I know it, I'm not stupid, but when I feel the pull it's like," she took a breath, "it's like home, and I can't help but think it's Alec."

(Panadrome has never talked about being tied that way to someone; there's nothing about it that he wants to say out loud.)

He said instead, "How does she feel about the wings?"

Elena looked up with a thin smile. "Worships them," she said, and then with no smile, "She doesn't expect to have them long, you know."

Panadrome was impressed with Bird's foresight, and felt a

little pang for Elena, to be so sharply tuned to something so empty of comfort. He sighed a minor chord.

"What if Boss is dead when we get there?" she asked.

It was Panadrome's turn to put his hand to his chest (not where his heart was; he forgot his human body long ago. He put his hand over the clasps that fasten across his chest like a soldier's coat).

"I would know if that moment had come," he said.

(He did not say, I would have dropped dead if she had. He and Elena were made early, before Boss's powers were honed. They are held together by joined will, Elena and he, by the animal desire to live; he doesn't think, if they fall in this fight, they could be raised again by any skill the circus possesses.)

Elena nodded (she's always known what he really means, she's never been slow to catch the direction of the wind).

"Take care of yourself," she said. "Whoever doesn't die will need some music later."

It was the closest to praise she'd ever given, the most concern for him she'd ever expressed.

"You as well," he said.

She shrugged. "I have to tell women who swore off fighting to pick up weapons or run for shelter and hope they're not slaughtered," she said. "After that, the fight should be nothing."

"Nor should it," said Panadrome, roughly. "She deserves our fight. Without her, who of us would still be living?"

There was a little silence. Then Elena said, "They'll start without me," and moved past him, and was gone.

In the open yard, Jonah and George and the crew were raiding the tent truck and the props truck and the workshop for anything that could be a weapon. Into the cabs and the trailers went everything that could be used in defense. Even the strings of light bulbs were handed off; even the wrenched-apart pieces of the trapeze.

The first of the trucks were already rolling out, pulling away from the camp and back onto the road, mud spraying under their wheels as they turned. There would be no rest, Panadrome knew, from now until when it was over.

Elena leapt lightly into the trailer from the ground just as the truck lurched forward.

Panadrome's crewman knocked on his wall, and a moment later he too was rattling through the camp and out onto the packed-dirt road.

Panadrome sat at the dressing table and looked at the spears that Elena had gifted him, so he would have some means to protect himself that didn't require him to lock his hands around someone's throat.

(One thing Boss had never questioned about Elena was her ability to tell who had the heart for something and who didn't.)

She had always been of her own particular kind, Elena. There was never knowing what she meant, unless she was out to be cruel; anything else wasn't worth thinking about.

If Elena had brushed Panadrome's hand on her way out, it might well have been an accident; if she had grasped his metal fingers in her soft ones for a moment before she kept going, it wasn't for him to say.

73

Ying was the first one over the wall (she was lightest and most nimble, and the others wanted her safe inside the walls, just in case), and the first caught, and after the reinforcements had come she was the last one dragged down the stairs three at a time, nearly carried aloft by the soldiers who held her arms. She banged her ankles on the stones, slipped on the pavement of the courtyard.

She looked around for Barbaro (maybe he was hiding among them), but everyone was a stranger, and one of them slapped her, snapped, "Head down."

(I was a soldier too, she thinks. Is this how you treat a brother? Don't you know who you're fighting for?)

Ayar kept wrenching his head around to look back at her, like he wanted to make sure she wasn't going to disappear from the end of the line. The soldiers shoved his head each time, amid barked orders: "Look forward!" and "Keep going!"

One of the blows caught Ayar's shoulder, and the fist bounced off harmlessly; the soldier looked, for a moment, as afraid as he should have been.

At the door of the capitol building, the rest of the guards were waiting for them.

Halfway up the stairs, Brio balked and shouted and struck out at the two holding him, but after the first blow that took out one of his guards, a soldier struck him with the flat of his rifle butt and Brio slumped forward. Another soldier shouldered his rifle and took his place on Brio's unguarded side.

Ayar and Ying glanced at one another, and when Ayar shook his head, for the first time Ying despaired; so it was the two of them now with Barbaro gone, Brio helpless, Boss trapped in the city, and no help coming.

She thought dimly, At least we'll find Boss when they take us to the prison.

She thought dimly, Maybe they'll kill us right now, and we won't have to give way for the government man. Maybe Brio had been fighting to die before the government man got hold of him, she thought, and for a moment she went slack all over from horror. She wanted anything but what had happened to Bird; Ying would fight until they killed her rather than go into the dark of the cells.

The guards at the door were motioning them to the alley. "Take them down," said one, and the other said, "And stay with them until he comes, for fuck's sake!"

The soldiers dragged at Ayar as if at a bull, turning him away from the door and toward the tiny alley. Ying looked around for a tree, a fence, a wire, anything she could swing from.

Then the soldier in front of her collapsed.

There was a moment of confusion as they all looked to Ayar, who seemed as surprised as anyone.

A second later, the soldier closest to the alleyway choked and toppled.

"Sniper!" a soldier called (Barbaro, it was Barbaro), and the soldiers staggered back and shouldered their guns in that moment before retreat that Ying knew was the tipping point.

Without thinking, she struck.

The soldiers had loosened their grip on her (fear has strange effects), and once she was moving she knew they would never catch her. She wrenched backwards and cartwheeled twice, out of the center knot of soldiers; behind her the gunfire trailed as Barbaro clipped them down one at a time as soon as she was beyond harm. Now that there was nothing to lose, Ayar was wreaking havoc amid the soldiers, mowing through them to reach Brio. They flew from his swinging arms like rag dolls, knocking back the oncoming crowd.

(There were so many soldiers, the four of them would never make it out.)

Ying came out of the cartwheels already looking for an escape (she had to get above the street, she would climb anything). The soldier nearest her got his neck snapped for his trouble, and as soon as Ying saw the shop awning she was tossing the rifle on top, gripping the edge of the fabric and bending in half, legs up and over the edge of the support beam, then a swing up onto the awning proper and a scramble up the drainpipe, and she was up and safe, pressed flat to the roof.

The soldiers had come to their senses, and had swarmed Ayar and Brio, preventing their escape and keeping Barbaro from getting a clean shot.

Ying rested the gun on the edge of the roof and resented that Boss hadn't allowed weapons. She was out of practice, and if she couldn't hold steady for the shot—

They were firing back at Barbaro now; they couldn't see him, but from Ying's height she saw him crawling to the next roof, trying to get two more shots from the new vantage point before they caught on.

Beyond Barbaro, Ying saw the clusters of soldiers on top of the capitol roof, guarding the bell tower. She could guess what had happened after Bird escaped; no clever man left a prisoner where there was a known escape.

"Get them inside!" the guards were yelling; the doors of the capitol were open, and the soldiers were shoving Ayar and Brio forward.

Through the open doors, Ying could see a sliver of a cruel face she recognized as the government man, and Ayar and Brio were sinking into the shadows under the lip of the capitol. Another moment and they would be out of reach.

"Brio!"

It was Barbaro calling (he had never cried out like that for anyone, but then Ying remembered they were brothers).

Ying looked over as Barbaro fired the last of his rounds into the crowd; then he was standing up to jump down from the roof, into the knot of soldiers dragging at Brio.

There was the sound of a shot; Barbaro shuddered and sank back, and Ying realized he had been struck.

She had to reach him, she had to, but what now that the government man was in sight?

Ying lifted the rifle. She'd take out the government man— she'd strike Ayar if she had to, but the time was short and the government man was almost too far, she'd have to take the chance and fire—

The night pressed suddenly against Ying, and the air was filled with a triumphant, trumpeting sound, and even as the adrenaline pounded through her she thought wildly, *It's Alec*, and then, *No, it's the wings, it's the wings.*

74.

Boss spends the first hour of that long dark night looking over the city, out past the last lights and into the blackness of the wild.

The last time she had been in a city at night, it had been the night of *Queen Tresaulta*, and she had stood outside the opera house with the last inch of a cigarette, watching the street lights snapping to life one by one down the line, a line of bulbs fighting the dark.

(The wreaths of lights have always been her favorite thing about the Circus.)

The cage they've put her in is for a soprano bell; she can't fully stand, can't sit, and she knows this position will eventually break her legs, having to bear her weight in this half-bent way. The government man probably teaches his soldiers how to choose these things. There's no reason to value her comfort; she can do her work just as well without working legs.

She panics a little. (It's quiet, thank goodness, so they don't get satisfaction. When you live in the open, you learn that your doubts have to be silent or the whole thing falls to pieces.)

The cold wind numbs her, eventually, which makes her happy. At least she won't feel her legs give out.

From beside her, Alec says, "They're coming. It won't be long."

"I hope not," she says, fear seizing her. "The Minister will be looking for them—he'll know if anyone has come into the city after me."

"Too late," Alec says with a grin. "You know who's come, don't you?"

She does know; it's the same as listening to the camp as darkness falls and the rehearsals end, and knowing the footsteps of everyone coming home for the night.

Ying and Ayar and Brio are near (Bird is gone, near dead), and nearer than all of them is—

"Barbaro," she says, wrenching her eyes open. Her body is tight with sleep, and her throat burns. "He knows you're here, get out. Alec," she says, looking over, "you have to get him out—"

But of course, there's no Alec. The cold and the fear are pushing her into dementia. She thinks about giving in (she'd be useless to the government man if she was out of her mind), but to give in after all these years, for something like him, seems cowardly. She must push forward; she must find what will make him give way.

She wonders if Panadrome is all right, but she would know if he had died; she would have known. She knows how her children are.

But she is weary and cold and weak with terror, and when she feels Barbaro coming for her she presses herself against the bars (it cuts through the skin on her knees) and wills him to come closer, to climb the tower and break the cage, and it's only after the fear buffets her does she realize it's not all her own, that Ayar and Brio and Ying have come too soon (or too late).

She sags against the bars of the cage. The government man will make her work on Ying first, probably. He'll think Ying can be wasted. He'll want Ayar whole. Barbaro can make it out, maybe, if he waits, if he's careful, but for the others it's too late.

Why did they come back? How could George have let it happen?

He would never have sent them. They must have split; the circus must have fractured.

Her heart breaks.

Below her, there's a smattering of gunfire, and Boss opens her eyes to look down on the square and see which of her children has been executed. But the soldiers are milling, there's retaliation from the ground. Boss looks closer (the bars are ice-cold against her forehead) and sees that Barbaro is firing on them, that Ying has broken free of the knot of soldiers, and she thinks fiercely, These are my children, this is my circus they're fighting; she looks at her children and thinks, Take as many with you as you can.

Ying has reached the roof, Ying has managed a gun on top of everything, and she takes aim at the capitol doors. Boss can't see, but there must be something there that terrifies her; Ying lines up the shot and holds and holds and holds.

Just shoot, Boss thinks, why are you hesitating, and even as she thinks it Boss knows it must be the government man (that's a shot you can't miss, strike the heart or lose your chance).

Then Barbaro stands. (Barbaro falls.)

Boss strains against the bars, once, but he's too far to catch, and Boss sucks the cold air into her lungs, trying for some trace of him she knows will never reach her.

She hears the music of Alec's wings in the distance, growing closer, and thinks, So this is it, trapped here while they fight, the cold freezing my reason. She thinks, *Let Alec come, I'll take the madness, I can't go lower.*

Then Bird flies across the moon; her feathers catch the moonlight, flickering in and out of Boss's vision like the last lights before the wilderness.

Bird is the one carrying the music with her; Bird is folding her spread wings for the dive into the tower. Boss is horrified, relieved to tears; her heart aches that George has done so much so soon with what she gave him.

The soldiers below her on the roof are firing up into the darkness (the stray bullets ring off the bells, and Boss covers her head), and then she hears a the chord shift to a minor key as Bird angles the wings and dives, feathers out like knives.

Boss hears a short series of screams, then a moment where not even gunfire rings out over the sound of the wings, and then she hears the thunder of boots as the living soldiers panic and flee.

(Alec would never have used them for this, Boss thinks even as she knows she shouldn't look a rescue in the mouth. She must forget they were Alec's; the wings he wore were of a different kind.)

Bird appears, so close that Boss startles; Bird wrenches off the rusting cage door, lifts Boss into her arms. Boss wraps her arms around Bird's shoulders, out of the way of the sharp wings. (Bird will not take care, so Boss must be careful on her own behalf.) There is the fleeting spark that Boss gets when she touches one of her make, and just before she can form the thought with it, she's in the sky and the stars are getting closer.

"Where do I carry you?" Bird asks.

"Barbaro," Boss gasps, and Bird dives.

Boss is wrenching out of Bird's arms before they've even landed, she's running as fast as she can without thinking of the bullets (Bird draws fire from above her); she drops to her knees in front of Barbaro and holds out her hands to trap whatever's left.

But it's too late; there's nothing left of him but meat and smoke. He struck out to save his brother and has suffered for it. There is nothing now but a body like any other body that sleeps in the ground.

Bird has swooped lower; Bird is watching for signs of life that will never come.

Boss stands up, says, "Take me to the capitol doors."

She must fight where she can fight, and there's a man she wants to see.

75.

Ayar is lost in the battle-sounds, the pang of bullets striking his ribs and the crunch of bone under his feet, snatching Brio back from the soldiers who have dragged him to the ground to slide him into the building.

(There is too much gunfire around him for him to hear a single voice, a single shot; he will not know until the battle is over that Barbaro has died.)

Ayar doesn't notice the music until one of the soldiers on the stairs lifts his gun upwards and then freezes, staring, until Bird dives into the fray.

The soldier goes down under her wings, and that's when Ayar really sees her.

He can't forgive her (can't forgive Stenos), but he sees Boss in her arms and thinks, that's one good deed she's done us.

The soldiers are, for a moment, struck dumb, and the only sound is the fading chord of the wings.

Then the chaos begins, and someone from inside shouts, and the soldiers at the top of the stairs fumble to reload.

(It was the government man shouting, "Kill the one with wings," because even then he had not given up hope—they had loyal fighters, but he had numbers on his side, and he knew that her soldiers could bleed as much as his—but Ayar did not hear. Ayar only knew they were in danger, and feared for them all.

Ayar did not hear the Minister's voice shaking, or he would have taken heart.)

"Get her out," Ayar calls, moving between Boss and the soldiers. If she gets shot, it's all over.

But Boss has a hand on his chest, in the center of his woven ribs, and it stops him as if her arm was made of iron. She says,

"I'm here for the Minister," in the voice he has come to recognize (for that voice, all things give way).

He steps back, lets her walk past him and into the dark of the capitol.

There's a shot.

Ayar, panicked, thinks it's Boss who's been struck. It's Bird (she cries out, and Ayar thinks it sounds like a falcon), but it must be a glancing blow, because she fans her wings to take off; a soldier grabs for her wing and draws back a bloody stump, screaming.

"Give him here," Bird cries to Ayar, her arms out.

Ayar shifts Brio off his shoulders and hurls him as gently as he can, watches as he flies ten feet above the soldiers' heads; Bird catches him by the waist, sails out of sight.

Free of his burden, Ayar swings his elbow out to test his new reach; it connects, and he hears a neck snapping. The others are trying to edge away enough to lift their guns, but he pushes back against the tide, keeps them too close for them to get an angle, and for ones farther to get a clear shot.

In the little space he's made, Boss walks forward, up the stairs, her dress fisted in two hands, her face trained on the government man, who is standing behind a clump of soldiers and looking as if he's deciding how to flay her if the soldiers manage to catch her.

(The soldiers should have caught her already, Ayar thinks, but they fall back as she walks; this is a fight they cannot win.)

Ayar shoves his way through them to block their shots at her; no soldiers will get through to her if he can help it. He fights them as they dare come, grabbing at guns, punching ribs out of whoever's close enough.

Bird swoops back, scoring the edge of the crowd, picking up a straggler and carrying him a hundred feet up before she drops him into the fray again.

The soldiers surge forward on Ayar, half-angered and half-panicked.

(Some of the soldiers in the back, safe from the wings and from Ayar's arms, are hesitating; they are waiting to see how the river flows before they wade into it. They may be fighters, but they're not fools.)

Ayar does not see this; he only sees that Barbaro has given up shooting, that Ying's shots are far between, and come only to save Ayar from harm. When their bullets run out Ayar will be here alone with the crowd of soldiers, and Boss will be trapped inside, beyond Bird's reach, and they will all die together, which he thinks is better than it could have been.

Better to die here than in a cell; better to die fighting, no matter what comes.

Inside, Boss has been surrounded; she does not struggle against the soldiers who hold her, and when the government man pulls out his knife she does not look surprised. (She must know what she's doing, Ayar thinks, but below that is fear, and fear is his master; he has done hasty things before, when fear takes him.)

Ayar turns and moves for her without thinking; he doesn't understand the sting of the bullet that strikes his leg as soon as his back is turned, until he moves to step on it and the leg gives.

He crashes to the ground, and the soldiers descend.

His heart is thudding against his ribs, his ears are stopped up from panic, and he is so intent on keeping back the crowd that he doesn't hear the pounding at the gates as Big Tom and Big George use their arms as a battering ram; he does not hear the tiny pings as the strings of lights hit their marks and shatter.

He does not realize, until he sees Jonah and the dancing girls running into battle with copper pipes as lances, that the circus has come at last.

76.

This is how the circus enters the city:

Big George and Big Tom are lashed to the tent truck, their long arms lying along the top of the cab and out in front as a battering ram. That truck takes the main road straight into the gates, which groan and cry out with every blow as the truck backs up and drives forward, four metal fists crashing against the wood.

The other trucks have fanned out, and the Grimaldis and the aerialists screech to a stop at points outside the city walls. The tumblers run out and stand in pairs with their hands in a porter's hold, and the aerialists step onto the locked wrists and are flung clear over the wall, their bodies tucked for speed. They unfurl at the top of the soldiers' walk, landing lightly on their feet on and charging in a single motion at the soldiers keeping watch, who stagger back from the onslaught of impossible motion and fall too fast even to scream a warning.

When there are no more aerialists the tumblers launch one another, and Elena and Fatima catch their outstretched arms, swing them safely onto the stone. Alto and Stenos come last, jumping one at a time straight from the ground.

One by one they jump from wall onto the roofs of the city— Penna and Elena aim for the trees, which form a lacy fence along the main road, nearly to the open square.

Fatima stays alone on the wall, securing the ropes when the crew tosses them over. (This is how the crew must climb until the gates are open; this is how they will all escape if the gates are blocked.)

When Fatima has attached them, she crouches in the shadow of the wall; she will wait for them here.

("I don't care who fights," Elena said, "so long as you pretend to be useful, for once," and when she turned and said, "Fatima, you can still tie a knot, I hope?" Fatima took her first breath in a long time.)

The gates at last give way, and the soldiers there have lined up ready to fire.

But Boss's trailer is close behind, and as soon as the tent truck has driven through the soldiers and scattered them, three soldiers find themselves on the wrong end of javelins.

(Panadrome is the only one of them who was never a soldier. He is surprised by his aim, and thinks no further; as the truck drives past the dead, he forces himself not to pity them. If he is sorry to have to see battle after so long without, it's not his nature to say.)

As soon as the road is clear, Jonah and the jugglers and the dancing girls grab whatever weapon is at hand and pile out of their trailers. As the smaller trucks roll into the city they run alongside and grab the rails; they enter the city hanging one-armed off the sides of the trucks, their eyes scanning the dark streets, hammers and planks and lengths of light bulbs coiled like rope clenched battle-ready in their hands.

This is what they see as they close in on the capitol:

(The ones on the roofs see it first, and Stenos stops short when the battle comes into sight. Behind him, Nayah and Alto and Altissimo land heavily with the shock of it.)

There is no open square; it is a sea of soldiers, a carpet of men, and for a sickening moment they see only that Bird is drawing their fire and she can hardly get close enough to do harm; they see only that Ayar is sinking under their outstretched arms.

Stenos watches Bird dodge the soldiers' shots and says quietly, "We're too late."

Then Nayah says, "No, look," and starts again leaping from edge to edge; then Alto and Altissimo see Ying with her rifle, and Barbaro and Brio lying farther off, and they're running off across the roofs.

Stenos sees only that Bird is bleeding. He scales down the wall to the ground, scoops up a rifle, runs.

Elena is sailing between the trees (easier than running), picking up power and speed, and she sees the battle only in impressions between swings; the surge of uniforms, Stenos's face as he disappears into the fight, a flash of wings as Bird sees him and pulls her sharp feathers back.

(Elena sees the red stains spreading from between Bird's ribs, and before she can help it she thinks, At least this one won't live long enough to go mad.)

The truck reaches the top of the hill, but before it can turn onto the road to the capitol Jonah sees Ayar sinking under the soldiers. He jumps down and runs, and Sunyat and Minette are close on his heels, the copper pipes gripped in both hands. The truck follows, and the others take up a whooping cry as the battle comes into view.

This is what Ayar sees when his rescuers come, and even though Stenos is the one who clears the way when the soldiers cover him, Jonah is the one who reaches Ayar in time to offer his arm up and stand at his back.

The circus joins the fight in earnest; as the acrobats drop from the roofs, there are bursts of gunfire from the street below, and someone screams, then another. Then the jugglers and the crew are coming. Some of them carry makeshift flails; one of them has found a welding torch.

Then it's nothing but the sound of flesh giving way and the glint of rifle barrels, the battle without quarter from two sides who can't risk mercy.

77.

Elena watches from the tree above the square until she sees where she's needed.

She is close to the city roofs; she hears the shouts of Alto and Altissimo when they cannot wake Barbaro, and long before they give up trying, Elena guesses what has happened. (Boss has to be close to take hold of you, the moment you go. She remembers that.)

Then she drops from the tree and leaps through the battle, snapping one neck every time she lands, until she's taking the capitol steps. They crumble underneath her; she was never a soldier, not like the rest, but she knows how to kill as well as anyone.

The mass of soldiers are beginning at last to fall back, before an army which must seem immortal, an army designed to terrify, and the last few yards of her way are clear, except for the bodies.

She and Stenos reach the doorway at the top of the stairs at the same time, ready to face the government man and the soldiers holding Boss.

But the soldiers inside have vanished, and only Boss is left, standing with her hand outstretched over the government man's fallen body. Boss looks ill, as if she's eaten something rotten, and Elena wonders what happens when Boss takes a life she doesn't plan to give back.

Stenos gets closer, points his rifle at the body as if there's a chance the man is still alive, and looks at Boss for orders.

Elena hangs back. She still remembers the moment before she died the second time, Boss holding out her hand this way and Elena not believing what Boss meant to do until the world went black.

Stenos looks impressed by Boss's skill; he half-grins up at her as he says, "Did you wait to kill him until he saw we were coming?"

But Elena knows better. Elena recognizes Boss's expression just before she speaks; it's regret.

(Boss regrets things so rarely that it takes Elena longer than it should. Elena was never a soldier, not like the rest.)

"I should have killed him before you came," she says, as if to herself. "I was waiting for the soldiers to give way and run, so he would know he was without help. But it was too long; it was too late."

For a moment Stenos doesn't understand what she means. Elena waits for him to realize; when he does, his face gets set and grim. He looks down at the body; the gun trembles in his hands, and he doesn't speak again.

(Elena knew, as soon as Boss spoke, what the matter was.

In the moment before Boss killed him, the government man had seen Boss's army come to her rescue. Before he died, he had a glimpse of the circus performers descending on his soldiers and fighting as viciously as he'd always dreamed they could.

Just before he died, he had seen that he was right.)

Around them the battle rages, but in the marble vestibule where the three of them are standing, it is as safe and dark and quiet as a tomb.

78.

The two hours I spent under guard in the workshop trailer were the longest I remember. With the griffin on my arm I was too valuable to lose, but it was agony to be trapped without a thing to do. I could only listen to the bustle of the camp as they prepared for the casualties; covering trailer tables in canvas, setting out wrenches and nails and bandages for the living, and needle and thread for the shrouds.

At last Fatima climbed down from the walls and came through the woods to the workshop, and quietly we laid out what copper pipe was left, and marked with grease pencil the lengths of a finger bone, an ulna, a femur.

After a long silence I asked, "Could you see Ying from the wall?"

"I couldn't see any fighting," she said, and something about the way she said it (relieved, maybe) kept me from asking any more.

(Once I pulled down a copper bowl and frowned. "What's this for?"

"A pelvis," she said, and placed my hand on her hip so I could feel where the rim would curve out and around her, and I thought, I must be a different person than I used to be, for her to be at ease.)

We worked until we heard the first shouts from the camp.

They were driving out of the city in the truck—too slowly to be in retreat. They were dangling from the sides if they were well, stacked up in the open bed if they were injured, and Boss standing in the center of them all like the captain of a ship that's coming home at last.

As soon as she was on the ground again I ran towards her without thinking and embraced her for the first time in my life; for a moment she was pressing me back, her cheek against my hair, and then she was stepping away and walking for the work-shop trailer. I fell into step beside her (I was home again).

"How many are injured?" I asked. I saw Fatima running with supplies from the workshop to one of the trucks with an empty bed, so both Boss and I could work at once.

"Most of them," she said. Her face was drawn. "Two are on the edge; I don't know if I can save them. It will have to be you."

"Why?" I asked without thinking, but when she looked at me I saw that glimpse of the graven image that had frightened me when I first had the tattoo; she looked shaken and cracked, and I didn't know what she had done in that city to be so drained of her power.

"Is anyone gone?" I asked, already dreading.

"Barbaro," she said, and I stopped walking and looked back at the truck. (I thought I had seen him, but there were only seven brothers; I had seen what I wanted to see, because I couldn't yet imagine that Barbaro had died.)

But mourning would come later, and as Jonah and Minette leapt off the truck to unload the others, I called, "Bring the worst to the workshop."

When Ying was helped down from the truck (her leg looked wrenched, but she was here and that was all I needed), my heart smacked twice against my ribs.

As I motioned the truck to drive Ayar to the workshop, I did a quick count, frowned. There were fewer, too few—Moonlight and Sola were gone, and more of the crew then I could even look for.

I saw a silhouette far off on the edge of the wall, and even in the thin light I recognized Elena's profile. She must have come over the roofs, making sure there were no last-ditch fighters hiding in the alleys. Nayah and Mina came after her, flickering at the top of the wall like shadows, appearing moments later at the end of the ropes, feet hardly touching the ground.

"And Stenos?"

Boss's mouth went even tighter. "Bird is missing."

My skin went clammy. I thought, No, she's all right, because if she was dead I'd know.

But Boss was too far ahead of me, her shoulders sloped for the first time I could remember, and they only lifted when she opened the flap of her half-made tent and Panadrome stood waiting for her. He spoke, and she spoke, and they stood together for a long time before the flap dropped closed behind them, and the work began.

I tried to hold on to the idea that Bird was alive like it was something I'd have to prove, but I was choked with so much loss and relief and emptiness that I could hardly notice a little more. The ache increased as I worked on Ayar and on Brio and Ying, and long before Stenos came out of the city (his eyes haunted and his hands empty), I had accepted that Bird was gone.

Stenos was the last of us, and we took all our dead with us when we drove away from the walls; this city was no place for a performer.

When we stopped for the night to bury the dead, we lit fires and gathered to keep warm, because even though we were still too close to the city we were a free circus now, and who did we fear?

(Boss didn't join us. She closed the door of her trailer every night for a long time.

Later, she and I would talk about what sort of government springs up in the void. She never got over the death of the government man. He had been cruel, but it was another hundred years before anyone else made half the progress he made.

"This world is so fractured and so slow," she said. "It's why we can go so long without growing old."

As if to prove it, the griffin on my shoulder never healed; the edges stayed singed and raw, and it ached until I learned to ignore it.)

That night Stenos was apart from the fires, as always, but he seemed so stricken that I left my seat beside Ying and followed him into the dark.

He was sitting on the trailer steps. I saw what must have driven him out; in the lamplight, the table was stained the purple-red of old blood.

I wanted to say, She might be all right, but I didn't believe it, and I didn't want to insult him with the lie. He had suffered enough without false hope.

Instead I said, "Why don't you come to the fire."

"So you're still the little ringmaster," he said, glancing up at me.

I grinned. "Not if I can help it," I said.

He asked, "What will I do now?"

It hadn't occurred to me that he was without a partner, that there was no place for him without an act.

"We'll find something," I said. "Now come on to the fire. You need to eat something, at least."

All that night he sat at the fire as if he'd been ordered not to leave. No one spoke to him; Elena didn't even look his way, as if she was afraid to catch his eye.

She needn't have worried. His whole attention was on the sky, as if he was just waiting for the first notes of the wings.

79.

Panadrome greeted Boss, under the flap of the medic's tent, with, "I was afraid we'd lost a good alto."

(He can't say what he wants to say. There are no words invented yet.)

She says, "I killed the man who could have brought the opera back."

There is a new ache, suddenly, that Panadrome didn't know he had room left for. It's easy not to want what is impossible, but to know that Boss had seen the possibility almost drives him into the city walls, just to see what she had seen.

He wants to put his arms around her, but they're as cold as the air, and no comfort to her.

Instead, he says, "Who's first wounded?" and turns to the workman's table.

(His hands are still a musician's hands, and when it comes to sewing up wounds, he's deft with a needle.)

80.

Elena refused, point blank, to be the other half.

"He has no place here without Bird," Boss said.

Elena folded her arms and said, "I stood on your doorstep and begged you to destroy the wings. You didn't, and this is what comes of it. Figure it out yourself, or give him to the Grimaldis."

(They would never take him, Elena knew. Not after what had happened to Barbaro.)

"One of the others might partner him, then," Boss said. "He needs something to keep him from going mad."

For one long, nauseated moment, Elena thought about Bird going mad in her hands on the trapeze, about Bird with one eye gone (horrible, horrible), Bird whose madness had never been a worry. How could Boss trust so much in one of them and not in the other?

"Make him some wings," she said.

Boss frowned and stepped forward, her bulk seeming to fill the air around them, and her voice was at its most commanding when she said, "You'll partner him."

"What am I," Elena said, "an animal?"

(She had loved him, and it was over.)

Fatima was the one who offered, at last.

"He never dropped her," she said, not looking Elena in the eye. "One could do worse, I think."

"The more fool you," Elena said, but she didn't fight it.

(She was afraid what Boss would do if it went on like this; she imagined Boss turning to one of the dancing girls, passing her hand over Sunyat's eyes, making whatever she couldn't find.)

Fatima suits Stenos.

She's as tall as he is, lithe and strong, and when they walk together into the ring they look like one of the peeling marquees for a romance. Their routine is choreographed; when he throws her into the air she flutters back down like a ribbon, confident and light.

Elena thinks Panadrome must be disappointed; now he has to play the same song every night.

It takes some getting used to that when Stenos gathers Fatima into his arms, she looks like an acrobat at rest and not like an animal in a cage.

Stenos never utters a word about Bird, after that first night. Whenever George mentions her in passing, Stenos looks up as if George has spat on the ground, turns away again.

No one else in the circus mentions Bird, because they don't think of her. (She can't have lived long, wounded and so far away from home, and she could not be mourned as much as Barbaro; there were no seven mourning brothers waiting for her coffin to be set into the ground.)

Elena doesn't mention Bird because she fears that to say her name will pull that little string that ties her to the wings. It lies silent, and that's all Elena requires. If that means Bird is dead, then that's what it means; Elena is finished with being compelled.

(Sometimes when it rains, or in the winter, Elena feels a lonely pang along her ribs. She ignores it; you get all sorts of pains in this line of work. There's nothing else to be done.)

Now the tumblers go after Ayar. Stenos and Fatima take the ring after the tumblers have gone, and on their heels Elena and the others drop from the ceiling onto the trapeze, as soon as the applause has faded.

Now when Stenos leaves the ring, people applaud.

Elena thinks he must be happy.

(It isn't true.)

81.

This is how you silence a pair of wings:

You find a barren plain on a windy day, and you sink to the ground as low as you can, and you bathe in the dust.

The first time is like resting your hand over guitar strings; you feel the vibration deeper than before, but the sound is softer, humming instead of singing.

The second time you bathe in the dust, it's like setting down a guitar when you've finished playing; there's the hint of motion, the echo of the song, but if you didn't know what to listen for, you'd never know.

The third time, they are downy as a sparrow's, and make as little noise, so no one can hear you passing overhead.

Then you can spread the wings as wide as you like, catch the wind without singing a note, go so high that the ground has no more hold on you.

Then you are the bird, and the bird, and the bird.

82.

This is what George sees, years later, when he comes into the city carrying his rolled-up poster and his bucket of glue:

The old poster is still there, though it's gone yellow with age and the once-rich green has been gnawed away by rain and sun. ("Been a while since we hit that city," Boss had said when they stopped, and George can only imagine what that means.)

No one has pasted over it or torn it away or scorched the wall; the whole city seems on the verge of being civilized, down to the concrete streets that make it easy for him to walk through it in his brass casts. (No power or amount of his working on them can make them more comfortable.)

Inside the sickly-pale cameo of The Winged Man, someone has drawn with grease pencil over one of Alec's eyes; now he wears a quarter of a skullcap, and has a wide bright eye that never closes.

George looks at the poster for a long time; then he turns around and peers up into the sky.

It's a cloudy day, the sky as flat as a sheet of lead, but if he closes his eyes, he imagines he can hear music.

Ying meets him at the edge of camp and takes the bucket out of his hands, and they walk together around the empty, flattened ground where the crew is already setting up the tent.

Ayar and Jonah are helping, driving the stakes so far into the ground that the sound of the hammer is swallowed up by the earth.

(George can never shake the feeling, now, that they move like soldiers. The circus hasn't been itself since the day in the capitol city. It's clear now that it's a shelter for fighters from a war they can't ever escape.

It's as if a sharp light has been turned on over the circus that can never go out, and now all their shadows are different.)

Outside her trailer, Boss is talking with Panadrome, sketching plans in the air with her expansive hands—a map, maybe, or a tent with a new shape. Maybe someone has been to audition while he was plastering the poster to the public board. (He doesn't worry. Boss will tell him later; these days she's more his partner than his master. She doesn't tell him why, and he doesn't ask. If her powers are diminished for being shared, he doesn't want to know.)

The acrobats are practicing on the grass, and the aerialists in a nearby tree, except for Elena, who stands at the bottom and barks out the orders.

Stenos and Fatima have finished training; they walk back across the camp to the aerialists' trailer. At the door Stenos nods and keeps going, to the edge of camp and beyond it, out of sight. George can't see if Stenos looks at the sky or not.

Ying says, "He looked. He always looks."

George grins at her. "I have to put these inside," he says, taking back the bucket and holding up the broom. "I'll meet you at the wagon, I'm starved out."

The inside of the supply wagon has a window that faces the little trailer, and George looks through the grime and wonders what to do.

(It was right to tell the truth, he knew; but he was learning how to play the truth against the circus. What good would it do Stenos to know she was alive if it would only drive him back onto the road, and then what would happen to him, alone and empty, looking for a bird who might not ever pass this way again?)

When he comes out, Ying is waiting at the food wagon, talking with Ayar. She says something and jerks her head at the tent, and Ayar throws back his head and laughs.

George glances at the sky, and for a moment he watches a

little silhouette too far off to see, unless you know what you're looking for.

Then he joins Ying and Ayar for the meal, on his way to meet with Boss and make plans for the road ahead.

There are things about the circus he is beginning to understand.

❧ THE END ❧

ACKNOWLEDGMENTS

This book would not have been possible without the contributions of many people whose dedication has delighted and amazed me throughout this process. I would like to thank everyone who has been interested in the book, at any stage; nothing pleases a writer like the idea that someone else might actually want to read it.

I'd like to thank Kathy Sedia, who encouraged me to begin. I'd like to thank my agent Jennifer Jackson for her sage advice along the way, Paula Guran for her insightful editing, and Sean Wallace for putting his faith in both the process and the product.

I'd like to thank Kiri Moth, who was able to conjure so much with her artwork, and Stephen Segal for his cover design.

I'd like to thank John Joseph Adams for believing in the book, and for all his advice and support.

I'd like to thank (and apologize to) all the friends who have been remarkably patient with me long before I started in with specific annoyances related to this book, particularly Eileen Lavelle and Veronica Schanoes.

Special thanks are due to Anna Psitos, Stephanie Lai, and Elizabeth Story, who are the most enthusiastic and dedicated readers and friends in or out of the business, and to whom enough gratitude can never be rendered.

And last of all I'd like to thank my family, who first took me to the circus.

ABOUT THE AUTHOR

Genevieve Valentine's fiction has appeared in *Clarkesworld, Strange Horizons, Fantasy Magazine, Subterranean,* and others, and in the anthologies *Federations, The Living Dead 2, Running with the Pack, Teeth,* and more. Her nonfiction has appeared in *Lightspeed, Tor.com, Weird Tales,* and *Fantasy Magazine*; she co-wrote the pop-culture book *Geek Wisdom,* coming from Quirk Books in summer 2011. *Mechanique* is her first novel.

Genevieve lives in New York, where she has discovered a rather counter-intuitive wariness of the theatre district. Her appetite for bad movies is insatiable, a tragedy she tracks on her blog at: genevievevalentine.com.